Praise for Maggie's Tree

'Told through flashbacks and nightmares, it's a gritty, addictive read' *Company*

'Walters can really whip up pace and rake (both movingly and wittily) through the deranged psychology of her characters ... I must admit to being gripped as the dénouement hurtled into focus' *Daily Telegraph*

'A darkly funny tale' *Bella*

'An extremely dark, complicated, literate emotional roller-coaster' *Daily Mirror*

'Her use of language, especially her talent for finding highly original metaphors and similes that conjure perfectly the emotional climate, is as good as you'll find anywhere. A stunningly assured, delightful debut' *Daily Irish Mail*

'Knockout stuff, the work of a writer who knows what she's doing' *Independent*

'This is a disturbing and thought-provoking novel about mental torment and the often blackly comic, mixed-up ways we view ourselves and misread each other' *Guardian*

'Lots of eccentricity with shades of Woody Allen and *Valley of the Dolls* ... wonderfully atmospheric debut novel' *Eve*

'The emotional issues are addressed tenderly and with feeling' *Daily Express*

'This would be a perfectly reasonable first novel even if it were not by an actress who is a National Treasure. It is set in the theatre, but mainly concerns the tragedy, black comedy and sheer chaos of mental illness' *The Times*

'A spirited novel that captures some of the careening terror of mental illness. It's not without a certain deadpan wit, either' *Observer*

'Walters's prose style is likeable and bright' *Sunday Times*

Julie Walters was born in Birmingham and went on to become a nurse before joining a Liverpool theatre group. Since then she has been nominated for an Oscar for *Educating Rita*, having made the part her own on stage, and starred in Billy Elliot for which she also received an Oscar nomination. She is Mrs Weasley in the Harry Potter films, and starred in *Calendar Girls*. Versatile enough to appear both as Mrs Overall in her friend Victoria Wood's Acorn Antiques and the sexy Wife of Bath in the BBC's adaptation of *The Canterbury Tales*, she is the recipient of six BAFTAS and is 'arguably the nation's best-loved actress' (*Sunday Times*). She lives in West Sussex.

Maggie's Tree

Julie Walters

PHOENIX

A PHOENIX PAPERBACK

First published in Great Britain in 2006
by Weidenfeld & Nicolson
This paperback edition published in 2007
by Phoenix,
an imprint of Orion Books Ltd,
Orion House, 5 Upper St Martin's Lane,
London WC2H 9EA

1 3 5 7 9 10 8 6 4 2

ISBN 978-0-7538-2173-2

Typeset by Input Data Services Ltd, Frome

Printed and bound in Great Britain by Clays Ltd, St Ives plc

The Orion Publishing Group's policy is to use papers that
are natural, renewable and recyclable products and
made from wood grown in sustainable forests. The logging
and manufacturing processes are expected to conform to
the environmental regulations of the country of origin.

www.orionbooks.co.uk

To Grant and Maisie

The Beginning

ℛ

Maggie is missing: within an hour of her arrival. One moment there, the next gone, like a death she had slipped away into a freezing Manhattan dusk, leaving Luke and Cissie turning circles on the spot in bewilderment. Leaving them spitting expletives and accusations at one another.

'Christ! Well didn't you ...?'

'I thought you said ...?' then wandering along the vast sidewalks in the descending darkness, yards of angry space between them, like lovers in a tiff. Peering through the windows of bars and restaurants, fairly certain that she wouldn't be inside. Now four hours have passed and they stand on the steps of the Elmscote Hotel staring at the traffic hoping somehow that their very anxiety will draw her back to them.

'Cissie, why on earth did you bring her in this state? You must have known she was heading for this?' Luke is now staring down at his feet, holding his glasses in place and his face is flushed as he speaks. 'I mean for heaven's ...'

'No! She was a bit quiet last week, that's all ... and I suppose coming here was a bit ... spur of the moment ... on my part ... so I probably wasn't concentrating. She just very quickly went downhill on the flight.'

'Well, if you can locate a few fellow passengers with similar symptoms – you know, paranoid delusions, hallucinations, general insanity – we may have a case for litigation ... But I don't think you can blame everything on the airline food.'

Cissie slumps down onto the step, eyes gritty with jet-lag, her small, dark head falling heavily into her waiting hands.

'And goodness knows what Dame Helena is going to make of all this.' He joins her on the step and Cissie slips her arm through his and shuffles her body into him. 'She's hardly going to want to spend the last week of the run in pursuit of Maggie. Friend or no, I'm afraid her patience has just about run out with regard to Maggie's bouts of insanity.' He then jumps up abruptly. 'Oh good God, Cissie, that step is freezing, we really don't want to be adding piles to our problems.'

Cissie gets up with a little grunt of strain. 'Oh Luke, what have I gone and done?'

'Well . . . she can't have gone far.'

But Maggie is in another place, where the disappearance of her friends and the falling darkness are special indicators. She has been watching the entrance of a bar for several minutes and she can smell its beery breath from across the street. Now, as she enters, a tiny voice informs 'and it's getting colder, folks!' and the barman reaches up and turns the television off, showing her a sweat-soaked armpit. She tries to catch his beady swivelling eye as she approaches the bar but, with the briefest of glances, he turns his back on her. She stares at the large expanse of beige polyester as if it were a computer screen about to display urgent information, but all there is is another small, spreading stain sitting in its centre. Then without warning he whips around, like 'Grandmother's footsteps', his red face shining and expectant.

Suddenly there isn't enough air; her lungs are filled with panic; she flares her nostrils to suck in the scanty stuff and gulps at it, frantically, like a stranded fish. Oh no, they cannot give up on her now, not on the brink of her deliverance! Bringing her hand up to sweep the hair from her clammy forehead there is a startling crimson flash. It was, and it is, her hand, bright and burning like a scarlet glove. The other one, the same, instantly joins it. She spreads her fingers and gapes.

'WHAT CAN I GET YOU?' his voice, booming and distorted somehow. Despite her heart hammering at her throat and a cool film gathering on her forehead, she manages a smile and says,

'Ahhh ... You tell me.'

With a slow, world-weary blink of the eyes the barman suggests, 'Beer?' She feels a little spasm of anger in her stomach. How dare he? knowing all he knows.

'Vodka! neat! no ice!' She wants to add 'you arsehole!' but thinks better of it. Before showing his back to her again, he returns a small smile and in it Maggie is sure she detects a hint of admiration. 'Thank you!' The sheer volume of her voice spins the barman round on the spot.

'You're welcome.'

Is it the slight shock in his voice that makes her want to laugh? All at once the panic leaves her chest and turns itself into great walloping bubbles of mirth hooting out and halting every bit of chatter in the place.

Into the silence comes the clunk of her glass as the barman places it on the bar. She reaches for it, at the same time checking her hand. It is quite an ordinary pink now, as is its fellow and both are tingling with a friendly warmth. Putting down the glass, she spreads her fingers and examines her palms, little maps of her life, and in an instant her throat is bunched with sorrow. 'OH, Maggie, Maggie, MAGGIE.' She downs the vodka, to stem the flow. She cannot give vent to this now, not with all she has to do. It would pour out of her, on and on, taking all her precious strength with it, leaving a damp, empty sack. The vodka slows her heart. After several strangled sobs she is calm but overwhelmed with tiredness. She longs to thump her head down on the bar and snore her way to oblivion, but she can't let herself be taken, for fear of where she might go.

'Same again, Mack.' The voice is low and throaty and pure Raymond Chandler. It reverberates through her body to the point of thrill. She knows this is right. She doesn't need to check out the barman's smile, but she knows he's smiling and now he really is of no more use to her. He's saying something but it drops down into the gloom behind the bar. With a practised toss the second vodka is gone, and exhilarated by her performance she slowly turns to face the room. And they are waiting for her, everyone is staring, not like on the street where not a single pair of eyes dared to look. Now unbelievably, as if on cue, in unison they turn away, back to their chat, back to their drinks, eyes to the wall, eyes to the floor, to their shoes, their nails, their newspaper; muffled giggles and whispers and sneaky backward glances. God! She wasn't ready for this. Far from being Lauren Bacall in *The Big Sleep*, she is a tiny frozen thing in a vast, unfriendly landscape. Her skin ruched into a million goose pimples, she begins to shiver. This cannot be happening. The arms which a moment ago had been stretched sensuously across the bar in a crucifix pose of supreme confidence now recoil and wrap themselves around her, a voluntary straitjacket to quell the shaking. Her right foot begins to tap, and then to stamp, keeping an angry rhythm with the rest of her body. STAMP IT OUT. STAMP IT OUT. STAMP IT. STAMP IT. STOP IT. STOP IT. STOP IT.

She looks down at the workman's boot going up and down, up and down, furious little thing, mutinous and strong. It makes her laugh – it's Charlie Chaplin, it's Minnie Mouse. She buries her chin deep into her chest and laughs and laughs and laughs. There is so much laughter she has to scream to get it out; but she knows that really she is crying. Then a quick involuntary burst below sends a hot rivulet down the inside of her other leg. She waits to see if it will get as far as her little girl's white sock and sure enough it streaks straight across the cuff, leaving behind its yellow trail, and trips cheekily over the boot and onto the black rubber mat, to become a small round pond next to a flattened cigarette butt. She stares down at it, her mind vacant from exhaustion.

At a loss as to how to prevent some horror filling the vacuum, she is relieved when at the periphery of her vision she sees a pair of feet. They are in well-worn brogues, brown and shiny and cared-for. She drops down onto her haunches, joints cracking like sticks on a fire, and sits on the thick brass footrail that runs along beside the bar. She has an urge to touch the leather and squeak her fingers along the creases of these shoes. She can smell the polish and she begins to cry. She reaches out and gently rubs the back of her fingers down the soft black corduroy of his trousers.

'My favourite pants.' He bends down onto one knee and startles her, his face only a foot or so from hers. It is pale and freckled, with very round eyes. The eyes have the same colour as the shoes, a warm, reddish brown. He is smiling.

'Would you care to sit down?' A gentle hand is at her elbow.

'Come on,' almost a whisper. He hauls her to her feet and Maggie allows herself to be steered towards a nearby booth. She bumps her damp bottom down onto the thinly covered seat and he sits opposite her. On the table, alongside an almost finished glass of beer, is a copy of *Time* magazine, carefully placed, angled towards Maggie, the letters juddering and jostling. She quickly switches it back to face him.

'Are you alright?' He is handing her a handkerchief, one corner frayed, but it is freshly laundered.

'Am I going to need this?'

'I just thought you might want to blow your nose.'

She lifts the soft square to her face and breathes in its clean washing-powder smell. She sees her mother's quick arm at the ironing board, the worn pink hand sliding the iron skilfully back and forth, and again sorrow rises in her throat. Swallowing it, she looks across at the man, his soft dark curls, his face creased with concern. 'Is this it? Is this my *Time*?' She lifts the magazine up in front of him, careful not to touch the pulsating letters.

'Sure, it's yours, take it. I don't want it.'

She takes a huge breath and in a voice so low it barely leaves her lips she says, 'O.K., I'm ready.'

'Excuse me?'

How long had Maggie been looking for this moment? Was it all her life? However long, it had dodged and evaded her. It had hidden round corners and appeared in disguises that she had blundered past, only to recognise them long after the opportunity was lost. And now it has finally come. She has cornered it, here, in this bar. 'Am I supposed to fuck you or something?'

The Darkness

❧

'She's probably out fucking Brad Pitt or somebody in his private penthouse, while we're here, playing worried aunties, and not getting our beauty sleep.' Helena lands with a bounce in the unwelcoming armchair that smells vaguely of cigarettes and people, long gone. 'I don't suppose there is any chance that she has been sensible enough to have her mobile on her is there?' No one speaks. 'No … silly me, what a daft question.'

She swings her long white feet with their darkly painted nails up into the air and brings them down with a crash onto the sticky surface of the coffee table; the cups and saucers jump and jiggle in surprise. She begins to towel dry the thick, shoulder-length hair that she swears takes twenty-four hours to dry and eyes Cissie who is slumped opposite, her head bowed. She could be asleep but Helena knows that she isn't. She feels a wave of annoyance as she looks from Cissie to Luke who is sitting on the sofa poring over Maggie's lunatic ramblings, his mouth a wet pout of concentration. A brief scenario plays itself out in her mind: she lunges across the table, crockery and spoons flying, rips the notepad from his hands and beats him savagely about the head with it. She is ecstatic as she pictures his startled, hurt expression, the large eyes larger, the pout dropping into a gape. She snatches at the round, gold-rimmed glasses, the frightened eyes trapped behind, the lashes like spiders under glass, and rips them roughly from his face. She will smash them underfoot!

'Oh God my feet are ugly.' She reaches down beside her chair for the bottle of Bulls Blood and lets out a whoop which cracks into tinkling giggles.

Luke's voice a monotone: 'What's got into you?'

'That's for me to know darling and for you to only guess at.' The wine gushes and bubbles into the cheap tumbler. Luke stares at her, frozen in his moment of bewilderment. Staring straight back at him, she addresses Cissie.

'Oh, come on, ickle Ciss, have some more wine, for God's sake, it's Saturday night.'

Cissie's head snaps up as if someone had unexpectedly entered the room, her face momentarily blank. 'Oh, oh yeah, go on then.'

'Don't look now, darling, but Lukey is doing his "reptile at the zoo" impersonation.'

They both look at him. In freeze-frame he continues to stare at Helena but his eyes have darkened.

'It hasn't moved, you know. Is it real? Oh! No, wait a minute it just blinked, I saw it blink! Ahhhh, it's quite sweet really ... for a lizard.' Luke shifts his gaze from Helena down to the uneasy clutter of the coffee table, a piece of newspaper ingrained in its veneer, where something has been spilt and not cleaned up. He feels his face go hot, and without a word he stands to leave the room.

'Oh Lukey, don't be such a Nelly.'

'Have you not an iota of concern for that poor girl?'

'Oh for God's sake you don't honestly expect us to go scouring the streets do you? I have just done two bloody shows and it's midnight – in Manhattan! Oh, Ciss, cue for a song.' Helena sings out, a high, lilting voice:

'This ain't no time to get cute.'

Cissie joins her in strident discord: 'It's a mad dog's promenade!'

Then they wait. Looking up at Luke. Faces like children's at a puppet show. He is motionless. Looking down at them. Then almost imperceptibly a smile disturbs the thin straight line of his mouth; he closes his eyes and cocks his head as if listening to the perfect plan. Nodding his agreement he taps his foot; head and foot exactly in time, now joined by the clicking fingers of his left hand. The women click too, eyes shining, smiles spreading as they watch the long awkward body convulse; sucking in air, the narrow shoulders gather up, the head drops back and out of the mouth, now wide and sensual, comes a clear, sweet note.

Helena closes her eyes and allows his voice to fill her. She thinks of a small dark room in the eaves of a tall Victorian house and a thin young man talking about blackness and inertia into the small hours of a bitter Sunday morning. She thinks of a tiny disused church, its floor and walls occasionally spattered with pigeon droppings; lit by a thick shaft of hot sunlight. In the corner is an old upright piano, behind which sits Miss Hyland: great white hands hovering like birds of prey above the keyboard; her large, plain face a picture of encouragement, with its half-open mouth poised for song. Next to her, in an agony of self-consciousness, stands a pale, uncoordinated beanpole of a youth, with nothing to recommend him. She plays again the opening bars of Paul McCartney's 'Yesterday', and, when nothing happens, pings out a note repeatedly as a reminder of the key in which it should be sung.

Several snorts and titters can be heard as the boy's face turns purple. Then suddenly he strikes a pose more reminiscent of being shot in the stomach than of singing a song. One of his fellow students tries to muffle an embarrassed screech of laughter and the look of kind coaxing in Miss Hyland's small blue eyes rapidly changes to alarm; but then in turn to a kind of rapture when up through the lanky throat, with its shaving scars and spots, comes a sound so unexpected she is simply paralysed, the birds of prey momentarily suspended, before diving down in a panicked chaos of fingers and notes. After this, whenever they met unexpectedly in the tatty corridors of the All Saints School of Theatre, Miss Hyland would blush.

Helena throws her head forward with such force that the thick, damp swathe of hair sends a pair of spoons skidding across the table, and grabbing up the towel she begins to rub at the hair ferociously; until the singing stops. Then through its dark curtain she watches Luke. He has removed his glasses and with his eyes closed he has that inert Buddha look about him. And then with some alarm she sees that Cissie is staring right at her through the damp strings, eye to eye, like a hunter peering into a lair.

'. . . What?'

'. . . Nothing, you just made me jump with your hair.'

'. . . O.K. kiddiewinkies, matinée tomorrow, time for mega-bobos.' Dragging the large white bathrobe around her Helena bends down and takes Cissie's face firmly in both hands.

'We are not going to let her do this. This is your holiday. This is my time. We are not going to let her do it. Not this time. The buck stops wherever she is.' Then squashing the small even features into a fleshy gargoyle, 'God you're beautiful!' She plants an extravagant kiss on her forehead and one in the air just above Luke and leaves.

Energy rushes from the room, like the last dregs of a bathtub. Nothing now, just the hum of the building, a low, migraine hum. Cissie's head is heavy and thick with fatigue. Then through the grey slot of a window, from somewhere out in the darkness, comes what sounds like a distant yelp of pain. Her heart instantly quickens. But there is nothing again, just the hum; no sound of rushing feet, no cries of 'Stop him! He went that way!', no police sirens. Just the hum and the darkness.

Cissie considers for a moment that the noise had been inside her head.

'I'm going to call the police.' It is Luke, myopically holding Maggie's spiral notepad about a quarter of an inch from his face. Cissie can't decide whether this is comical or not. It certainly had been on many an occasion in the past, but the pale eye mechanically scanning the tangled letters of each and every line is somehow unnerving. Putting the notepad down, the eyes collapse into puffy slits as he gropes for his spectacles amongst the debris of the coffee table.

'You can't call the ... they're not going to turn up because somebody shouted somewhere. There are people shouting all over New York.'

Spectacles in place, the eyes focus on Cissie; they look blank or full of hatred, she cannot see which.

'What's the matter?'

'"What's the matter?"! Your very, very dear friend, of God knows how many years' standing, is missing, in a strange city, in a very, very strange state. Has it not occurred to you that she may be in some need of assistance?'

It is hatred. And now there's a self-righteous anger, which brings her own shooting to the surface.

'Fuck you!' and then with a face purple and quivering, 'Maggie, Maggie, Maggie, Maggie, Maggie, Maggie, Maggie, MAGGIEEEEEEEE!, I couldn't give a flying bollock if she's been shagged senseless by King Kong and impaled on the Statue of Liberty's fucking torch! I was thinking about me for once! MEEE!' She stabs a bruising finger repeatedly into her own chest. 'Have you any fucking idea how many times I've run myself ragged, this last couple of years, getting that cow out of one bleeding mess after another?' Luke's face is again blank, or hateful or perhaps fearful; to be decided. She cannot wait and stomps from the room, blundering into the unexpected darkness of the bedroom.

She stands there for a moment disorientated by its complete blackness and its heady mix of warm body and Chanel Number God knows what. Helena's breathing comes deep and rhythmical from the direction of the bed. Cissie is startled by the desire to get in with her, to bury her face in the damp hair, to cry and rage and lose herself. Instead she feels her way to the bathroom, stumbling over one of Helena's shoes.

Once inside she pulls the light cord and is plunged into a series of nightmarish flashes as the cold fluorescent strip stutters into being. The room is damp with washing. Tiny pairs of coloured briefs hang like bunting; underneath, the bath is filled with washing, suspended in murky-looking water. She turns to look at her reflection in the small rectangular mirror, the unkind light throwing into sharp focus the dark circles beneath her eyes and draining the colour from her face. Behind her the jolly rows of panties mocking and crowding. She checks her watch and whilst doing so, sees that her hands are still shaking from the outburst.

It is twenty past six in the morning in England. Jenny will still be asleep. Or perhaps not; Cissie can quite easily see her standing barefoot in the kitchen, a Pooh Bear figure in her striped winceyette pyjamas; a cigarette burning lazily in a saucer, she is leaning forward, her palms against the worktop. With shoulders hunched and head bowed she stares at the kettle as it builds to the boil. Cissie tries to catch a glimpse of her face, but her mind's eye refuses to conjure it. Instead, alarmingly, it throws up Frances: her older sister's face looks hard and grim. And then her mother's. She yanks at the light cord. Standing there in the darkness, she realises that she has been holding her breath and lets it out with a dry little sob.

She opens the bathroom door and silently makes her way through the bedroom. About halfway across, a long, rattling snore comes from the bed; at its crescendo it is exhaled with a great wet puff and a flapping of lips. Cissie imagines Helena's appalled expression at hearing such a snore from anyone else and goes back into the living room smiling.

Luke is standing by the telephone clutching a pencil and paper, he too appears to be smiling and, strangely, blushing.

'Was that Miss Helena regaling us with one of her farmyard impressions?'

'Yes.' She giggles and then, 'I'm really sorry about that; it's not that I'm not concerned about Maggie, it's . . .'

'Say no more. I've got a number for the police from the little man on the desk, so I'm going to telephone them now. Meanwhile I think you should read this.' He hands her the spiral notepad.

The Cross

This has not been a good day for Michael. He had woken just before dawn in the grip of the old recurring nightmare. He hadn't had it for nearly a month, but until then Dominic's bruised and lifeless body being pulled down into the ground by some unseen force had stalked him nightly. All through the day there have been endless sightings of the boy and any gap in his concentration has been flooded with images that made his stomach lurch. Now he watches through the window of the bar as tiny flakes of snow meander towards the sidewalk, and he steers his memory sharply away from the day snow first fell that winter.

She had simply appeared in the bar, a welcome and oddly moving distraction with her bright bleached hair and her old velvet cloak, muttering and laughing. In dealing with her, the barman's straight-faced impatience had made him chuckle. Then when she turned round he had been shocked by the pale skin and the vivid green eyes. He had expected a gaunt, ravaged countenance, soiled and weary and a good deal older. This was a lot more exciting and he was enjoying the spectacle of this odd beauty spinning and reeling from one emotion to another like some bizarre audition. It was when she began to shake that his enjoyment stopped and the stamping of her foot and her loss of control drew him in. He had felt himself attracted to the strange, darting thoughts and the extraordinary eyes with their massive pupils; great black wells that went down and down; inviting him in.

Outside snow is falling and is sticking thinly to the windowsills of the huge grey edifice opposite. He sees Dominic's gloved hands scraping a snowball from the stoop on McDougall Street and seconds later the burst of blood from his nose. The shocking red stains in the snow. He downs the rest of his beer and looks at his watch. It occurs to him that she might not come back and he is surprised by a sudden dart of anger at the thought of her dissolving away into the night. He swings round to look at the restroom door. It is slightly ajar but the two people next to it think he is staring at them.

He swings back and comforts himself with the sight of her crumpled blue cloak and she is there! A faint odour of stale urine as she slips silently back into her seat. A ravishing smile.

'O.K.?' There is a note of irritation in her voice and he cannot answer her for a moment, his thinking is frozen as he stares at the bright crimson cross in the middle of her forehead. She giggles excitedly.

'I don't think you realised, did you?' He is still speechless. It is not the cross but the eyes that are disconcerting him. The long black tunnels have diminished to tiny pinpricks in a sea of impenetrable green marble.

'O.K. Over to you.' The smile has gone. His chest begins to tighten and he reaches in his pocket for the inhaler. Shit! He must have left it at the loft. The face is still straight and challenging, but the mouth is something else, a law unto itself. She has no jurisdiction here; it is made in the shape of a smile and full and pink. He is distracted by the creak of his lungs, a tiny orchestra tuning up, and he moves his gaze upwards, blurring over the eyes to the forehead and the cross. He reaches for his glass and it is only when he gets it to his lips that he remembers it is empty. He manages to giggle and swallow at the same time, resulting in a painful gulp of air which seconds later erupts in a large, beery burp making his eyes water. He claps a hand over his mouth and lifts the other in apology.

'What is this?' The face creases with irritation, but the eyes remain unmoved.

'Yes! I'm sorry. Look . . .' He glances at his watch.

'Precisely! Isn't it time we moved on?'

'Well . . . where can I take you?'

She frowns, the eyes look like glass. Then that delightful, lilting laugh. 'You really are something,' she says.

'Oh! please don't misunderstand me. I merely want to help.'

And within seconds she has the face of a child. 'Yes I believe you do.' She reaches out a surprisingly large white hand with ragged nails and he immediately clasps it between both of his. His instinct is to press it to his lips but he stops short at his chin and smiles. Carefully he places the hand down on the table and rubs his thumbs over the rough knuckles.

'Why don't you sleep on my couch for the night? It's very late and we can sort things out in the morning.' There is a minuscule narrowing of the green eyes. 'But you know I'll . . . I'll take you anywhere you want to go . . . well, in Manhattan anyway . . . Look, I'll make sure you get home . . . wherever that is . . . Well, I suppose it's England, am I right? Well . . . I can't ensure that you get *there* but . . .'

'I'm coming with you.' The voice has lowered and the little girl has gone.

After a deep breath he gives her a determined smile and signals to the barman that he wishes to pay the bill.

Maggie watches as he goes over to the bar and in an excited flurry of words, on a single breath, she whispers, 'It's now or never, shit or bust, rapture or rupture, love me or leave me, kill or cure, do or die.' And then under her breath without moving her lips, 'Oh Michael, you are so clever, you have given nothing away. You are subtly guiding and bombarding with countless clues, but are you Jesus or Beelzebub?'

The Waiting Room

Purgatory or deliverance!!

IN THE NAME OF THE FATHER AND OF THE SON AND OF THE . . .!

Your poisoned river runs through me, snaking and slithering, dropping its evil seed into the pink, moist innocence of my soul. Already I hear the oily flapping of the great black wings, trapped inside the very core of me. I will expel you oh not so holy HOLY GHOST, I will have your heart on a skewer, oh yes please!! and I will feed the filthy writhing thing to the hounds of hell!

Beware of sabotage in all its forms.

Beware the alien who will interfere with the process.

Beware the HOLY GHOST!!

Who is the Archangel?

Succour or destruction.

Only the moment will tell.

'Jesus Christ.' Cissie is sitting cross-legged deep in the corduroy jaws of the old brown sofa. 'This is seriously Doolally Tap. I mean this is classic barmy, isn't it?'

Luke lets rip a short high-pitched giggle whilst his face shows nothing but a slight blush. 'Well it's certainly not *The Country Diary of an Edwardian Lady*.'

'"*Who is Cissie?*" Well I've spent most of my life trying to work that one out, darlin'. Who is Cissie! She's the small dark-haired woman that runs around after you with a pooperscooper.'

Cissie is shouting at the notepad, holding it inches from her face. 'The one that's not going to do it any more. You must remember her?'

'Oh dear. Do I detect a faint ripple of unrest in the calm waters of friendship?'

'Who is Cissie?!' At this point the writing becomes illegible, it swings and scratches erratically across the page, a lie-detector catching out its victim.

'Huh! She's obviously as confused as I am.'

'Goodness me, it's snowing!' Luke is opening the window. Cissie drops the pad and springs over to join him. Great uniform flakes are falling thick and fast and have completely covered the clutch of pipes that shoot diagonally up the wall of the building opposite. Cissie plunges her hand out into the freezing air to feel the flakes land and melt.

'Oh, this is brilliant!'

'Not if you have no roof over your head.' She withdraws her hand rubbing it to restore its warmth and longs for Jenny. The ubiquitous police siren wails and fades but the great throb of the city is muted under the deadening effect of the snow. Even the hum of the building seems quieter and somehow more distant.

'So the copper had absolutely no concern then?' A shudder runs through her and she moves away from the window.

'It was exactly like reporting a stray dog. What does she look like? When did you last see her? Tell us if she turns up.' He turns away from the window and lollops into the armchair. She can't see whether he is looking at her or whether his eyes are open or closed.

'So a total fucking fruitcake roving round New York wanting to take a knife to the Holy Ghost when she sees Him didn't seem to present any particular problem down at the precinct then?'

'It seems not.'

Someone is playing music somewhere. Vague strains of it are flitting through the open window on draughts of frigid night air and it is familiar; but before she can name it, Luke's sweet voice is there, quietly bringing it to recognition: 'No woman no cry.'

Cissie swings her feet up and stretches full length on the sofa. 'No woman no cry.' She checks her watch as he continues to sing.

'Everything's gonna be alright.'

It is five to eight in the morning in Putney.

'Why didn't Miss Jenny accompany you, Cissie?'

Hands behind her head Cissie stares up at the yellowed ceiling and wonders if the effect has been caused by years of nicotine. 'I would have thought that no-nonsense approach of hers is just what this situation could have done with.'

This is a room no one has cared about, it has been passed through and tolerated by those who dreamt of better things. It has been a waiting room, a stale setting for depression and disaster.

'God! I've got to get out of here.' A twanging of springs and Cissie is up, standing dazed in the middle of the room like someone just woken from a coma only to find themselves on the other side of the world.

'Do you fancy a walk, Luke?'

'No, but if you insist . . . I shan't let you go alone.'

'Oh God, I'll be fine, I just need some air.'

'Yes, and I suppose there is just the remotest of chances that we may happen upon a certain mad person.'

The Body

&

Cissie and Luke are standing in silence, watching as the giant flakes swirl and dive to their extinction on the black, oily surface of the Hudson. It is uncertain which of them sees her first but neither speaks as the pale form floats into view: a strange shape, encrusted with snow and illuminated by the cold grey night lights of an empty pleasure-cruiser. It could be a bag of rubbish, it could be; but that is unmistakably a shoulder and that is unmistakably a neck, a jawline, an upper arm. They both step forward at the same time, their right feet in unison, and lean over the balustrade, destroying its snowy cover.

'What's . . .?'

'It looks . . .'

It is now bobbing and bumping against the pleasure-cruiser, nudging for attention, a helping hand, a drop of kindness. Cissie spots a set of steps leading down to a lower landing stage, but the way is barred by a thick chain fluffed with snow. She leaps it without disturbing a flake, leaving the thing hanging motionless like some bizarre Christmas decoration, then springs down the steps, landing perilously on the wharf. She is now only four or five feet above the water, and leaning as far forward as she safely can she peers out into the darkness. The water is bringing it closer. She can see the long hair just below the surface. It is blond.

'Nooo!' Her voice is small and gruff.

'What? For God's sake be careful.' Luke has stayed at the top. 'Look, we can call the police.'

The snow is now darting aggressively, hitting her eyes before she can blink; she doesn't hear Luke, she remains fixed, unable to avert her gaze from the body. It is now just ten or twelve feet from her and is moving from shadow into light; at last she can see it. It is floating rigidly on its front, the head is tilted round to the side but the face is obscured by snow, the right arm is partly raised as if she were doing the Australian crawl and has become frozen in midstroke.

'It's a bloody shop dummy.'

There is no left arm. There are no legs. All at once a tiny avalanche and one side of its face is visible: the lips are a full cupid's bow, a perfect button nose, and the right eye partially closed, the lid trimmed by thick black lashes. There is something caught in the stiff, pale fingers which are delicately waving, pinky outstretched, just above the surface of the water. Cissie slowly lowers herself onto her haunches as the thing moves ever closer, the hand seeming to offer up its find. And there it is – a used condom, sparkling with snow.

'Well it couldn't have been Maggie anyway. She was never so practical.' Cissie speaks quietly to herself and then she begins to laugh. It is dry, unfulfilling laughter, which causes her whole body to shake, and it is soundless apart from sharp little expulsions of air erupting in the back of her throat. These come faster and faster and faster and faster and then her mouth explodes with vomit, the bitter residue of an evening of cheap red wine and pizza eaten hours before.

'Are you alright?' Luke is stamping his feet and rubbing his hands. She doesn't look up, but looks back and down into the water, her nose and eyes running. The plastic hand is still holding up the condom, triumphantly, for all the world to see.

'Well, that didn't do you a lot of good, did it, dear? I don't think you should see him again . . . bit too rough.' She stands up wearily and begins to mount the steps. Luke is standing at the top, his blue and white bobble hat, his duffle coat, trousers and shoes almost entirely covered by a layer of snow; even his eyebrows and glasses have not escaped.

Cissie looks up and stops in her tracks. 'Bloody hell, it's "Where's Wally This Christmas? It's a game! It's a cult! IT'S A WORLD-WIDE OBSESSION!!"' She lets out her trademark honk, the result of vocalising an intake of breath and laughing at the same time.

'Josh away, Miss Cissie, but you may well have to rush off for towels and hot water. I'm frozen to the spot.'

Cissie is on her knees halfway up the steps and the laughter that now comes is raucous and full-throated. She looks up again, her face crimson. 'You look like you've just fallen off a bloody Christmas cake!' Still laughing she climbs the steps on all fours. When she reaches the top Luke has pulled his hood up, but is standing in the same position.

'If ever they do the musical of *The Snowman*, Luke … Luke Boileau *is* The Snowman.' She straddles the chain, wiping it free of snow with the hem of her long leather coat, and comes to stand directly in front of him, mirroring his stance. The snow is blowing harshly into their faces and she gives him a stiff hug. She suddenly feels weak and deeply cold: her teeth begin to chatter. 'Where the bleeding heck are we? Apart from standing by the Hudson that is.'

Luke lets out a long sigh. 'Where the bleeding heck is she?'

The Holy Ghost

&

The drums are beating for the chase; a hot, dark rhythm accelerating along with her terror. She has no way of knowing how many of them will join in, but one thing's for certain, the archangel has deserted these streets; these streets that look so innocent in their pretty white shroud. The stage has been set with masterly skill, perfect little eddies of swirling snowflakes effect their own tiny whirlwinds, dramatically lit beneath street lamp and shop window. The sidewalk, pristine, virginal, waiting to record her every move. Nothing is beyond them, the artifice is stunning. Even the air through which she moves seems real, except that it is here that their skill falls down, for no matter how much she gulps it back into her desperate lungs, this poor substitute is no life-force. It hovers stagnantly in her chest, a leaden pollutant bringing her body skidding down onto the sidewalk with a painful crash. The drums hammering at fever-pitch fill her head, the omen of her own extinction. She watches her own arms flailing; white and spastic trying to disturb the sterile scene in which nothing can survive.

'Pleeease noooo!' But no one can hear this, the words are stifled and drowned in her throat by the hysterical battering of the drum. She feels him before she gets the courage to look. A crawling sensation on the back of her neck and up across her scalp. She twists her body stiffly round and there, in this Christmas card setting of soft white streets and falling snow, a black, malignant thing appears but a couple of hundred yards from where she lies. It is momentarily still whilst the drumming reaches an excruciating tattoo. Sitting up, she slaps her hands across her ears, useless hands! They have erased all feeling from them. Is this it? A creeping paralysis of all her senses? She throws the hopeless extremities into the air, her crossed forearms coming down and resting protectively on top of her head, allowing her upper arms to guard the bursting ears. But it is too late; drum and drummer have entered. For who else needs to hear this? It is written for her; her very own solo, her very own beat.

Slowly the creature begins to move towards her and then with a little arachnid leap it starts to run. The drummer is ecstatic. It is then that she sees the wings, ragged and flapping. The Ghost is almost upon her, she must be defeated. The drummer is orgasmic, something has to give and surely it will be her. She crashes her face down into the dark folds of her skirt and waits. Waits for the process to take its course.

'Are you taking her with you, or do I get the pleasure?' The barman's podgy hand snaps up the two twenty-dollar bills, checks their authenticity and slides them into the cash register in one fluid movement. Michael laughs conspiratorially and, male camaraderie established, he waits for his change.

'No, I'm taking care of her.'

'Whoo! Rather you than me, pal,' and with that the barman turns his back and walks away. Michael waits for a moment. Clearly the barman thinks the transaction is finished. Michael stands a moment longer hoping that something might happen. Perhaps the fellow will remember and come back to put things right or maybe ...? Maybe what? At a loss he turns to look at her; and she is gone. During that brief interchange with the barman she must have left without a sound. Again he feels the little spasm of anger at the thought of her disappearing and again he is comforted by the sight of her blue velvet cloak, lying crumpled where she had been sitting just moments before.

'Did she go to the rest-room?' but the barman is on the phone, with his back to the room.

'She went out the door.' A loud, rasping voice. Michael turns around but the place is now empty.

'Left! Gone! Vamoosed!' Then he sees her, a tiny woman, her head bundled and wrapped to twice its size in a big woollen scarf. Sitting in the corner, her hands clad in large brown fur-backed gloves, she is smoking a cigarette with difficulty.

'Oh thank you.' No time to lose. Michael rushes over to the booth to collect his things.

'Don't mention it.'

Picking up the cloak he notices a book sticking out of a pocket in the lining. He cannot resist.

'She had a bellyful of you, Big Boy.'

It is a copy of Shaw's *Man and Superman*.

'Why don't you leave her alone?'

Inside is an envelope, being used as a bookmark. It has a name on it: Helena Cassidy. The voice is getting louder.

'Preyin' on innocent women!' He quickly reads the name and address and puts it back.

'Death Row is full of bozos like you! They ought to cut your stalk off!'

'Alright, Gracie, turn the volume down.' The barman has interrupted his call.

'They ought to cut his stalk off and stick it up his ass!'

Michael gathers his lighter and cigarettes and picks up his long black overcoat. 'Yes, yes, maybe that's just what they should do. Good night all.' And without stopping to put his coat on, he leaves.

'Goodnight, Asshole.'

He spots her some way down Seventh Avenue as he slides to a halt at the corner on Fiftieth Street. She seems to be lying on her back and with jerky, angular movements is lashing out at the air, fending off some unseen attacker. He notices a taxi shark its way out of the snowy gloom, the little light on its roof offering him a simple conclusion to events; and for a brief speck of time he longs for his now nightly routine of brandy-induced oblivion and is back in the familiar normality of his loft on Collister Street, making hot chocolate in the tiny warm kitchen downstairs; then upstairs, drawing the long, heavy curtains against the night. And from somewhere incredibly close, that particular scent of Dominic, of his skin, his hair, his clothes, his inescapable presence. But anyway he has the poor girl's cloak and should at least return it to her. He begins to move towards her, then all of a sudden her struggling arms freeze, mannequin stiff, in mid air and she shoots upright into a sitting position then almost immediately collapses into a small, dark ball like a spider under threat. He thinks of the flimsy top and the thin crêpe skirt and runs towards her. He is speechless for a moment as he stands over her, his lungs squeaking and complaining with every breath. He crouches down and reaches out to her, but stops short of touching her, for fear of the soft ball exploding into a mess of flying, frenzied limbs.

'Hi, it's me. Michael. You can't stay out here, you'll freeze to death.' And gently he wraps the cloak around her. Very slowly, the small blonde head twists round and gives him an odd sidelong look, the eyes black with fear.

'Is it you? Is it? Is it truly you?'

'Well . . . it was the last time I looked.' He drapes his overcoat carefully on top of the cloak.

'Michael . . .'

'Yes?'

'Michael! . . . Michael of course! Oooooh I should have known, I'm so sorry. I think I expected something more obvious; but not a white feather in sight!' And that brilliant smile again and at the same time the black eyes filling up with tears.

'Come on let's get you home.' Taking hold of her icy hand, he helps her to her feet. An unhailed taxi pulls up alongside them and without a word he steers her towards it.

'Wow!' she says. 'Oh wow!'

25

'Collister Street, Tribeca.'

'Sure, peoples. We'd be better off with Rudolph and his pals tonight, huh?' The cab is being driven by a young woman. A jingle of earrings are pierced around the edge of her right ear. There must be at least seven or eight from lobe to temple and a tiny crucifix is bashed and jostled by an even tinier ball and chain as she turns to clock her passengers. On her head is a dark green porkpie hat, pulled roguishly down at the front to just above her eyebrows. She must only be twenty-one, twenty-two at the most. Michael studies the back of her head, the thin, greasy tendrils of mousey hair, curling stickily over the black turtleneck. Had he been alone, he ponders, he might have invited her back to his loft.

'Where are you guys from?' The little ball and chain has wrapped itself around the crucifix.

'Originally, Baltimore and er ... my friend is British.' She erupts into something that sounds South African but is obviously meant to be a 'Cockney' accent. 'Cor luvva duck, governor! Are you a limey?' She laughs with glee at her own expertise, then slips back into the comfort of her native Queens.

'My family were originally from Ireland, way back.' Michael clocks her identification on the dashboard: Madeleine Court; he feels he can detect a genetic Irishness in the pale, gamine features.

'Whereabouts in Ireland?'

'Oh, close to the border with Scotland.'

'... Right.'

Maggie listens. The drummer has retreated, the invisible herald of her homecoming, the last lap, the final shaking off of the chrysalis. And even now as she watches his profile, she can feel the fire consuming her skin, and her hands and feet are bloated with pain. She struggles to free herself from the soft heavy confines of the overcoat, eager to see her transformation, her hands burst out from the darkness, blood-red and throbbing. She hadn't bargained for this.

'What's happening to me?'

26

Michael turns to her, his hair sparkling with melting snow-flakes.

'Mmm?'

'What's happening to me? What am I going to be?'

'What are you going to be? … You're going to be … home … dry … warm and safe in about … oh, ten minutes or so.' She watches the lips moving, she watches them smiling as he turns to talk to whoever is driving. She wants to feel the tip of her tongue touch them lightly, then to run around the edges and down onto his neck. She watches his Adam's apple, flecked with dark bristle, moving as he speaks and laughs, and a sharp little spasm of lust darts through her belly. She thinks of her tongue finding the collar of his coat and she can smell him on it from where she sits, his pure, unique essence, a mixture of stale and fresh, his past and his present: she would know it again anywhere. The pain having left her hands and feet, her body is immersed in a delicious warmth and she slips a hand under the waistband of her skirt. She watches his hands, strong-looking hands with a smattering of dark hairs gathering and leading off under the thick plaid cuffs. No sooner does her own hand reach its destination but her back is arched and she lets out a low, soft moan. 'Aaaahhhhh!'

Michael looks towards her. She has almost entirely disappeared inside the cocoon of his coat. Just the damp, dark roots on the top of her head are showing. He can hear muffled sniffs and snuffles coming from inside and he sees Dominic's tired and puffy face crumple with sorrow. This time without hesitation he places a hand on the top of her head. Her face appears, like a Russian doll, made ghostly by the cold city lights flickering haphazardly through the snow-covered window and she begins to laugh, her hands coming up to cover her face.

'What's gotten into you?' He lightly touches the back of her hand with the back of his, again experiencing the surprising roughness of her knuckles. Her hands shoot apart like a pair of mechanical shutters to reveal a cold direct stare, the eyes restored to their exquisite green.

'Obviously you.'

Michael feels himself pulled towards her, until he topples sideways into her and there is a painful crack of foreheads.

'Oh I am so sorry.' He pushes himself upright just in time to see the back of the taxi complete a silent glide to the right and then continue to slide, broadside, towards a set of traffic lights showing red.

'Whoa! Ride 'em cowboy!' He watches helplessly as the diminutive shoulders hunch and the tiny hands wearing frayed fingerless gloves grapple with the wheel. As they pass through the lights the thing grinds to a halt.

'Holy shit! I think this old girl should be wearing her chains.'

'No, no please. I know I have overstepped the mark.' Maggie is now sitting bolt upright, the cloak and coat having fallen down around her waist.

'What did you say, honey? Are youse O.K.?' She turns around to look through the grill, her elfin face just able to see over the divide. Michael chirrups nervously with laughter.

'Oh, we're fine.' The lights change and the luminous face disappears to continue her battle at the wheel.

'This is going to bring the City to a standstill.'

'Oh my God what have I done?' Maggie tries to swallow, her throat has dried to cracking, her tongue is shrunken like a dried chilli pepper inside her mouth. He puts a hand on her shoulder. He can feel through the thin, silky material of her blouse its hard angularity. It is a thinness that comes not from illness but from neglect, from a dearth of love and nurture. He has an almost unstoppable urge to crush her to him, to take her inside himself.

'Hey come on, you're responsible for the weather now?' and he lightly touches her cheek. She sits looking at the rattling cage that separates them from the keeper. Below it, the black divider is covered with scuff marks, wheeling and swooping; where some poor soul has railed against their imprisonment; each mark a story, a history, ending God knows where.

Looking down she sees a discarded tissue, blotted with blood. What kind of meat wagon is this? This confined space! This is no ordinary taxi, this was never designed to ferry civilised folk to a happy ordinary destination. This was for the dispossessed, the pariahs, the ones who would never make it no matter how many chances you gave them! She looks up as the windscreen wipers are fighting a losing battle with the elements and flings her door open. Michael throws himself across her. Her head and shoulders are hanging out of the cab, one hand clutching the door-handle.

'What the freakin' hell is goin' on?' Again the taxi slides a quarter circle round to a stop. Michael grabs hold of her wrists but not before the ragged nails have seared two bloody tracks across his cheek. Madeleine Court jumps niftily from her cab: she would normally stay put during a ruckus like this, and order them out, radio for police assistance or simply wait until the situation was resolved. But it was ten past five in the morning and she had had enough, and besides she didn't feel any great threat from the kindly, well-mannered man and the strange spectre of a girl he was appearing to help.

'Come on, lady, you're nearly home. Now get your head in, or you're gonna get it smashed by the door.' With that she crouches down and with both hands under one shoulder she heaves Maggie upright. Maggie's knees swing up to her chest and the two black boots land squarely on the partition, whereupon she arches her back and lets out an almighty screech. Michael tries to push her back down with one hand, at the same time attempting to suppress the savage, struggling arms. One of them jerks free and the fingers go straight for his hair. Madeleine Court, about to shut the door, sees this and grabs hold of the offending hand. When it won't let go of the hair, she sinks her teeth into its fingertips and after several seconds it loosens its grip. She then catches the wrist and pushes the hand painfully deep into Maggie's stomach. The screaming stops with a small whimper and Madeleine Court, her face but an inch from Maggie's, speaks in a low controlled voice.

'It's been a long night, lady. I don't want your fighting in my cab. I don't want your screaming in my cab. If this guy's keepin' you against your will, I'll call the cops. If not, shut your freakin' beak and get your boots back down there where they belong. Now which is it going to be? You gonna get out and walk? I call the cops or you shut the fuck up and I take you to Collister Street?' Maggie's boots slowly slide down the partition to the floor.

'I take your silence as meanin' you're gonna behave yourself ... O.K.' With that she lets go of the wrist and slams the door. Michael gives Maggie an odd kind of guilty schoolboy grimace and he too finally lets go of her.

The two sit in silence, admonished children, as the taxi moves carefully along in the ever thickening snow.

'O.K. Where on Collister are we headed?'

'Between Jones and Cornelia.'

'Right.' Madeleine Court watches them through her rear-view mirror. An intriguing pair, the woman obviously out of her brain on some drug or other, the man having picked her up in a bar somewhere. She is rather beautiful if you get beyond the manic eyes and the stale body odour. The man gently touches the woman's arm, an attractive man, a man not afraid of his feminine side, Madeleine Court could sense that, just like she is not afraid of her masculine side: the kind of man that in another situation she might make a play for herself.

'O.K. Collister Street! ... Give me a clue again?' There is something in the man's eyes that makes her feel uneasy.

'Just over there on the right, number fourteen.' He is wrapping the woman up in the cloak and placing his big overcoat around her shoulders. It is like parent and child, but the child is terrified, and the parent blind with need.

'Are you sure I shouldn't be taking you to the hospital with her? She doesn't look too good to me.'

'No, no, she'll be fine, she'll be just fine in the morning.' He is fumbling for his money.

'What's her name?' She cannot tell whether he is stalling or just concentrating on counting out the dollars. He finally hands them through the grille.

'I think you'll find that's right. I don't want any change ... Helena ... is her name ... thank you for your concern. Goodnight.' Before she can thank him, the two are out on the sidewalk and again he is fumbling, probably for a key.

'Goodnight. Take care of her, she's in a lot of pain ... but then, I guess you know all about that.' And she drives off with a slight queasiness in her stomach. It's been a long shift.

The Fall

❧

Luke is watching the waiter: he is slumped in the corner, chin on chest, a vast man with a huge goitrous neck and a face speckled with warts.

'He'd make a marvellous Toad, don't you think?' A dribble of saliva has left a wet trail down his chin and a little damp patch on his brilliant-white shirt. Every few minutes the great head jerks upright and the tired dark eyes scan the room for customers, but no one has been in or out for at least half an hour, the last person being a tall, sickly looking youth with bright red spiky hair, who came in and stood near the counter, swaying for a few seconds before he let fly a string of completely unintelligible abuse and left. On the wall, right next to the sleeping waiter, is a photograph of Rock Hudson, inscribed: 'Dear Frankie, Thanks, I'll be back! Best regards, Rock Hudson.'

'God! Do you think he's still waiting?' Cissie is spooning the frothy dregs of a cappuccino into her mouth, a habit Luke does not care to watch. They had walked for almost an hour, through snow that flew horizontally into them, blinding and disorientating them, until they had finally stumbled upon Frankie's Deli, *open 22 hours a day! Cholesterol free fries!!* As they walked into the little Sixth Avenue sanctuary, fluorescent-lit, smelling of coffee and frying and some unidentifiable food, boiled long past nourishment, Cissie had slipped on the linoleum, made wet and dirty by the snow that had melted from people's shoes, and had landed unceremoniously on her bottom. There had been three men sitting at a nearby table who had turned and tittered, their faces garish with make-up.

'See you next fall.'

Now the place is empty but for a thin, elderly man, sleeping in a seat by the window; his pale unshaven face, looking like a mask, his head wedged uncomfortably askew like an abandoned puppet, between the freezing window and a wall wet with condensation.

'Bloody hell, it's like the night of the living dead in here! And you look like you've just been dug up.' Luke lets go a weak little snort and, removing his glasses, pushes the knuckles of his forefingers deep into the corners of his eyes and goes at them roughly with big circular rubs.

'He's probably been dead for a week.'

'I thought there was a whiff of something I couldn't quite put my finger on,' and Luke replaces his knuckles with the heels of his hands for a final rub round the sockets, leaving his eyes looking angry and wrinkled.

'You look like you've had enough.' Cissie prods at the back of his hand with her forefinger as if trying to remove a stain. He stares blindly at her, the pale grey eyes disconcertingly larger without the glasses, and now beginning to water. She cannot tell whether it is just tiredness or whether he has been moved by something.

'Oh, how right you are, my darling girl. How right you are.'

'Well, we have been up all night looking for a mad woman, so it's not surprising really.'

Luke massages the livid dent left by his glasses on the bridge of his nose. 'Well actually, worrying about what Lady Macbeth might be up to has become a rather welcome distraction,' and he replaces his glasses.

Cissie has located something small and sharp in the right-hand pocket of her coat and is dragging her thumb repeatedly across it. Without warning the waiter snaps awake and his head springs into action, mechanically pivoting from side to side as

33

he scans the room, the jowls wobbling like a cockerel's comb.

Cissie in a stage whisper, one hand cupping the side of her mouth: 'Ooh eh up! You've woken Speedy Gonzales. He's just checking to see if Rock's popped in.' Luke allows himself a soft little giggle.

'Has the Queen of Mean been giving you a hard time then, Lukey?'

Luke snorts abruptly, his face again reddening to beetroot. 'Oh, you really don't want to know, Ciss.'

Cissie gives him a long, twinkling look. 'Since when have I not wanted to know other people's personal business? Listen, I could do with a couple of diversions myself. In fact I've been diverting all over the shop. I am diverting from so many things at the moment that shortly I shall be taking refuge up my own bottom.'

They laugh; meanwhile, deep in her pocket, Cissie is sticking the point of the small, sharp object into the tip of her thumb. Luke stares down at his hands, the long white fingers, the nails bitten down into grimy little ovals, how unsavoury they looked. Then slowly and in measured tones:

'It's the same old carry-on but the owner of the penis is different.'

'Oh Lukey . . .' She too looks down at his hands. They ought to be elegant but they somehow never looked clean. 'Have you talked? Or is that a daft question?'

'It's a daft question.'

'Well, who is it? And is it of any importance?'

'Of course it's of importance!' Luke is shouting; a large blue vein has dilated in the centre of his forehead. 'What do you think this does to my feelings of self-worth!' Spittle flies, a white, frothing missile, crashing onto Cissie's lapel, and simultaneously the waiter and the old man awake.

'Shoot!' says the old man.

'Who?' says the waiter, jowls wobbling, ready for anything, and then, 'More coffee there?' The old man is up.

'Nah, I gotta get out of here, she'll be waiting.'

'Sure,' says the waiter and all three of them watch the old man prepare to leave.

Suddenly, he is elegant. Tall and slim in his long, dark overcoat, Russian hat and leather gloves; chairman of the board of directors, a judge, a relative of David Niven. He approaches the door with a 'Wagons Ho!' lift of his arm, by way of 'goodbye' and they see that on each foot he is wearing a plastic bag, tied with string.

'Hope he's got shoes on under those.' And the waiter waddles over painfully on surprisingly small feet to wipe his table.

The snow, no longer driving across the window, is falling directly down in soft giant flakes and all is white. Suddenly through the battered swing doors in the corner comes an almighty crash of what sounds like several saucepans, followed by a high-spirited whoop and a joyful, tenor voice singing, 'La la la la la la la la la iiiit's amoreeee.'

'Ha haaaaa! It's Tony, when Tony comes I see the light at the end of the tunnel. I see my bed!' And the waiter waddles back as if barefoot on a gravel path, laughing a big fat man's laugh. He stops by their table.

'What can I get you?'

'I think, most probably, the bill, unless you want something more, Cissie?'

'No, I can see my bed as well. I don't know where the bloody hell it is but . . .' and she is overtaken by a huge, shaking yawn. Dragging her hand from her pocket to check her watch she sees that her thumb is bleeding; she thrusts the hand back in and fingering through the tattered lining she finds again the small sharp object and defines it with the sore tip of her thumb; Christmas Eve two years ago, she sees Jenny stretch across the crowded dinner table, pointing the big red cracker at her like a sword, the tip of her tongue touching her upper lip. During their time together, it was this moment that Cissie revisited most: it was, she said, definitive. A tiny red object shot from the cracker and landed in her coffee cup. On fishing it out, she found it to be a small red whistle. Jenny was laughing, with a candle flame reflected in each eye.

'You do know how to whistle, don't you?'

She stares down at the several jagged pieces of red whistle, at once both worthless and precious while her thumb continues to bleed onto her leather coat. She can smell Jenny's hair and neck. Another epic yawn overtakes her.

'What's that?' Luke has paid the bill and is brandishing a map of Manhattan.

'Oh . . . it's just something I broke when I fell on my arse.'

The Wound

♧

Maggie is staring hard at the photograph and what she sees is a poor, half-formed thing with huge, cavernous eyes peering directly back at her. The great orb of its head is bald and little more than a skull. And next to it there are more of these creatures, with their stick limbs; laughing; neither male nor female, not yet born, yet older than the world. From some other life, from a life between lives. And there is Michael! He is clutching one of them, the hunter triumphant! A victorious smile stretching his mouth from ear to ear. The creature looks weak and detached, resigned to its fate and unutterably vulnerable. And there the creature is again, trying to be human and worse ... trying to be American! A baseball cap placed, skewiff, upon its head, a cruel parody of a wholesome American child. Then something in its eyes and in the twist of its mouth draws her closer to the glass. She somehow knows the lie of its features and she tries to touch the little face with the tip of her forefinger. The eyes are becoming clearer, they are searching, searching her eyes. And asking something, asking the unanswerable. Each eye an abyss of want. She can hear the child breathing, she can smell its breath, acrid with need. She has an overwhelming compulsion to say ... to speak ... but there isn't a word that will cross the chasm. Instead she touches the glass with the tip of her tongue. And then she hears it, it is the child. At first not much more than a whisper and then a long, soft, 'aaaaaahhhh' growing in volume and in it she can hear a tear.

And it is getting louder, filling her own head to bursting and her throat with bile.

Michael is just behind her in the kitchen, making a herbal tea for her and brandy and hot chocolate for himself. He hears something that at first he struggles to identify: a low keening. He spins around as he realises its proximity and there on the stairs leading down to the kitchen is the girl, her back is turned towards him and she seems to be pressing her face into a photograph that is hanging there on the wall, at the same time letting go a long, mournful wail.

'Oh please, be careful.' As the cry reaches its crescendo, there is a sharp crack and she springs back from the photograph with a gasp. It is shattered from top to bottom.

'Oh no! What have you . . . For Christ's sake!' It is a photograph of special intimacy.

He wants to grab her by the hair and drag her from the stairs. He sees himself smash her face into the kitchen wall. Smash it! Smash it! Smash it! Smash some sense into her stupid, befuddled brain. Then she turns and blood is streaming from a cut in the middle of her forehead, at the very centre of the lipstick cross, through smudging and smearing it looks like it is ablaze.

'My God!' He sees himself wipe the blood from Dominic's face. 'Here, let me look at your head.' He whizzes round in the hot little kitchen, looking for something to clean the wound. Eventually he pulls a drawer completely off its runners so that it swings down and bashes him painfully on the shin and a pile of clean tea towels tumble to the floor. Wincing and hopping he chooses a white one with thick black lettering on it, which reads: '**If you can't stand the heat . . . fuck off.**' When he turns she is still standing in the same position, motionless, the stream of blood on her face untouched. There is a small triangle of glass sitting on the pale grey velveteen of her top, next to two perfectly circular spots of blood.

'Here, let me wipe your face. You have blood on your blouse.' He holds out his hand to help her down the last two steps. She takes it and steps down, never taking her eyes off his. He dabs carefully at the cut with the towel, inadvertently turning the cross into a smudgy-looking swastika.

'Oh my, what were you doing?' He spins round and runs the towel under the tap. 'I can't take my eyes off of you for five minutes.' He wipes away the already congealing blood and presses the wet towel onto the wound. Standing there for a moment, he feels a sudden rush of something. It is the same something he experienced in the taxi cab, a compulsion to wrap himself around her, to crush her into him to the point of consumption. He had felt this before but his mind bolted from the memories and anyway the black channels have all but obliterated the green of her eyes and he senses that this is not the moment, but that the moment will come, because he wants it to.

'Who are you?'

'Oooh, O.K., let's see . . . I'm . . . my name is Michael Spence. I'm thirty-six years old, I'm a photographer . . . eerrrrm . . .'

'A photographer of souls.' Her voice is low and contained. He lets out a soft ripple of nervous laughter and then holds her gaze for a moment; his eyes, a warm brown, smile.

'Photographer of souls . . .' he says slowly. 'I guess that's what I try to be, yeah . . . that's really neat. I should have that printed on my calling card, huh?' He removes the towel from her forehead. 'I'm going to get you a Band Aid for this, hold on.' He leaps the stairs, tossing the bloody towel onto the worktop.

She watches it for a moment, intrigued; crunched up and abandoned, a moist crimson stain shifting and creeping over the distorted lettering like a bloody amoeba. She takes in the little windowless room avoiding the wall by the stair. There is a door and on it a bright, dancing sign. Against a turbulent blue background, loud red letters proclaim, 'DAD'S DARK-ROOM!' She repeats it under her breath. 'Dad's dark room', and she watches the letters shimmer and wobble. Taking a quick step backwards, she stumbles over the drawer, still lying on the floor with its contents scattered, then losing her balance she crashes backwards into the worktop and lands on her bottom, amongst the tea towels. As she catches her breath she feels the black, oily beat of the wings within and a sickly feeling comes over her, causing her to clank her head back on the steel cupboard behind. It is then that she sees the towel, lying next to her outstretched leg on the pale, wooden floor and from its clean linen folds the words WATCH OUT scream their urgent warning in thick scarlet characters.

She stares as the words buzz and glow, and then flicks her eyes upwards to the poster, its letters wriggling and laughing. She closes her eyes tight and covers her ears and then she remembers something. It was under the towel, she can see it now in her mind's eye: a thin black line, running dead straight along the floor and turning left by her knee. With her eyes open a fraction, she stares down through the filter of her lashes and the image is confirmed. Drawing her knees up to her stomach, she throws them over to the right and watches the dark crevice run along and make another left-hand turn and come towards her. She pulls herself up, dragging several clattering items off the worktop and sees the crack disappear under the fallen drawer. Pulling the drawer out of the way, she can see the complete rectangle that has been cut into the warm blond wood; a brass ring-pull, inlaid to one side. And the drummer is back, his warning beat bringing bile into her throat again. The sudden unbearable heat in the tiny room dries her throat and burns her eyes.

She wheels round and dares to look at the photographs on the stairs, but they seem somehow distant and insignificant. She feels she can detect a stench seeping up from the floor, something rotten, rancid. She can see it rising up and distorting the air like heat on a motorway. She makes to grab the handle of the door, but the letters on the poster are giggling and squirming like small children in fat red babygrows. She hears a distant thud, somewhere above, and again she wheels round to face the stairs, but this time she skids on something hard and metallic. Then, regaining her balance, she peers down, the drummer reaching a bludgeoning crescendo. There on the floor is a large kitchen knife, its lethal point towards the stairs, its black, shiny handle half hidden under her right foot. As if the little black boot had flicked it out at will, a terrible and ingenious weapon. Over the insane drumming, she hears the muffled fall of feet on the floor above and snatches up the knife. Glancing at it only briefly, she plunges its impressive triangular blade into the side pocket of her skirt, and he is on the stairs.

'Alright, how ya doin'? I finally found a Band Aid.'

She is standing in the middle of the kitchen floor, surrounded by tea towels and cutlery. Like a poster for a horror film, her face is white and moist with sweat and in the middle of her forehead a globule of blood sits, poised to dribble from a burning swastika down the centre of her face. Her chest is heaving up and down, the glistening hollows in her neck sucked in and puffed out with every desperate breath. He grabs the damp towel and tends the wound.

'Whoo! you're perspiring. Let's get you upstairs, it's cooler up there. I can show you the bathroom and then we can get you settled for the night.' He takes her hand. It is icy and trembling and he has noticed that the small triangular piece of glass is no longer attached to the pale grey velveteen top.

'"The night" ... so this is finally it!' Her voice, high and breathless.

'Well there's not a lot of night left. It's ... er ... 5.45 a.m., but let's see if we can't get some shut-eye before it gets light.'

The drummer is beating a victory march and the great wings are steadying as the mighty talons take a painful hold of her gut. 'You've got me.' Her body is weakening, bubbling and choking on the writhing parasite within.

'Sure I've got you.' He gives her hand a squeeze. Oh, the assured note of sweet triumph in his voice. She falls to her knees, her legs elephantine sacks of useless blubber, refusing to carry her further; every cell of her body taking secret orders from

41

another voice. 'Hey ... don't give up now, we're nearly at the top.'

She grabs hold of the black corduroy leg. Then, from deep within her, the beak opens and lets out a savage roar, the likes of which her body can barely tolerate, but using its manic, alien energy she scrambles over Michael, hauling and grasping on elbows and knees to the top of the stairs and out into the long high room she had first entered on her arrival. She lies there; outstretched. For how long? Was it yesterday that she found the trapdoor? How long has she lain there, helpless? She can see herself, a huge, inflated thing, with tiny useless limbs, flapping, futile; a dull, heavy ache in her gut and bile in her mouth and something clutched in her right hand. It is a small navy-blue button on a jagged piece of thick green cloth. She stares at it, alarmed that she has no memory of it. She puts it to her nostrils and there again is the clean washing-powder smell from the handkerchief but mingled with that other essence. She rolls uncomfortably onto her back, disturbing the parasite within and causing vague waves of distant pain to drift up her abdomen.

Michael is sitting on the top step, right at her feet. He appears breathless, his eyes huge, his thick plaid shirt pulled open to the waist; underneath it he has on a white singlet which throws into relief the ragged space where the button had been.

'You are so clever.'

'Come on, we're both exhausted. Let's get you to bed.' As he helps her to her feet she tries to fit the little piece of torn material back into the shirt like a jigsaw puzzle.

'It's O.K. I can fix that.' He removes her hand.

'Can you?' Some of the green has returned to her eyes and her left hand is grabbing his arm in a bruising pinch.

'Hey, let go, it's O.K. Come on.' He leads her over to a long, deep sofa and pulling back a duvet he has placed there, sends up more of the trademark scent. She falls to her knees and buries her face in its blue striped cleanliness, touching its powdery dryness with her tongue.

'There, you can cosy down ... Do you need to use the bathroom? Well if you do, it's right over in the corner.' He's pointing to a door next to a spiral staircase which leads to a mezzanine floor above, but she does not look up, or even lift her head. 'I'll go fetch your herb tea.'

He passes the shattered photograph on the stairs and without looking at it slumps down on the penultimate step in the kitchen, elbows on knees, chin in hands; and fingers the two deep scratches on his cheek. He stares down at the mess of scattered cutlery and tea towels on the kitchen floor and for once he simply hasn't the will to clear it up, but wades through it to pick up the two mugs and stumps back up the stairs, passing the photograph without so much as a glance and thinking of nothing but his eyelids and the bliss of closing them.

She is asleep, all rolled up in the big puff of duvet, one heavy little boot poking out from underneath as if ready to repel unwanted bodies. He considers removing it, but something in the angle of its upturned heel stops him. She is facing away from him, just a few oily blond curls stick up between the pillow and the duvet, and he recognises the long drawn-in breaths then the heavy collapse of the ribcage as sleep born of exhaustion. He puts her tea down on the floor next to the sofa and squats on his heels to watch her, swaddled there in the great roll of air and feathers. The fine blue and white lines of the cover were his choice and his alone. He remembers the little thrill when buying it, knowing his wife would have walked past it in the store, for Elizabeth certainly would not have chosen it. She would consider it dull and functional. For a moment he tries to imagine Elizabeth's head on the pillow, the wilful auburn hair that she could do so little with, but somehow his mind's eye can't get it right: the little thatch of unclean, brittle curls refusing to disappear. He finds himself smiling at them and he leans forward and puts his nose amongst them. He can smell her, there is something other than the odour of her unwashed skin, something sweet; or maybe it isn't a scent but an instinct; or perhaps a confusion with another

43

body that had lain rolled in that same duvet, on that same sofa. Suddenly all there is is the stale, unsavoury smell of neglect, and he jerks his face away as if surprised. He stands and switches off the light.

'Goodnight,' he whispers and continues to stand there in the dark.

The Avalanche

❧

The landscape is confusing, he cannot tell where the mountain ends and the ravine begins. He hears the sound of speeding skis on perfect snow, but cannot see who it is that slides expertly by, spraying his face with powdered ice. The skier disappears into the whiteness; deleted, like a figure from a painting. He hears a sudden awful creak above his head and feels the ground beneath his feet vibrate. He turns to see the great white peak riven in two by a startling jagged crevasse, its two halves moving independently, like bad scenery in a school play. People are laughing; someone's hands are on his head, fingers are in his hair. He is lying down, an icy blast freezing his face and neck. She is a blurred image, darting, naked pink, in and out of vision. He knows the small high breasts and the fine square shoulders, the slippery cruelty of her laugh. She is carrying something and there is someone else present, he cannot make out who. Now the laughter is screeching and coarse. The familiar breasts are dancing in front of his face, the arms are lifted and all of a sudden his breathing is paralysed in one choking gasp and all is dark. He spits the snow from his mouth with one almighty gob.

'Oh! Jesus Christ!' Luke wipes the rough, icy mass of snow from his eyes and face with his sleeve. Now he is up from his bed, lurching blindly and thrashing about in the semi-darkness, his feet bedevilled by objects thrown in his path, his fingers outstretched, hoping for the touch of something he knows. He bangs his shin painfully and topples hard onto his knees, then he recognises the vague outline and dimensions of the coffee table, and realises that one hand has landed in the ashtray and the other in something wet. 'For Jesus' sake!' He scrambles back onto his feet and stands there, gangling and helpless.

'He looks like Mr Pastry!' An explosion of shrieks and titters and he can make out the hazy shape of Helena in the doorway to the bedroom. She is doubled up, still naked and breathless with laughter. As he stumbles back to the sofa to retrieve his glasses Helena lets out a high excited screech and disappears into the bedroom banging the door behind her. He hears a tiny, rodent-like squeak, and glasses in place he turns to see Cissie, lying on the other little fold-down bed, propped up on one elbow, with a corner of the duvet stuffed in her mouth. Her face is flushed full to bursting with an unexploded laugh. Luke sits and stares, his features dragged down by the weight of his misery. Cissie lets the duvet drop, and the laugh seeps away in a scatter of giggles.

'Snow's still here then?' He does not move, his body rigid with resentment, then with voice raised, 'Well thank you, Helena, and good bloody morning to you too. I hope you got *your* beauty sleep! We just happen to have been up most of the night looking for your potty friend. For whom you obviously have no concern whatsoever!' All this is addressed to the coffee table and with the large blue vein dividing his forehead in two. Then without waiting for a reply he swivels his legs up onto the sofa and turns a hard, angry back to the room.

'Oh Lukey . . . come on.'

He reaches out and drags the tangle of bedclothes right up around him, shielding his back from sly daggers and his head from further avalanche. They're the bedclothes from Maggie's bed. She had insisted on the faded peach bedspread with the lilac zigzags across it when Luke and the odd-looking porter from downstairs had brought up the beds, or cots as the porter had insisted on calling them. Maggie had stood there, mutely jabbing an aggressive forefinger at the bedspread. Cissie had grimaced at Maggie behind the porter's back, wanting to share the fun of his 'Lurch'-like appearance, but Maggie had retreated into the corner, an admonished child, isolated and confused and Cissie had wanted to slap her. Now she swallows down a tight small knot of sadness and is overtaken by one of panic and leaps from the bed.

The bedroom seems unusually bright. Helena is sitting on the end of the bed, amidst a freshly sprayed cloud of the mystery Chanel. She is vigorously lacing up a pair of knee-high sheepskin boots whilst a tinny radio scratches away from the bathroom floor with near-hysterical reports of airports closed until further notice, the city at a virtual standstill and more snow to come!

'You're an evil cow . . .' Cissie has closed the door and is leaning back against it, wearing her Minnie Mouse all-in-one pyjama suit.

'Good God, I didn't know they made those for adults.'

'They don't.'

'I take it Maggie has not graced us with her return? Fucking hell! I could ring her bloody neck!'

'Well for all we know somebody might already have done just that.'

'Oh no, no, no, no, not Maggie. Maggie the bloody cat? She'll have picked up some lonely zillionaire in some bar . . . by now he'll be besotted and she'll be in the process of breaking his heart and coming away with half his fortune . . . Jesus! I suppose we'd better ring the bloody plods.'

Luke can hear the echoey drone of their voices out on the landing, then the metallic clank of the lift door opening and now closing. It is safe to pull the covers from his head but somehow he can't, not yet. He listens in the darkness to his own breathing; long, soft breaths, deeply drawn, in and out, rhythmical, inevitable, and he can detect the faint whiff of something bitter. Helena had once referred to his breath as smelling like a 'horse's arse'. He had never really kissed her properly since and she had never asked him to. A year or so ago when a tornado of a row had ripped through a quiet Sunday morning he had confronted her with this remark, the insensitivity of it and its resulting pain and Helena couldn't remember having said it. This had enraged him, that she couldn't even remember the thing that had caused him such distress. Later, by way of an apology, she had said that anyway she adored horses. He exploded. 'Well I don't see you kissing their bottoms very often!'

'No! That would be too much like kissing you!' And so they were off again.

He brings his hand up in the warm damp space between his face and the sheet and tests his breath against it but there is nothing now. The illusive little stench has disappeared, saving itself for some vital moment where just one puff of its equine bouquet would destroy an intimacy in seconds. He remembers buying sprays and tablets to suck, and then one night, sprawled out on the prickly sofa, in the Lettice Street flat, he had confided in Maggie. What subsequently occurred was, for Luke, like visiting another country: distant, tropical; surrounded by warm, perilous seas and with an exciting but inexplicable culture and an unfathomable language. He had stayed in that place for just two weeks while Helena was filming in Dublin, waking up with a rude jolt to the icy London winter on her return. There is little evidence of the trip now, except for the odd brush of Maggie's big, rough hand and the occasional eye contact which pinned him to the memory and caused him to blush. He had considered telling Helena, throwing in her face the complete, unexpurgated version, in all its vivid detail; he had stood on many occasions before the long narrow mirror on the back of the wardrobe door spitting out the lurid details at his own reflection and thrilling at the thought of Helena's incredulous face. For once the clever, cynical babble stopped in its tracks, those hurtful, sneering eyes, themselves full of hurt and shock, the pout abandoned, hanging in disarray, agog: the word gobsmacked came to mind and was perfect. But he never did tell her because he was unsure of what had happened, of the nature of it; he preferred to keep it in a dark place that he could visit at his leisure; and anyway sometimes he was unsure whether anything had taken place at all.

He throws back the covers with some force, sweeping the ashtray off the coffee table, and swinging his legs down onto the floor he stubs his toe on the armchair. 'You bloody whore!' He stands there for a moment on one leg, clutching the toe and waiting for the pain to truly register, and when it does he lets out a long mournful howl of agony.

The Conundrum

The exhilaration in Dominic's eyes as he lay dying was at the forefront of Michael's head; even before he was properly awake and the image of the boy's delicate features, puffed and bloated beyond recognition, had brought him to the verge of tears. Most mornings he would wake in heavy confusion, uncertain of where he was and what he was to do. His feelings a dark conundrum, with which he himself had somehow conspired. The conundrum would gradually unfold during the first minute or so of wakefulness to reveal the thing that lay at its centre. This morning, however, there was no conundrum; the heavy pall of mourning was on him, defining him and his world, before he could even think or move: pinning him to the bed with its devastating weight. Now a further image of Dominic presents itself. He is lying on the big sofa ... the BIG SOFA! In one sickening jolt he is upright. Briefly he considers whether she had been part of a dream but before coming to any proper conclusion he is out of bed and into his study, peering over the wooden railing of its mezzanine floor, down into the space below. The duvet has been thrown back, frozen into a plump pile at the end of the big sofa and the girl is nowhere to be seen.

He listens for a moment; there is no sound, just the big, steady tick of his wall clock, a great circular specimen, with a plain face and a dark wood surround – a wedding present from his father ... 'don't waste my time' ... 'time is money' and 'time will tell'. He hurls himself down the small spiral staircase into the room, skids on something and lands with a soft thud onto the polished wooden floor. There, his outstretched hand detects something wet. What has she spilt? There is a cold sensation beneath his right hip and as he gets up he sees there is more of the stuff: what's more he has lain in it and his nightshirt is soaked.

'Oh Jesus ... Hello ...?' No answer; he stares at the dark, thick liquid, dripping stickily from his hand in the half-light and sniffs at it.

'... Oh no! ... Oh no!' Rushing at the bathroom door he finds it locked. He hammers on it with the sides of his clenched fists, so as not to get more of the stuff on its newly painted surface.

'Hello ...? Can you open up please?' He listens, his ear and cheek squashed against the door, the smell of fresh paint pricking his nostrils. There is a distant, thudding sound which he quickly realises is his heart, and there is the familiar laboured wheezing beginning to build in his chest, but otherwise there is a silence which causes him to swallow hard. He scurries across the room to the two huge windows that stretch from floor ceiling. Then wiping his hands on the front of his nightshirt he drags back the heavy curtains.

A shocking screen of brilliant white blinds him for a second or two and sends a stab of pain into each eye. He had forgotten about the snow and he is mesmerised for a moment by the unfamiliar magic of the scene. The view that greets him every morning totally transformed, nothing left untouched, the tiniest branch on the tree delicately balancing an inch and a half of snow. There is a child in a bright red ski suit, vivid against the white, pulling a smaller child along on a sledge in the middle of the street. They are squealing and laughing. A perfect snap for a Christmas card; and tucked around them is a great wad of silence, no drone of cars and taxis, no clanging of trucks as they find the massive and unnegotiable pothole on the other side of the street. Silence; they could be the last three people on the planet; the two children and himself; the only survivors of some mystery holocaust.

He wheels round on the spot like a dancer, and there is an audible creak from his lungs as he takes in the huge crimson stain covering the seat cushion where the girl had slept. Then down on the pale cotton rug a great red-brown patch, still moist. He stares at it for a moment and sees a map of North America. Leading off from it a messy series of puddles and splodges make their way around the sofa along the wooden floor to the bathroom door.

'Jesus!' He can barely squeeze enough air from his lungs to say the word. He scuttles around the other side of the sofa in order to avoid the bloody trail and heads for the bathroom. Changing direction almost immediately his feet find the cool silk of the Afghan rug and he wonders briefly whether he should check it for spots or stains, then landing on the safe solidity of the wooden floor he shoots down the stairs to the kitchen. There, his eyes take a moment or two to accustom themselves to the relative gloom of the electric light as he clatters through the spilled cutlery and towels of the previous night and grabs the small blue container lying on its side at the edge of the worktop. Two long, desperate drags from its thin silver stem, followed within seconds by the ecstasy of normal breathing, and he is back up the stairs two at a time clutching his inhaler like a weapon. At the top he stops for a moment, suspended somewhere out of reality, and coolly considers that this may be nothing more than a nightmare, an aberration born out of grief. He surveys the room for a moment and waits: waits for the true nature of things to emerge, but instead the scene becomes more blatant and vivid: he feels he can smell her blood: animal-sweet; and vomit lurches into his throat, burning his tonsils before returning to his stomach.

'Oh Jesus, come on, man! Hello ...? ... Please ... are you O.K.?' He is back at the bathroom door and again, straining to hear the slightest sound but his ears are filled with nothing but the panicked beat of his heart and the strangled squeaks of his lungs. Again he tries to open the door, and applying some pressure finds that it isn't locked but that something is against it, preventing it from opening. He pushes harder using his shoulder and opens it several inches, then wedging his body between the door and the wall he can see her.

'Oh my sweet Jesus! ... Hello? ...' She is lying on her back, her head rammed up against the toilet bowl, one knee pushed back by the door and lolling against the shower cubicle, the other splayed the opposite way, leaning nonchalantly against the wall. The little black boot toe to toe with his bare foot. It could be a wanton pose, a centrefold with beckoning eyes, but the eyes are shut and the smell is of death. Great bloody handprints smudge and slide their way around the walls, the toilet is full of blood and spattered to the rim as if it has poured out from a great height, and the floor is awash. She is completely still, a stillness he recognises; her face white and shiny.

'Oh no ... Oh no ... Oh God ... please no!' He pushes the door further, and by lifting her leg opens it fully. As he crouches down beside her he notices that one sock is almost completely blood-soaked, whilst the other is untouched. He tries for a pulse. Her wrist is cold and clammy and her hand hangs stiffly over like a chicken's claw. No pulse. Nothing. Not a hint of the buzzing insanity of the night before. Empty. She looks like someone else, he cannot think who.

'Hello ... it's me, Michael ... please, please wake up ...' He is rubbing her cheek with the backs of his fingers and he sees that they are shaking, that he is shaking, a steady whirr of vibrations throughout his body.

'Oh Jesus ... come on ...' he races to the phone and dials 911. Somebody answers, a woman's voice, saying something.

'... there is a girl dead in my bathroom!!!' He is fascinated for a moment by the sound of his own voice, frightened, high and childlike and he scans the room for his inhaler. The woman is talking again.

'Sir? Can you tell me where you are?' The voice is small and remote.

'I'm downstairs by the phone ... she must have killed herself ...'

'O.K., now try and stay calm. Can you give me your address?'

'There's blood everywhere ... she can't have any left in her.' His voice having risen slowly in pitch explodes into a huge falsetto sob and he feels himself holding Dominic's freshly washed body, the smell of the sandalwood soap, the cold touch of his cheek.

'O.K. Sir ... What is your name?'

'Michael Spence ... I'm in Tribeca, Collister Street, number fourteen, apartment 2a ... Please, please, please come ... somebody ... please.'

'There is an ambulance coming to you now, Michael. You say there is a dead girl there? Are you sure she's dead?'

'Oh yes, there is no life left in her ...'

'Have you checked for a pulse, Michael?'

'Yes, she is cold and covered in blood.'

'Where is she, Michael?'

'She's ... she's ...' Another huge sob is blocking his throat.

'Take a couple of deep, deep breaths. That's good. Now, I think you said before that she was in the bathroom. Is that close by?'

'Yes, it's the downstairs bathroom.'

'Now, Michael, I want you to do something for me. Would you cover her with a blanket? Not her face, Michael. Now don't hang up, just go and cover her with something warm, a towel even. Will you do that?' He runs skidding through the blood to the bathroom and stretching around the door he pulls the big grey bath sheet off the hook and lays it carefully over her, tucking it in around her, a child being prepared for her bedtime story. He stands up and stares down at her, and says under his breath, 'Who are you?' And then, a sudden surge of anger in his chest, 'Why have you done this?' He stamps his foot and sees that his feet are covered with wet and encrusted blood.

He doesn't know how long he has been staring down at his feet or where his mind has been, but he knows that Dominic is near, he can hear his footsteps in the study above, his voice upon the stairs, the squeak of his hand on the hand rail.

'Dominic?' It is almost a whisper. He can hear his laugh, light and unfettered.

'Oh my darling ...' He can smell him, that sweet smell that seemed to be concentrated just below his ear, the smell that has kept Michael out of the little bedroom for months. Now the boy's breath is on his cheek, his sturdy arms hanging on around his neck. Michael can feel the weight of him on his back. He is whispering and giggling in his ear.

'Dominic ... what? What are you saying?' The weight is lessening.

'Just let me hold you.' The weight has gone.

'Wait!' He can hear the little voice urgently whispering on the stairs and he scrambles from the bathroom to the foot of the spiral staircase. Then there is a banging on the door which batters shockingly through his chest. He whips around – the whispers are still on the stairs and fading.

'No ... Dominic ... please ... come back!' The battering is more insistent.

'FUCK YOU!' He rushes to the door and opens it.

'Michael Spence?'

A small navy-blue posse files past him and scatters into the room, bringing with it icy wafts of freezing New York air, mingled with alien aftershaves and fried food. Their shoes squeak on the wooden floor and their heavy tread causes the boards to vibrate. Michael has an urge to cover his balls, which he half does with a hovering hand; with the other one he points.

'She's ...' Two of the posse, a squat, sweating man with a huge gut and a diminutive Hispanic-looking girl, walk with what seems like little urgency towards the bathroom.

'What happened here, sir?' Michael turns and catches sight of his own reflection in the long mirror by the door. He stares at the bent figure, the huge, cavernous eyes, staring back from the milk-white face, its cheeks blotched with congealed blood, like misapplied make-up; the dark unbrushed curls standing up on top of his head. A cartoon of a frightened man: Macbeth, the comedy. He cannot decide between anger or laughter.

'Oh ... I'm sorry what did you say?' The other half of the little posse is standing by the big sofa.

'I said, what happened here, sir?' This from a tall red-haired man. Another man is sauntering to the top of the kitchen stairs and is now peering down into the kitchen. They are police officers.

'You are ... you are police officers.' The words hiss and wheeze through his teeth.

'That's right. I'm Officer Crowley and this is Officer Boyle. Are you alright, sir?'

'... I just need my inhaler.'

'Is this what you're looking for?' Officer Crowley picks up the little blue canister from the arm of the sofa and hands it to him with long, delicate fingers.

'Sir?' It is the young woman calling from the bathroom. 'What is her name, sir?'

'Her ... n ...' He stares at Officer Crowley, as if somewhere in the pale, freckled face the girl's name will be written. Officer Crowley's face is a blank. Michael looks back to the woman.

'Her name?' She repeats her question with insistence and he can detect something else in its tone. The black eyes look coolly back at him, unwavering in their certainty of something.

'No ... I know what this ... it's not what ... it's not ... HELENA! ... is ... is ... is her name.' He looks around at the two policemen and then back at the woman, an idiot grin of relief on his face. Now he can hear the big, sweating man talking to 'Helena', softly calling her name.

'Is she alive?! My sweet Jesus. Is she alive?' The woman stands between him and the bathroom, feet apart, challenging, protective.

'She's hanging on in there. Is she pregnant? Do you know?'

'Oh . . . look . . . I . . .'

'Are you her boyfriend?'

'No . . . no! I har . . .'

'Is she pregnant?' Again the tone is of judgemental insistence. Michael wants to slap the tiny woman's face.

'Look! . . . I . . . I have no idea. I just met her last night . . . I gave her a bed for the night. I . . . I found her like this . . . this morning . . . I've no idea what has happened here.'

'Did you have intercourse with her, sir? We need to know, it's important.'

'Jesus no no . . . I didn't touch her . . . NO. Listen she was . . . she was disturbed . . . I felt sorry for her.'

'O.K., sir. You didn't have a fight?'

'No! . . .' From the corner of his eye Michael can see Officer Boyle's stocky figure hovering near the little bedroom. His hand is on the handle.

'Don't even think about it.' A thrill of anger surges through his body, and he knows beyond doubt that should Officer Boyle's hand drag that handle down, something will explode from him, a dark thing, the nature of which he is fearfully uncertain. 'I don't want your fucking big boots in there.' He can feel it now rising like milk in a pan. 'I don't want your smell in there.'

Officer Boyle removes his hand from the handle.

'I don't want you in there!'

Officer Boyle raises his hands, a placatory gesture, but Michael is sure he can see a sneer of insolence drift across his face.

'And I don't want your stupid smirk in there!'

'O.K., Michael, simmer down. He's not going in there.' It is the soft voice of Officer Crowley and something in its softness triggers a spasm of grief in Michael's throat. He lets out a little yelp of sorrow, followed by a series of silent, shaking sobs.

'Come on, come and sit down, we'll get you a coffee.' Officer Crowley is steering him towards the other sofa.

'O.K. let's move it. Is she on any medication, sir?' The

paramedics are coming from the bathroom with the girl on the stretcher. Michael spins round.

'Oh Jesus . . . I don't know. I know nothing about her . . . she was very disturbed . . . is she going to be alright? . . . Where are you taking her?' He avoids the young woman's gaze and addresses the man.

'We're taking her to Bellevue. She's lost a lot of blood. They'll need to find out what's going on inside.' His breath is rank with stale coffee and cigarettes and his face is red and shiny with a rivulet of sweat running down his temple. The woman is saying something to Officer Crowley in a low voice.

'. . . But . . . I'll need to come with her . . . she's English . . . she . . . she won't know where she is.'

Officer Crowley is now right behind him. 'We'll give you a ride down there later.' The woman then speaks in a tired voice, without bothering to turn round. 'They'll take good care of her. We got to get through this snow.'

They are already out of the door and into the covered passage at the side of the building. Great soft drifts of snow have snaked their way along the walls, blown in by the Arctic blasts that always seem to find refuge there. The ambulance, lights still flashing, is virtually on the sidewalk and the two children with the sledge are standing watching as they load the stretcher on. As Michael goes to close the door, he hears the bigger child say, 'Is she dead? Did that man kill her?'

The Form

❧

'She's completely deranged, Lieutenant, and what's worse, she's a very beautiful girl. My blood runs cold at the thought of the kind of attention she might have attracted.'

Cissie watches Helena's profile. Every time she stops speaking, she pushes her lips into a rosebud pout, moistening them occasionally with the tip of her tongue. She is leaning her elbows on the heavy oak counter and now she is lifting her heel behind her and leaving it to dangle there like a fifties starlet being kissed in a comedy.

Lieutenant Lorenzetti's steady gaze has not wavered, apart, that is, from a momentary shift, every now and again, when his eyes flick down to the moist cupid's bow; and despite her answering several of his questions, he has never once, not even for a second, turned the sparkling gaze onto Cissie. She considers that in some animal way he can smell her sexuality and has therefore mentally erased her from his presence. If he was asked to describe her later, he would be unable to. All he would have in his memory, would be a small, dark, blurred female. Whereas he would have a photographic memory of Helena's face: the sweep of her eyebrow, the line of her mouth. Cissie makes a decision to disengage from the encounter and half turns her back on them.

Sitting in the corner, handcuffed to a radiator, is a young black man. He is wearing a dark-grey, expensive-looking suit with a pair of new white trainers. His head is bowed and he is tapping his foot and humming tunelessly to some private melody. Next to him is an open door through which a huge black woman can be seen at a desk. She is taking down details from a tall, scrawny-looking woman, with long, badly bleached hair, whilst a tiny mixed-race child bashes a plastic hammer on the floor at the tall woman's feet; its face flushed with the heat of the precinct after the cold of the street; a snail's trail of snot leading from nose to mouth.

Cissie regards the woman's back, the gathered hunch of her shoulders as she towers over the black woman and her desk. She sees her mother's back at the kitchen sink, long and thin, the outline of her shoulderblades clearly visible through the blue nylon overall she always wore for housework. She feels the little knot of apprehension in her chest that she always felt on entering the kitchen each morning. The lie of those shoulders was the barometer by which the emotional outlook of the day could be judged. The higher they were, the more you kept out of her way. Cissie sees that the child has stopped hammering, and having wedged the thing into its mouth is sitting staring out of the room at her. Its ink-black eyes are huge with amazement, as if she had just appeared from thin air. Then the woman turns, bends down and expertly swings the child up onto her hip, whereupon it bashes her abruptly on the cheek with the hammer. She roughly grabs the hammer from its tiny fist and shouts into the little brown face.

'Fuckin' quit! This is goin' in the garbage! I've had it wit you!'

The little face explodes into sobs of purple anger, and Cissie wants to grab the hammer off the woman and ram it down her throat. She is on the verge of saying something, she doesn't know what, but as the woman storms past she beats her to it.

'You got a problem, lady?' Cissie opens her mouth and nods and then shakes her head at the same time, anything she might have said having been scrambled into a mush of useless verbiage by the woman's simple vitriolic question. She finds herself still nodding as the precinct door slams shut.

'Nice!' It is Lieutenant Lorenzetti. He is nodding, one eyebrow raised in irony. He has clear grey eyes and white teeth made brilliant by the olive colour of his skin. 'We get a nice class of person in here. This is how I got this. Dealing with these people.' He is pointing a forefinger, its nail scrubbed white, at the neat thatch of prematurely grey hair on top of his head. Another younger officer with a round cabbage-patch face is now hovering beside him and joins him in comradely laughter. He warms to his theme.

'Yeah, all this was jet-black before I came here.' More laughter. Cissie is irritated by him, his swaggering masculinity and his deluded attempt at comedy.

'Oh my aching sides!' She mutters this half under her breath and Helena flashes her a warning glance, at the same time kicking her with the side of her foot. Now Lieutenant Lorenzetti is ushering them towards the complaints room, where the large black woman will fill out a missing person's form. He tells the young officer to fetch another chair so that both 'ladies' can sit down. As they wait for her to start her questioning, Cissie hears the men talking in low voices and laughing; dirty male sniggers. She swivels round in her chair to shoot them a withering look, but their backs are turned. Meanwhile Helena crosses her legs and relaxes her pout. The black woman speaks, loud and mechanical.

'Name?'

'Helena Cassidy.'

'Middle initial?'

'None.'

'Address here in New York?'

'I'm staying at the Elmscote Hotel, West . . .'

'Not you, the missin' person. You ain't missin' are you?' And the black woman bounces with laughter in her chair.

'We know where you are . . . You are right here and staying at the Elmscote Hotel.' A torrent of little high-pitched screeches reverberate through her Michelin frame.

Helena sits high in her chair and reins in her full mouth to a flat straight line. Then, in a quiet, measured voice, 'The address is the same, no middle initial to speak of, and the name is Maggie Salt. Maggie as in Margaret and Salt as in the condiment.'

'Salt?' The woman sounds as if she is offering it at the dinner table. 'Is that an English name?'

Helena stares at her for a moment. 'It most certainly is.'

The black woman repeats it quietly as she writes it on the form, 'Maggie Salt.'

The Discovery

❦

'Helen Cake.' Luke's voice is soft with nostalgia. Helen Cake, wearing a blue- and white-striped bikini, is lying on the ground, partly sprawled over the legs of another girl, a girl he cannot quite put a name to. Huddled close behind them are several young men in swimming trunks, jostling and grimacing. It is to the one on the end, the one with the pale torso and puzzled smile, that his attention is now drawn. The young man's hair is bleached by the sun and he is squinting.

'Why aren't you wearing your glasses ... you soft berk?' His attention returns to Helen Cake.

'Come back, Helen Cake.'

Helen Cake has had sexual encounters with all of the young men, all six of them, but at this time she only has eyes for the gangly boy on the end who cannot see.

'Oh you poor bastard.' Luke brings the tattered photo up to within an inch of his face and removes his glasses. He beams the searchlight eye across each and every face, letting out little sighs of loss. Then it lands on Helen Cake and he does not breathe at all for several seconds. Then letting the photo drop he takes in a deep, faltering breath as if he were about to sob, and lets out a tiny moan on a long, long sigh. He returns the eye to the photo and focuses it again on the boy with the unseeing eyes. It was a photograph he had always adored, thinking himself to be attractive in it, almost handsome. He studies the details of the tiny image, searching for signs of his sexuality, of his appeal; but all he can see is a child standing there, with a group of men; a lost child, a blind child, a great, big, awkward, sexless kid.

'You poor, poor little fucker.' All he sees in the image of his twenty-year-old self is unutterable pain. The others in the photograph are adult, amused and tolerant of him. Except, that is, for Helen Cake. Helen Cake connected somewhere, somewhere dark. They shared a special darkness. She sought him out. In fact, looking back to that time, finding that connection with Helen Cake was like finding another child to play with at a grown-up party. But Helen Cake is no more. With a flash of panic he considers that Helena is an entirely different person – an interloper, a cuckoo, an intruder; that when she changed her name she got rid of more than a surname; by adding that A she had got rid of an innocence. She had destroyed Helen Cake, his intimate, his first love, and now there is Helena Cassidy. Helena Cassidy is like a long-lost sister, brought up by a different family on the other side of the world. Yes, the early years had formed a bond, but in essence she was little more than a stranger. A grown-up; long gone. A speck on the edge of the desert, it was no good shouting: she simply couldn't hear.

Luke sinks back onto the pillows of the unmade bed amidst a cloud of Helena's perfume. He sniffs at it, twitching his nose like a rodent, trying to identify her under its heavy sweetness. He cannot, and the perfume is unfamiliar, it had always been a fresh, uplifting scent, designed for men, the same one she had used for years, the one he had bought her for birthdays and Christmas, but this was much more heady and earthy. It put him in mind of ripe Italian women, olive-skinned, with disturbing cleavages and a display of heavy gold jewellery. He didn't care for it at all. It put him in mind of his mother. He brings the photograph up for one last glimpse and with his other hand he finds his penis.

He had not intended looking in the drawer of her little beside cabinet, but on his way to the bathroom he had noticed that it was open. He had stood for some time staring at it. Then he had ventured forward and hovered over it, holding his hands up out of the way, lest they should touch. To one side, next to a biro and a bottle of what was more than likely sleeping pills, was a corner of the photograph. It was upside down and he could just see a man's head and most of his torso. He had become almost light-headed at the thought of some kind of discovery, at finding some irrefutable truth, at pinning it to the deck, wriggling and writhing, a stake straight through its centre. His hand had been shaking as it carefully lifted the photograph out of the drawer. He stared at it for some time, his heart leaping in his chest, before he could really see the faces, then he had slumped down onto the bed in a deflated heap. He had felt like crying, but somehow the tears wouldn't come. Now they are coming in torrents and collecting in a tiny pool at the base of his neck. His right hand is now hanging, discarded, over the edge of the bed. His other hand still holds the photograph. He sits up slowly and places it in the middle of Helena's pillow.

The Butcher

𝒫𝒶

M ichael is bewildered by the pain in his left hand, before he realises he is burning it on his mug of coffee. He transfers it roughly into the other hand and burning that one he bashes the mug down onto the glass coffee table, scalding himself in the process. The steaming brown liquid having splashed over his knees and hands then glides swiftly over the shiny surface to find Officer Crowley's black leather gloves, whereupon some of it settles comfortably into the fleecy white lining of one of them, while the rest rushes over the edge of the table; a steaming cataract cascading onto the wooden floor and splattering Officer Crowley's highly polished shoes.

'Arrrgh! Oh I'm so sorry . . .' Michael is on his feet trying to pull the burning trousers away from his legs. Officer Crowley's long fingers delicately fish the gloves out of the runaway coffee and he too is on his feet.

'No problem.' He is holding the gloves over the coffee table to allow the coffee to drip off the leather and splash into a little lake that has formed there.

'I'll get a cloth.' It is Officer Boyle, who has been loitering by the outside door and glancing at books in the bookcase there. Michael had noticed him doing this and had laughed cynically inside his head at the thought of Officer Boyle sitting down to enjoy Bertrand Russell's *History of Western Philosophy*.

'Do you need to change your pants?' Officer Crowley's voice

couldn't be kinder, a father dealing with his three-year-old's potty training.

'No ... no ... thank you ... I think I'm fine ... thank you.' Michael slumps back down onto the small sofa with a twinge of anger and stares at the pink scald on the back of his hand. Then he notices that, despite washing his hands and a careful inspection, there is a tiny speck of the girl's blood lodged at the edge of his nail. He marvels that it has managed to stay there and has an urge to lick it off.

'Do you need something for that?' It is Officer Crowley, still dangling his gloves over the coffee table, and now Officer Boyle is back mopping around his feet with loop upon loop of kitchen roll.

'Pardon me?'

'You burnt your hand with the coffee. Do you need something for it?'

Michael puts his head in his hands. 'No ... I just need to drink my coffee.'

'Sure.' Officer Crowley sinks back down into the old leather armchair, causing it to creak comfortingly. Michael adores the sound and smell of this chair. It was a present from Elizabeth for his thirtieth birthday and he had loved it on sight. She had found it in an antique shop whilst visiting her sister in England and had had it shipped home. It had apparently come from a gentleman's club and did indeed smell faintly of cigars. Officer Crowley should have looked at odds with the chair, but somehow it suited him. Even the dark blue of his uniform and the red of his hair looked well against the faded blue-green of its leather and Michael is surprised to find that he doesn't mind him sitting there; in fact the opposite is true. The sight of the big, soft, lumpen form trapped within the squeaking confines of this old armchair is rather comforting.

Many a night he, Michael, had sat in it in the dark small hours cradling Dominic's thin little body. It was in this chair that they had first talked of death. Michael had been taken aback by the boy's pragmatism: what would happen to his stick insects? His Superman outfit was to go to his cousin, Dorian, but he would take Geoffrey, his beloved toy rabbit and Lucien, his toy mouse with him. Daddy was to see that they both went through the washing machine before the day came.

Michael looks across at the chair with its worn discoloured arms and his chest fills up with sorrow. He needs to take a deep breath to blow it away, but his lungs refuse to let him and so his eyes fill with tears.

'Kevan, will you make another cup of coffee for Michael? I don't think you have a lot left in your cup there.'

Michael is beginning to be slightly irritated by Officer Crowley's easy concern.

'Can you just ask me what you want to ask me and then perhaps we could go to the hospital?'

'Sure. O.K. So ... well all we have is her name is Helena Cassidy ...'

Michael had not shown them the envelope with her name and address on. Without stopping to think, he had slipped it between two books in the bookcase and had watched the prowling Officer Boyle like a hawk whenever he went near. Officer Crowley continues his summary of the facts whilst taking tiny sips at his coffee.

'She may be English and she may or may not be on medication of some description. Leastways she was confused you say.' Michael releases a tired sigh.

'Yes.' He looks around for his inhaler.

'And you say you met for the first time last night in a bar you think is on Madison and 59th, but you can't be certain?'

'Yes ... no ... yes, that's, that's right.' He is staring down again at the speck of dried blood on his cuticle and he remembers that he left his inhaler in the upstairs bathroom.

'Tell me again how you got the scratches on your face.' A fresh cup of coffee is placed down in front of him by the thick stubby hand of Officer Boyle. It is in a white mug with the motto 'I'm

68

a sick bastard' emblazoned on it in thick black lettering.

Michael stares at it for a moment and then up at Officer Boyle who is now leaning loutishly against the bookcase. Michael is sure he can detect that same sneer crawling across his face. He suddenly feels utterly drained and goes to take a sip of his fresh coffee. His lips are instantly stung by the blistering heat of the mug, and he flings it away from himself with a yell, sending at least half of the stuff flying through the air in the direction of Officer Crowley. Officer Crowley leaps out of the chair, but not before being hit full in the chest by the burning liquid. In trying to back away he topples back down into the chair.

'Well you got me this time.'

'Whoa . . . here we go again.' Officer Boyle scurries down the kitchen stairs and Michael can hear him chuckling below and clanking about on the spilled cutlery as he no doubt locates fresh kitchen roll.

'Oh Jesus, I am so sorry . . . look I can't take much more of this . . . and I really don't care for that officer's attitude . . . I know what you're thinking . . . I have done nothing wrong . . . she tried to get out of a moving cab and when I tried to stop her she went berserk.' Officer Boyle is back with more paper and Officer Crowley is wiping spatters of coffee off his face.

'O.K., Michael, we won't keep you much longer . . .'

'I can even remember the name of the cab driver . . . Madeleine Court! She had to help me restrain her.'

'O.K., Michael, that's good. If we need to we may contact her.'

'But see, there's somethin' here we need to clear up.' This is Officer Boyle's deep monotonous voice. He is again mopping, this time around Officer Crowley's feet. 'What's the big kitchen knife doin' on the bathroom floor?' Officer Boyle's small dark eyes are verging on a smile. Michael's chest tightens further.

'What?'

'The big kitchen knife?' Officer Boyle stands up, allowing the kitchen roll to drip coffee onto his shoes.

'What kitchen knife ... I don't know what you're talking about.'

'Right where the girl was layin' ...'

'Kevan ... your shoes.' Officer Crowley indicates the dripping paper and gets up.

'Let me just show you, Michael.' Having one last dab at the front of his uniform, he shoves his piece of saturated kitchen roll at Officer Boyle and taking his time walks over to the bathroom. He stands in the doorway looking down, waiting for Michael to join him. Michael cannot move just yet. He stands for a moment feeling slightly nauseous and listens to the restricted creaking and whistling of his lungs. He looks at Officer Crowley's big broad back. He wants this man to believe him. More than that, he wants his respect.

'Michael ...?' Michael walks over without a word, a child about to be punished. His body feels heavy and invaded, his head sick and aching; he needs his inhaler. 'There, you see? Next to the toilet.' Once again he is sure he can smell her blood, sweet and metallic. He had expected the scene to be easier to deal with now that the girl had been removed, but somehow it is worse without her. There is a greater air of violence, of some untold butchery. He feels the coffee bubble in his stomach, preparing to launch itself up into his throat.

'Where did the knife come from, Michael?'

'The kni—?' He sees it, the huge triangular blade pointing towards him, its sheen dulled by smears of dark congealed blood. The coffee is at the back of his throat for an instant, burning and bitter. 'I have to get my inhaler.' The words are squeezed out on the thinnest of breaths.

'Sure.'

The air in the upstairs bathroom is stifling and oppressive, parching his throat, and the pinkish glow of the lights, normally cosy and kind, stabs painfully at his eyes. He has the sick, heavy headache he always gets from over-use of his inhaler and after two more desperate puffs he looks in the tiny bathroom cabinet for painkillers. As he turns to the basin for water, something on the floor catches his eye: it is the small, jagged piece of cloth that the girl had ripped from his favourite plaid shirt. He bends down to pick it up and the floor comes whizzing up to meet him. He steadies himself just in time to stop himself from toppling headlong into the wall, when the room gives another sickening lurch, causing him to stumble backwards and sit involuntarily on the toilet seat. He sits there for a moment and waits for the dizziness to settle.

'Oh God help me ... oh God help me.' For a moment he wishes Elizabeth were there, to put her cool hand on his brow and speak softly, but of course she would be appalled at his actions: picking up some strange, mad creature in some low bar, bringing her to his loft and then ... The nausea returns.

He turns towards the basin and in doing so catches sight of himself in the mirror above. He is touched by the image, the white, white face, his eyes great black orbs, their pupils stretched and immobilised by the terror of what they had witnessed. Then he stands and moves closer, for something else has drawn him in to the reflection. It is something in the eyes. He moves still closer to the glass and peers into them and there in the darkness at the centre of each eye he can see him! A sudden chill of anxiety causes his dry throat to crack into a painful swallow. He stares again into the endless blackness and now there is no mistaking him. The audacity of this fellow! The sheer nothing-to-lose brass nerve of the guy: he doesn't even feel the need for disguise! But then again why should he? All is out. He will never retreat into the shadows again. He has been set free like a genie from a bottle. Officer Boyle had engaged with him at first glance and now there he is, glorying in this recognition.

'Oh my God help me!'

'Michael?' It is the voice of Officer Crowley from the foot of the stairs, refined and tender, almost womanly. The voice of a man who would never see such an image in his mirror, who could never be party to such a thing as has happened here. Officer

Crowley could no more lift a knife against his fellow man than he could upon his own throat. Boyle of course is a different matter, it is easy to picture this brute of a man in some squalid dive, vicious and threatening, brawling over some whore. Yes, Boyle is a very different kettle of fish; Boyle knows the culprit!

'We have spoken with the hospital, Michael. Could you come downstairs please? We need to talk.'

Michael carefully places a hand over each eye. 'Mea culpa, mea culpa, mea maxima culpa.'

The Imprint

֍

'So, Cissie; how's the love of your life?'

'Oh, I'm very well thanks.' Cissie feels a small sting of pain in her right thumb and brings it out of her pocket to examine it. The tiny wound caused by the broken plastic whistle the night before is bright and angry. She sticks the thumb into her mouth and sucks at it, bringing an instant picture of Jenny into her mind's eye: Jenny sitting perched on the worktop at home has her forefinger doubled up and propped between her top and bottom teeth, something she does when she is bewildered. Cissie takes a deep breath in and drops her head into her hands.

'Oh, I take it we shouldn't be anticipating wedding bells then? ... The patter of tiny feet?' Helena is carefully rubbing moisturiser into her face, stopping every so often to examine her features at close range, widening her eyes and pouting her lips, tilting her head this way and that. She has the thick dark mane of hair scraped back and protected by a wide satin band. Above her reflection, written in emphatic red lipstick, is 'G.H. TUES 6 P.M.!', followed by a perfect imprint of what must be Helena's lips. 'What you have to do is get a nice, intelligent, good-looking young man, who is willing to pop a few sperms into a jiffy bag, borrow your mother's turkey baster and hey presto! you could have your very own nuclear family by next Christmas.'

'What if she's dead?'

'Well, you'll have to buy your own turkey baster.'

'Helena . . .'

'Cissie . . . We have spent the morning in the bloody police station! You and Luke have been up all night looking for the cow! This may seem harsh to you but there is nothing more we can do! And I for one refuse to give her any more of my rather precious time, thank you very much. At least for today. I've got a bloody show to do for Christ's sake . . . As soon as she stops being the centre of attention in whatever situation she may have got herself into, and just when she thinks we might have given up and stopped worrying about her, she'll be back. You see if she's not.' Helena seems to have said this all on one breath and her face has gone quite red.

'Yes . . . I know . . . I know . . . part of me just wants to bugger off home and leave her to it. I'm so fed up of fretting over Maggie . . . I've had a real basinful this last couple of weeks.'

'Well then don't. Don't fret. Don't fret, pet! This is where it stops.' Helena turns round in her chair, her face bare and shiny from the cream. 'Has it ever occurred to you that she may pick her time for these bouts of insanity? . . . Well, take this present "crack-up" for instance. I think it's no coincidence that it has happened at a time when we are both riding high. I've just won a Tony; you're, to quote the tabloid press, "the nation's darling", with your telly series, while La Salt's career is, let's face it, looking decidedly jaded in comparison.'

Helena draws one foot up onto the chair while a floppy pink sock slides down the long slim calf. Cissie looks over at her and feels her own face stretch wide into a great toothy grin, and as if tickled by some invisible stranger she collapses back onto the divan with a bounce, a deep scratchy giggle bubbling away in her throat. She continues to bob up and down for several seconds, the springs of the old bed striking up a tinny spasmodic tune as they reluctantly adjust themselves to the weight of her body. She can hear Helena talking but she is no longer listening, her eyes are fixed in a trance born out of exhaustion. They are set on a huge pipe that makes its way, solid and straight, along the wall, just above the skirting board; the smell of its hot paint heavy in the air, mingling with that of dust, dried and scorched, collected year upon year, in dark, impossible to get at corners, it blends roughly with the perfumes of heavy cosmetics and intimate sprays concocting a heady mix that is both cloying and seductive, and in turn competing with freshly washed costumes and the musty damp smell of neglected tatty furnishings, upon which decades of actors had laid and fretted over lines and moves and the next job. Cissie dislikes other people's dressing rooms; they make her feel uncomfortable, like getting fully clothed into someone else's warm unmade bed.

'. . . going to let her piss on my parade . . . thank you very much.' Helena has turned back to the mirror and is applying a pale foundation to her face and neck with a small triangular sponge. It has the effect of blotting out the shadows and lines of her features as if wiping them clean to start again. It leaves her face looking peculiarly lifeless.

'Blimey! What do they call that colour? . . . "Near-Death Beige"?' Helena snorts at this and lights a cigarette. 'That's better.' She twinkles at Cissie in the mirror.

Then with a terrible squeak the dressing-room door is flung open causing Helena's 'Good Luck' cards to flutter and flap from their blue-tacked positions on the wall above her dressing table.

'Flowers for you, Miss Blanche . . . oh *my*! Ah am soooo excited! Do you think they could be from the master, Miss Blanche? A dozen red roses! It's just too romantic! Oh my little old heart is just going pitter pat!' A tall reed of a man is hovering over Helena with a huge bunch of roses arranged in a scratched tin vase. He seems to have been blown into the room on the cold draught that rushed in as the door opened. He speaks in a high-pitched Southern drawl.

'Would you care to take tea now, Miss Blanche?' He has plonked the vase down on Helena's dressing table and is posing like a 1920s bathing beauty, both knees bent and swung over to one side, primly pushed together with his hands coyly crossed and resting on one thigh. He is at least six foot five, with short dark hair, the tips of which are bleached blond.

'Billie, you haven't met my friend Cissie.' Helena throws an extravagant arm out in Cissie's direction. 'This is THE Cissie O'Brien, stand-up comic extraordinaire, currently the toast of dear old Britain with her brand-new hit comedy series *Kathy Came Home*. And Cissie, this is Billie Rosenblatt, dresser to the stars, all the way from Auckland, New Zealand. The man who has single-handedly kept me sane throughout this not exactly uneventful run.'

Billie Rosenblatt has barely moved from his pose, except his head has swivelled round to take in Cissie, his jaw has dropped open and he has brought both his hands up to his face in mock horror. After several seconds he lets out a short, throat-tearing shriek.

'Eeeek! Miss Blanche! You should have told me you had a visitor! And me in my old rags!' He covers his mouth with long, flapping fingers, his large grey eyes widening to an impossible size, affecting a mime artist's pose of shame.

'Hello, Billie.' Cissie's tone is tolerant and weary.

'Oh please, miss, call me Wilhelmina.' His great long body collapses into a curtsey and he looks up shyly, batting thick dark eyelashes, a line of smudged shiny kohl defining blue-grey eyes that need no definition. 'Would you care for some tea also, miss?' His hands are now brought together as if in prayer, his head tilted to one side; his eyebrows, severely plucked into the thinnest of lines, are arched in an expression of pious concern. He is Joan of Arc in a silent movie.

Helena is up on her feet. 'Yes, darling, teas all round. We are in crisisville. Remember I told you about the other actress who was arriving yesterday? . . . Well she's gone walkabout . . . missing since last night and . . . there are kangaroos in the top paddock, as they might say in your part of the world. So yes . . . tea would be greatly appreciated.'

'Oh Jesus, you're joking . . . you mean she's disappeared?'

Billie's voice has dropped into a harsh Antipodean whine and he suddenly looks more like Bill than Billie. The arch of his brow has dropped into a thin straight line and his whole persona seems to have followed suit and sagged into a dull suburban normality which is disturbingly at odds with his appearance. Like seeing a pantomime dame take off her wig and talk about football. 'Have you called the cops?'

'Yes we've been down at the precinct, my dear, looking into the gorgeous baby blues of a certain Lieutenant Lorenzetti. Now, darling, I need to ablute.' A wave of Helena's arm sends Billie teetering across the room, again as if the simple movement of air had blown him towards the door. Then lifting one heel up behind him and throwing back his head he says in his finest Southern drawl, 'Oh, Miss Blanche, I simply love a man in uniform. Was he really so very, very handsome? ... Oh and by the way, Miss Blanche, at what time will you be requiring your sleigh tonight?'

'Oh God, Billie, I don't think there'll be any cabs around, there's absolutely nothing moving on the streets, it's like the end of the world. You can try for a cab if you like at the normal time, but I think we'll be walking or perhaps "trudging" would be more appropriate.'

'Very well, Miss Blanche.' And he is sucked through the crack in the door and is gone in an instant.

'God! Which Christmas tree did he fall off?'

'He's a life-saver.' Helena has pulled her kimono up around her waist and is hitching her bottom up onto the rim of a huge old porcelain washbasin. She supports herself by holding on to the two elephantine brass taps and lets her legs dangle, until the one pink sock gives up and slips to the floor. The ancient pipe-work groans as several flakes of plaster drop down to join others in a neat little heap at the base of one of the pipes, and there is a definite gap between the basin and the wall where it has been wrenched away by the sheer weight of endless actresses' bottoms.

'I simply can't walk up four flights every time I want a piss.'

'Well they do say "a dressing room isn't a dressing room until you've pissed in the washbasin".'

'Exactly, so do feel free ... though *you'll* probably need a mounting block to get on.'

'Who sent the flowers?' Cissie has sunk back down into the deep bouncing comfort of the old divan and is laughing as its odd medley of twangs ends with a particularly tuneless one from somewhere within its depths.

'Oh I know, you couldn't exactly have secret sex on that thing, could you? The whole of Broadway would know about it ...'

'Ooh you've given it a go then, have you, Helly?'

Helena is vigorously patting her face with a soft pink powder puff, giving it a thick matte finish which makers her impressive grey eyes seem small and colourless, as if they have retreated inside her head, wishing to disassociate themselves from the transformation that is taking place. She does not answer.

'Come on, who gave you the flowers?'

Helena turns round and leans her elbows on the back of the chair. She smiles directly at Cissie for several seconds and then, in a quiet voice, 'Guess.' Still smiling she rests her chin on her forearms. Cissie smiles back and raises herself up on one elbow, setting off another cacophony of pings and twangs. The two friends continue to smile at each other in silence, a game that has been played many times, comforting in its familiarity, something exciting in the predictability of its ritual.

'Well presumably it's old G.H. up there on the mirror, next to the big pink smacker.'

A warning squeal from the unoiled door hinge and Billie is back, having been swept in on another icy blast from the corridor outside. He is hovering over Helena holding a battered tin tea tray at shoulder height on the tips of his outstretched fingers.

'Oh Miss Blanche, the phone lines are down! We are completely cut off from the rest of the world!' He clanks the tea tray down on the dressing table and with a deep curtsey announces: 'Tea is served!'

'You may rise, Billie. So, we have no phones, but more importantly, do we have an audience?'

'Miss Blanche, we don't even have a leading man! Mr Todd has not arrived yet and he is usually up on the stage by now ... ooohing and aaahing ... warming up his voice ... stretching those gorgeous limbs and doing that exercise that makes a girl feel quite faint.' Billie has slapped both hands on either side of his face in a camp parody of *The Scream* and he has turned his tragic silent movie star eyes onto Cissie, inviting her to take part in his very own drama. She looks away, willing him to do the same, like a member of an audience hoping against hope that a performer will not pick on them to participate in some humiliating carry-on.

Maggie would have loved this man. Cissie can hear the high, soft hoots of her laughter like some exotic bird. Maggie would have been a willing audience revelling in his fantasy, absorbing his campery with total conviction, and in the blink of an eye the cocaine would be on the mirror, the dollar bill would be rolled and the pair would be off, arm in arm, screaming and jabbering into a night that neither would remember in any detail. Maggie's new best friend. Maggie's life was full of men like Billie, they seemed to be attracted by the fragility of her and the rollercoaster nature of her life. Droves of them had drifted in and out of friendships with her over the years, lifting her onto pedestals and adoring her. Only to withdraw quickly and quietly and inevitably after being dragged into some hell that she had created.

There is a picture now which stubbornly displays itself in Cissie's mind. A scene that she had witnessed just a few days since, but which now seems like a universe away. The door is opened onto a young man's bedroom. Maggie is lying on his bed, like something from a fairytale, one arm caught up under her tousled blonde head, the other stretched out invitingly. Her flimsy patchwork skirt, pulled up around her knees, is spread out to full effect, a small girl showing off her party dress. The sturdy white calves dangling over the side of the bed and ending in the inevitable little black boots complete a picture of blissful abandon. The young man claps a hand across his nose and mouth; the room is covered with her excreta. She is snoring and the hint of a smile loiters across her face. She will not be invited to dinner again.

'I'm leaving,' Cissie says to the floor. For a second there is silence, then Billie shrinking into Bill makes to leave.

'Oh ... O.K. ... I'll leave you two alone I guess,' and is gone without hardly seeming to open the door.

'What's the matter, Ciss? Was Billie a bit too much?' Helena has painted a thick, unwavering, grey-black line around each of her eyes, but the eyes still seem to be refusing to cooperate, shrinking back from the task in hand.

'No ... no ... nothing to do with Billie, I wouldn't want to be stuck in a lift with him mind.'

'No, well you never were a fag-hag, were you, Ciss?'

'No. I've just reached a decision. I'm going home.'

'... Home-home you mean or the fabulous Hotel Elmscote?' Helena has now painted half of her top lip with a shiny scarlet lipstick and has whipped around in her chair holding the tiny lip brush like a cigarette.

'I'm going to get the first flight out I can.' Cissie is still addressing the floor.

'Oh Cissie ... don't be silly ... you've only just arrived. You haven't even seen the show for goodness' sake ... It's fucking Maggie, isn't it? You really have had enough. Why on earth did you bring her? Why in God's name didn't you bring Jenny?'

Cissie still hasn't raised her head and is supporting it with her hands. 'Because I was running away!' This is hissed through clenched teeth and Helena is at her side in a swish of silk and a cloud of the unidentifiable perfume.

'But ... I thought ... you said ... everything seemed to be ... I thought this was the happiest you'd ever been. I just thought you were down because of Maggie going bonkers again.'

Cissie lifts her head, her face is flushed and then with a small gulp, words come tumbling out.

'I dragged Maggie here ... this is all my fault ... I knew she was in no fit state ... I knew she was heading for something ... and I left Jenny to face everything on her own.'

'Well ... face what for goodness' sake? What on earth have you done?'

'The bastards are on to us, Helena ... the low-life bastards ... they know.'

The Goodbye

ॐ

Michael opens the curtains only wide enough to look through with one eye. He is afraid. He is not sure of what exactly and he feels slightly sick. Inside his overcoat pocket he is holding his inhaler, though his lungs are calm and unusually silent. Someone is shouting.

'Ya yella belly bastard! ... Go see! ... Go seeeeeee!' It is a woman's voice, alarmed and shrieking. He turns in the direction of the voice and in a cubicle beyond the nurses' station, on the other side of the room, he can see a small, squat, oriental-looking woman. She is standing on top of the bed, feet apart, her short, powerful-looking legs braced for action.

'You! ... Go seeee! ... Yella belly bastard!' She seems to be pointing directly at him, but he cannot tell whether the eyes, puffy black slits, one of which is partially concealed by a thick white dressing, are looking at him or at a man in a white coat, standing in the nurses' station with his back to the woman.

Suddenly the man shouts without looking round, 'O.K. Calm down, Mae-Mae.' She begins to jump up and down on the bed and jabbing a violent forefinger through the air, apparently in Michael's direction, she continues in a very loud stage whisper:

'Go seeee ... big asshole ... go seeeee!'

The man says again, 'Mae-Mae ...' and she slips down onto the bed and out of sight. As he turns back, Michael can still hear her muttering.

'Lily liver ... you are big asshole of many weakness ... Mae-

Mae don't even get a cup of coffee.' Michael turns back and pulls the curtains together under his chin, so that only his face is showing through. Beneath the covers he can see Maggie's chest gently rise and fall, and he lets go a little sound, halfway between a laugh and a sob. He watches the pale pink mouth with its built-in smile blow open ever so slightly with each exhalation and he sees himself press his lips urgently onto hers. He can smell her skin and taste the warm slither of her tongue. He lets go the curtain and slips inside its cubicled privacy, pulling it to behind him and shutting out the ward beyond. He could touch her now, no one would see. He could put his face within a millimetre of hers. At the very least he could watch her, really watch her, every tiny detail of her face. He steps nearer the bed. He can hear his heart racing in his ears. Someone drops what sounds like an empty tin can on the floor nearby. Michael moves closer to the bed, leaning his thigh against it. He studies the minute blue veins under the thin, delicate skin of her eyelids and the dark puffy sacs under each eye, and Dominic slips a small frozen hand into his. He can feel the child's cold fingers intertwine with his own and he is afraid to move his hand lest one of them should snap. He can hear Dominic's heavy adenoidal breathing and he is comforted by the gentle rhythmic rise and fall of the freshly pressed coverlet.

'You come for me, honey? . . . You come take Mae-Mae home? . . . Mae-Mae good girl . . . she give you no shit.' Then from somewhere very close, maybe just the other side of the curtain, Michael is sure he can hear someone sobbing, voiceless and dry, a kind of soft ticking sound from the back of a human throat. He turns his head to listen; it is gone. He looks back to Maggie; he can no longer hear the breathing.

One short but violent intake of breath and Dominic was gone, it was like a sudden change of mind, a last desperate grab for his life. Michael can see Elizabeth arrive at the top of the kitchen stairs, a silent scream of realisation spreading across her face like an ink blot. She had simply gone down to the kitchen for some water and Dominic had seen it as his cue to slip away. She could never quite forgive Michael for her not being there. Dominic should have been at home, she had said, his proper home, not this excuse for a home. With an excuse for a father is what she meant. Even with their son lying dead between them there was blame and shame and judgement.

Michael sits down on a chair and Dominic's fingers slip from his. He grabs Maggie's unsuspecting hand like a drowning man grasping at the next floating thing he comes across and he spreads the large white fingers between his two hands. Her hands if anything are a little larger than his own, the knuckles rough and slightly grimy; not hands that you would match to the delicate skin and features of her face. It is as if hands and face had experienced entirely different lives.

Dominic calls him.

'Daddy ...?'

He looks up at her face and answers, his voice light and fragile, little more than a breath.

'Yes ...?' Her eyes are rolling rapidly from side to side, blind, frantic headlamps beneath the almost transparent membrane of her lids. He hears a tiny moan from inside her throat, but the perfect mouth remains closed.

Dominic whispers, 'Daddy ...' This time he moves closer to her face and answers more boldly, 'Yes ...?'

Now her mouth opens and he sees that the soft pink of her lips is cracked and darkened. Creamy strings of stale saliva stretch between top and bottom only to be snapped by a sudden gush of breath from within, unclean and acrid. On the breath is a sound, long and soft, like the beginning of a sad song, a lament, a dirge, ending on a little cry of pain.

Then from across the room:

'Mae-Mae go home now ... please? ... Mae-Mae go home ...'

Michael puts his face next to Maggie's, his chin touching her pillow. On her forehead he can see the remains of the bright lipstick cross she had drawn in another lifetime. Scarlet pinpricks of the stuff still sitting stubbornly in the pores of her skin and the little scratch where she had pressed her face onto his precious photo on the kitchen stairs. Again her mouth opens, new strings of mucus stretching like mozzarella as another breath is exhaled. This time her mouth shapes itself around the breath and a word is formed, drawn out and pleading. It sounds like 'Home ...' but he is not sure. He goes to push her hair from her forehead and in doing so he spots the tiny dark fleck of her blood still lodged at the edge of his nail like stubborn nail polish.

He puts his mouth next to her ear and whispers, 'Oh sweet Helena ... what is to become of us?' With his left hand he reaches into his coat pocket for the envelope with her name and address on.

'No, no ... put that away Mae-Mae.'

'Mae-Mae got her lurrrve to keep her warm.'

Michael lets go of her hand and sets it gently back down on the counterpane. Her other hand is strewn carelessly across her thigh. It has a dark-red squiggle of plastic tubing taped to its back, through which fresh life slowly seeps into her after flooding out so drastically; so finally for the child; hardly a child; the beginnings of a child. Unformed yet wiser than them all. A complete life in just five and a half months. Not a loss of a life, just the completion of one.

That is what Elizabeth and he had constantly told one another in the weeks leading up to Dominic's death, but it hadn't stopped either of them careering headlong into hell in the small hours of that grim December morning. A hell that neither one could share with the other. Each one jealously guarding their own personal abyss, lest the other should shine a light.

It was somehow fitting that Dominic should have died as winter came on. He had always seemed battered by the winter elements, always cold and tired and somehow shrunken, literally shrinking from the world like a small, weary animal looking for a dark place to lie down. Yet when spring arrived he seemed to grow both in body and spirit. He would stand taller and a smudge of colour would appear in the sallow skin of his cheeks; a delicate flower growing up through concrete. Both Michael and Elizabeth had felt that had he survived until spring he would have come through, but it is mid-March and there is no sign of spring.

Michael looks again at the envelope addressed to Helena Cassidy, at its bold stylish writing and slips a tentative forefinger underneath the triangular flap. Again he notices the speck of dried blood on his middle finger and with a twinge of impatience he plunges the finger into his mouth and scrapes at the nail with his two front teeth. Then on seeing it gone, he opens the letter and reads:

Dear Helena,

I've been off with laryngitis and I caught your show last night. You were quite simply superb. I hope you don't mind but I knew I'd be passing the Elmscote today so I felt compelled to drop you a line and pop it in. Enjoy the rest of the run. It is a truly fabulous performance.

Best wishes,

Monica Thornton

P.S. I believe our matinée days are the same, Thursday? If ever you fancy a bite in between shows just give me a ring at the theatre, I'd love to see you again, I so loved our stint at the Bush together and I'd love to catch up. Give Luke my love, I presume he is here with you. David is on tour with the R.S.C. I can't believe I'm missing him so much. Anyway this was meant to be a note not a novel! Hope we can get together, M.

P.P.S. My stage door number is 435 6697. Isn't New York wonderful?!

Michael feels a cold panic blow through his chest as he continues to stare at the letter. He goes back and reads it again, stopping at particular points and rereading them over and over. It is like staring through a series of keyholes into another world.

A world, he is surprised to find, he resents. 'Give my love to Luke, I presume he is here with you.'

'Oh my God.' The panic in his chest rises as he relives a moment of a couple of years back, when he had stood on the ground floor at Bloomingdale's and realised Dominic was nowhere to be seen. Michael, sick and sweating, scoured the shop, enlisting the help of several assistants. A stomach-churning forty-five minutes later he came upon the boy, standing anxiously by the main exit door. He had wanted to both hug the child and thrash him at the same time. Later, when recalling the experience for Elizabeth he had said that he never wished to go through anything like that again.

Without looking at the girl Michael takes her hand, squeezes it and whispers into it like a microphone, 'O.K., Alice, back through the looking glass with you. Safe journey, sweet girl.' And he goes to find a payphone.

The Call

Luke is lying in the deep sag of the old double bed. The same little valley of tired bed springs that inadvertently threw himself and Helena together nightly, in a tangle of forced intimacy. On first retiring Helena would perch valiantly on the top of her 'bank', reading some book or other, one leg almost out of bed to prevent the inevitable slide into the centre and Luke. He on the other hand made no attempt to scale his 'bank' but got in and lay where the bed naturally put him and looked forward to the time, after lights-out, when having fallen asleep, Helena's body would gradually relax and give in to the pull of gravity. He loved the feeling of their bodies hemmed together by the gentle pressure of the stretched old mattress, like twins in a womb.

He picks up the photo of Helen Cake and chums and presses it to his heart. He is lying flat on top of the rumpled chintzy bedspread, its large flowery pattern saddened by years of savage laundering. His legs are spreadeagled and his flaccid penis lies lifeless across the open zip of his flies like an uncooked pastry. He is in a kind of half-doze, dipping fitfully in and out of sleep. One minute consciously homing in on Helena, close up on her eyes, like a camera zooming in, desperate for her secrets; the next in some far-off land about to do something unspeakable to a woman he has never seen before in his life, but somehow knows. It is something angry and wrong and he jerks awake before anything occurs.

His mother has been there too, dancing in and out of both

conscious thought and snatches of dream. Her olive skin with its mystery sheen, her eyes promising and flirting. He has not spoken to her for three years and cannot even think of her without a spark of rage igniting somewhere within. Years of psychotherapy have not lessened his anger – in fact it seems to have sharpened it and set it into startling focus.

Now lying there with Helena's strange new perfume filling his head, and beginning unconsciously to crumple the little snapshot of his former self, he revisits the warm, bright room in which he had spent so many hours, crying and reliving painful segments of his life, examining his mother's behaviour and remembering with shame and hatred the many shadowy visitors who had shared her bed when his father had been away on one of his frequent business trips. Sitting there in the dark brown armchair on Wednesday evenings, the muffled sounds of his therapist's family life filtering up through the floorboards of the warm little house in an unfashionable suburb of south-west London, Luke would pick through the events of the previous six days. Most events, indeed most days, seemed to involve various degrees of pain, the worst of which he would describe as his 'Bechers Brook'.

'My Bechers Brook this week was . . .' and he would go on to describe a conversation or a confrontation or simply a feeling that had caused him distress. Almost inevitably this B.B., as it came to be known, involved his mother or Helena and the entire session was spent either putting him together after a disastrous fall or patting him on the back for staying in the saddle. Whatever had been revealed, barely a session would go by without some reference to the night of his father's death, and the telephone conversation that his twelve-year-old self had overheard; his mother talking in a voice only reserved for her 'men friends', dark and dripping and wanton. Just a few days later he had watched her as she wept over the coffin in the chapel of rest and he had wanted to bury himself in her bosom and then cut her head off.

The therapist had constantly referred back to that telephone

89

conversation as if it was somehow pivotal, and it was during their last session together that the therapist's persistent worrying at this particular memory, along with other memories of his mother's subsequent sexual habits, that Luke's tolerance for pain and rage snapped. He had stormed from the room, incoherent with anger and inconsolable, later telling Helena that he thought the man to be evil. When she questioned him about it Luke refused to discuss it further except to say that he thought the therapist had manipulated him somehow, planting false and devastating memories in his head. Luke would never go back nor would he ever forgive him.

Now he can see the man's face very clearly, sallow with those dark, deep-set eyes and a strong, square jaw. The sort of look that caused his mother to squirm and pout and behave like a six-year-old, and he can hear her now, the fag-stained voice pouring into the telephone on that desolate night.

'. . . but death is *always* inconvenient, my darling.' He hears her put the phone down and sigh to herself a light buoyant sigh. He can hear the swish of her dress and the clank of her bangles, her hot breath upon his face, mingling with the heavy, exotic scent of her perfume and the lingering smell of so many cigarettes. Suddenly, strident and shattering, the phone rings. Luke almost expects it to be his mother and hastily does up his flies.

'. . . Hello?'

'Luke . . .?'

'. . . Yes?'

'Jenny . . . Murdo. How are you?'

'Oh . . . erm . . .' Luke has no idea how he is, or for the moment, where he is or why.

'Is this a bad time?'

'Oh . . .'

'Look, if it's not convenient I'll call back later. I really just want and need actually to speak to Cissie if she's there.'

'Erm . . . no, she's not here I'm afraid. Oh God, Jenny . . . we're having a bit of a crisis here.'

'Well join the bloody club, Luke. I'm having my very own little crisis here as it happens.'

'Oh . . . really? . . . I am sorry . . . erm . . . shall I get her to call you back when she gets in?'

'Yes. What a good idea! That would be very kind. Goodbye.'

'Goo—' but she is gone.

After speaking with Jenny, Luke often had the feeling that he had been slightly wrong-footed and quite often that he had been slapped about the face with a cold wet fish, but what he always felt was that he was, in some small way, a disappointment. Her 'upfront' sexuality rendered him completely inarticulate: 'Hello! Murdo! Lesbian! Pleased to meet you' was how she greeted him at their first meeting. He simply stared, lifting a damp hand to be seized in her warm, firm grip and shaken vigorously. The scene sent Cissie and Helena into purple-faced hysterics and Cissie then replied on Luke's behalf, with a deep monotonous impersonation of his voice: 'Hello . . . Boileau . . . Church of England.' Maggie had giggled her tinkling giggle, slightly missing the humour of the situation and Luke had blushed. Now he touches his cheek with the tips of his fingers and springs to his feet.

'Bloody dykes!' The phone rings instantly as if in reply and Luke whirls round and stares at it, contemplating that possibility.

'Hello . . .?'

'Hello? . . . er . . . Do I have . . . Helena Cassidy's apartment?'

'You most certainly do.'

'. . . Might I be speaking to Luke?'

'. . . This is he.'

'I . . . I. I'm afraid Helena has been taken ill.'

'What?! . . . Where? Who are y—? Is she alright?'

'She's in Bellevue hospital, emergency room. I'm afraid she's . . . lost her baby.'

'. . . Lost . . .! . . . Lost . . .? What are you talking about? . . . Look, who *is* this?'

'Oh . . . I'm . . . no one. I was just there for her that's all. Look, she's going to be alright but she's had a pretty rough ride. They couldn't save the baby ... they had to ... well they'll explain all that. Sorry ... are you related to her at all? I'm assuming you are.'

'Related?! I'm her bloody husband! ... Obviously she hasn't told you about me! ... What I'd like to know is what relation are *you*?!'

'No ... listen ... like I said ... I was there for her ... she was in trouble ... and ... and ... and I was there.'

'... Yes! I bet you bloody were!'

'Well ... I wish her well. Please remember she's been very ill ... she's a sweet ... sweet girl ... she ... she needs a lot of help.'

'How dare you presume to tell me what my wife needs after such a brief encounter ...! Or was it so brief? Just how well do you know her ... you bastard?!'

And there is silence except for the lifeless whirring of the telephone line. Luke stares for a moment at the earpiece through which the news has come, and for a second is not sure of what he has exactly heard. He sits back down on the edge of the bed and speaks the words that he has heard quietly to himself, letting each word sit in isolation on his tongue, as if to somehow test its validity.

'She's ... in ... Bellevue ... emergency ... room ... I'm afraid ... she's ... lost ... her ... baby ... I ... was ... there ... for ... her.' He feels a smile, unbidden, stretch across his face and something like anger stirring deep within his gut. He continues to sit, the telephone receiver clutched tightly in his right hand as if he were still looking at it, and he savours this gut feeling that is something like anger. For it is not the insoluble, futile frustration that he normally associates with this emotion. There is a thrill involved here and an exhilaration and a sense of unerring certainty.

'Please replace the handset ... Please replace the handset ...' He does so. Then he goes into the bathroom to check out this maverick smile. He walks carefully, keen not to displace it in any way. Sure enough, it is there, and as he thought it is more than a smile and he likes what he sees.

'O.K. The fucking dénouement!'

The Lunatic

M ichael has replaced the handset and is resting his forearms on it.

'She is married,' he says in a small, wavery voice. He now rests his forehead on top of his forearms and stares down at his black winter boots, still damp from the snow. The sounds of the hospital clang and echo around him. His head feels heavy and his eyes feel raw. Like a horse, he could fall asleep right there where he is. He begins to imagine the possibility of doing so standing up, and his knees buckle beneath him. Then he tries to put Helena, vulnerable and wayward child, together with the thin, angry reed of a voice he has just heard. A voice that had sounded more irritated than concerned. He imagines its owner to be pale and blond with a moustache, a cross Leslie Howard. Michael had been taken aback by the man's outburst, by his anger and suspicion, but more importantly by his claim to be Helena's husband. He focuses back onto his boots and he sees her on her haunches at his feet, rubbing a shaking forefinger along the creases of his much-loved brogues. She looks up, her eyes threatening to cry, and the face is Dominic's, looking up for approval after tying Michael's shoelace on the stoop at Mc-Dougall Street, his face plump with life. Now it is Elizabeth, down on one knee at the side of the bathtub, one arm supporting Dominic's floating corpse, the other gently bathing the boy's bloated face, her own face bloated itself, with grief. Michael lifts his head and allows it to swim for several seconds. He considers calling Elizabeth, but instead he watches his boots as they make their way towards the waiting area, where he slumps down in the front of several rows of plastic chairs.

'See you ... I can see you.' The voice is unreal, it sounds like a voice a boy might give to a plastic action hero – Luke Skywalker or Captain America.

'See you, pal ... I can see you.' Michael whips round in his seat. There is no one in the seats directly behind him from where the sound seems to have come. Two rows back there are two Asian women. They have huge sheepskin coats over their saris; one is cradling a small child, the other is breastfeeding a baby, her modesty spared by the lapel of her coat. They stare back with blank faces. Directly behind them and to the right, a middle-aged woman sits alone, wearing what looks like a pink angora hat, pulled down around her ears. Her face has the purple discolouration of a drinker; chin on chest she is asleep.

'Stick around, they'll make you a star.' Michael catches sight of a small dark movement at the periphery of his vision. To his left, four or five seats along, at the end of the row, sits a ragged heap, a sepia bundle, at the centre of which something hibernates. A grimy knitted hat is stretched across its head, its colour obliterated by layer upon layer of grease and dirt, and from underneath matted pieces of dark hair protrude like a cheap, poorly made wig.

'I know you ... you want trouble.' Michael senses that it is in fact a man and in a face where the skin is indiscernible from the rags in which he is wrapped, the eyes are alarmingly clear and blue and very much awake.

'You ... you ... you ... want to get your act to ... to ... to ... together and leave us people alone.' Michael is hoping that the man is not addressing him and optimistically turns around to see who is sitting on the other side of him. No such luck: there is no one else in the row. The man lifts a bright-red Coke can to his lips and sucks the last dregs noisily into his mouth. Michael savours the image.

'Captain America is right,' he says with a smile and makes a mental note to come back here with his camera. He looks round hoping to share his joke with the two Asian women but they persist in staring back blankly and Michael gets the distinct impression that they share the same sentiments as the vagrant.

'Back o . . . o . . . off, Mister. P . . . p . . . p . . . people don't want t . . . t . . . to know y . . . you.'

'O.K. I got ya . . . I'm backing off. O.K.?'

The man continues to mumble and stutter but Michael can no longer make out what he is saying. Now he can hear Elizabeth: 'If there's a lunatic on the street you can guarantee he'll make a beeline for Michael. He just attracts them. He's a complete hazard on the subway, they approach him in droves. I refuse to sit next to him out of fear for my life.' Michael smiles to himself as he recalls a time not long after he and Elizabeth had started dating. They were on the subway when a well-dressed Wall Street type sat down next to Michael. There was a faint whiff of alcohol about the man but apart from that he seemed normal enough. Some minutes later he spoke in a low menacing voice.

'You fucked my wife!'

Michael wasn't sure of what he had heard to begin with but the man obligingly repeated his accusation in a slightly louder voice and continued to repeat it in an increasingly agitated fashion adding lurid details of what he claimed to be Michael's sexual preferences. Michael feels his face go hot as he remembers the burning embarrassment as the entire carriage turned their attention on him, and then subsequently his efforts to allay Elizabeth's fears of some sordid affair. The man had followed them down Park Avenue for several blocks haranguing Michael at screaming pitch and finally accusing him in front of quite a large audience of also having some liaison with his dog.

'You fucked my dog! You son of a bitch! The wife wasn't enough for ya. You had to have my dog as well. You fucked my little Mamie and I'll never forgive you for taking her innocence!'

After shrieking this proclamation at the top of his voice, the poor fellow was so distracted that he lurched into the traffic and was knocked down by a taxi cab. Michael to this day feels guilt as he remembers the sense of relief he experienced at seeing the poor creature prostrate on the street, and above all silent. For years after, 'You fucked my wife' had sent Elizabeth into hysterics whenever she thought about it. Answerphone messages for Michael frequently started with it and he still has an early Valentine card from Elizabeth which reads 'My innocence awaits . . . From your little Mamie xx.'

He thinks again of phoning Elizabeth, he feels a need to hear her deep-voiced, laconic message, 'Call me later' followed by Beethoven's fifth, but he would never be able to explain his predicament. He looks down again at his boots: the dampness appears to have gone, leaving behind a salty-looking thin line which zigzags its way across the toe of each boot like a river on a map. He rubs at it with his thumb and thinks of the small, polished wooden box he had made as a boy which now houses his shoe polish and brushes. It was originally intended as a Christmas present for his father, but Michael had become frightened of giving it, fearing his efforts might be thought substandard. At the last minute he had rushed out and bought a desk diary. He remembers the barely concealed look of boredom on his father's face on opening the present and how he, Michael, had cried himself to sleep that night clutching the little wooden box. He gets up to leave.

'Sorry? . . . Helena Cassidy . . .' The man is tall and bespectacled and wearing a blue and white bobble hat. '. . . She appears to have had some sort of miscarriage . . .' Again the dull drone of his voice is pricked by stress and impatience and he is about as far from Leslie Howard as it is possible to be – in fact it is the little cartoon character, Waldo of *Where's Waldo?* that pops into Michael's mind.

'. . . she was brought in this morning.' He watches the man's loping strides take him at some speed towards the ward and while Michael thinks of going home and polishing his boots and then perhaps calling Elizabeth, he is in fact following the man back to the ward.

The Loss

⁂

The corridor is long and dimly lit. There is a feeling that it is little used. There is no sign of life, no smell of life, just that of the stale air, disturbed by her movement. Distant voices echo somewhere beyond the blind windows that run along each side of the corridor, their panes thick and grey and impenetrable. Tiny blasts of freezing air stab at the small of her back and she can feel her teeth begin to chatter. She wants to stop, but there is nowhere to stop. This corridor is only for those moving on. No one must tarry. She knows that if she stops she will perish, alone. She can hear the wind beyond the windows, a high-pitched, woeful wail and then again it is the call of a child; lost and frightened, robbed of its warmth and nurturing; tossed out onto the Arctic winds to test its metal. But nothing is meant to survive here, there is no purpose to survival here. The air is scant, the temperature lethal; nothing lives.

Again she hears distant voices, separate and unaware; the anonymous, lilting cries of simple freedom. She is the forgotten one, scrabbling along some isolated outreach to nowhere, trying to unravel the inexplicable riddle of her existence. She opens her throat to let out one last almighty scream of despair, but the very air in her lungs is frozen, and the chattering teeth are gnashing together to their own crazy pace, like a set of clockwork dentures chomping their way across a polished surface.

Someone calls her name. 'Maggie? ... Maggie? ...' someone close by. She can almost feel their breath upon her cheek, but now her body is getting smaller as cell by cell freezes over, and in one last retaliatory gesture it begins to shake. Starting at her very centre with deep, painful spasms, it has taken charge of its own survival. Her head aches from the tumultuous crashing together of her teeth and she can see them smash cartoon-like into smithereens. Again the voice: it is someone she knows.

'Maggie ... for Christ's sake! ...'

And now they are turning down the lights. She can see her grandmother, lying in the dark wood single bed in the small back bedroom of the house where she grew up in Birmingham; her sagging grey skin, her mouth ajar with one yellow tooth clearly visible, her eyes not quite closed, with the chilling effect that from somewhere deep inside she was still keeping a surreptitious, to all intents and purposes blind, but secretly seeing eye on proceedings. She can hear the strange clicking sound in the back of her grandmother's throat as she breathes and she can smell the sulphurous odour of her breath and the sweet smell of her dying. She can see her own small hand pick up the tiny brush kept at the beside, dip into an eggcup of water and drag it across the cracked, discoloured lips.

More voices, close at hand: she searches for those she has known, for those she has held dear, but again it is this man.

'Maggie ... come on now ...' and a great weight comes down upon her and everywhere is turning red like blood through water. The tiny little thing that she was is growing again, no ... no ... no ... stop!! please ...

'NOOO!' Even beneath the suffocating weight, huge limbs are sprouting and the spasms at her centre are radiating out into great quaking shivers. A shock of white light shoots through the crack between her eyelids, causing her unprepared eyes to shrink back from the unwelcome pain. The voice again.

'I think she's coming to ... Maggie ...? Open your eyes ... can you?' There are others too, bustling. Someone has hold of her hand, whoever it is, is rubbing it between their own. Another voice.

'O.K., Maggie, can you hear me? . . . Open your eyes.' Strong, firm hands manoeuvre her efficiently onto her side and her arms flail like a newborn baby in need of swaddling and a warm bosom. The same strong hands begin to rub her back while others are rubbing her feet, and like a conquering army warmth begins to filter through the outer reaches of her body.

'Temperature's on the up!'

'Oh . . . thank Christ for that.'

'Is she going to be alright?'

'How ya doin', Maggie? . . . Ya warmin' up now? D'ya wanna check her B.P.?'

'Is she going to be alright? . . . What . . . What happened there? What was that?'

That voice again. She does not want to see the face, she knows exactly what the eyes will say and she can see, without opening her eyes, the faint curl of disgust around the mouth, the features hanging low in judgement. She cannot figure out and she does not wish to know why Luke is sitting at her bedside in this place. She tries to remember the cold grey corridor, to recreate its detail, but it slips away like sand through fingers.

'Yeah! . . . She's warming up alright . . . O.K., folks, keep an eye on her.' American voices, she is in her very own Saturday Night Movie, someone could possibly call 'cut!' at any moment, but she couldn't get up and her belly aches and anyway she refuses to come out of her trailer.

'Oh Maggie! . . . where the bloody hell have you been? . . . We have been up all night looking for you!' Luke is very close now, speaking in a low frantic whisper. His face must be almost touching hers.

'I know you're awake . . . why did you tell them your name was Helena for Christ's sake? . . . You know the police are looking for you?'

Somewhere, somebody starts to shout, someone frightened and in pain, someone with no one, an outcast, a refugee, and before she can stop them her eyes snap open. She cannot avoid the face, it is directly in front of hers and just as she had pictured; but no glasses so the gaze is myopic and watery. He lets out a deep sigh and says nothing for a moment, allowing time for his judgemental look to register to its full effect. She stares back and takes in the face and feels the energy seep from her body. She has seen enough and closes her eyes.

'Everyone is thoroughly pissed off. We are all quite simply fed up of you not taking responsibility for yourself and expecting others to do it for you. You have just put us through it too many times. You push people too far . . . I . . . I know you must be feeling lousy and this is probably not the time to say all this . . . but . . .'

'Anyway, you're safe now and you'd just better get some rest and I'd better go and see if I can't contact the girls and tell them where you are. Helena's got a matinée, she may still be on stage . . . You're going to be kept in apparently until tomorrow, so we'll pick you up around lunchtime. The roads might be in a better state by then. The girls may well want to come and see you later. But then again, they may not.'

She hears his chair scrape as he gets up and she watches his long, dark figure as he pushes the curtain back to leave. As he does so, she catches a glimpse of the ward beyond, and in the brief moment of the curtain being opened and then pulled back into place she is sure she sees a familiar face. It is a face she has no desire to recall, her memory an exhausting tangle of feelings and events. Michael . . . benign and terrifying. She still cannot work out which. New York . . . mysterious and grotesque. Has she been here half her life or just a matter of minutes? She does not want to know. It is a Technicolor blur and she feels queasy at the thought of it. She feels a warm, thick dribble below and a dull, drawing ache in her back and in her belly and out of nowhere a baby's scream shatters the air, long and piercing, made up of rage and terror.

'Shushhhhhhh . . . shush shush . . . now then, now then . . . shush now.' But the baby is having none of it. In fact the soft, soothing voice has merely served to crank its scream up an octave into murderous outrage; and then ... nothing. What brought that about? Maggie thinks about lifting her head. What? A bottle? A breast? ... A pillow?

Suddenly a cool, soft hand rests firmly upon her forehead and then upon her own hand. 'Oh my! Now you really have warmed up. Let's get rid of some of these blankets.'

The feeling of dream-like paralysis is gone and she can move her limbs but they are stiff and heavy. There is the sound of plastic curtain rings zooming along on their runners as the curtains are whooshed back in a couple of brisk movements.

'Are you going to wake up for me ...? Mm? ... and say "Hi".'

Maggie cannot. She cannot open her eyes. She has the sensation that if she does she will somehow be lost for ever, out into the world, that she will be giving herself up. That the very act of keeping her eyes shut will also keep her spirit safe within; and besides, she does not wish to see 'the man'; she does not wish to read what is in his eyes. Something hard is placed in her ear.

'Hey ... yer temperature's normal. Yer doin' great.' She can smell the fresh, lively perfume of the nurse and somewhere it makes her want to cry. She is a poor, stale, unwashed thing; only half alive. It would have been best all round if she had stayed in the long grey corridor, along with other human detritus. She is an empty sack, all the goodness drained from her. All the goodness. She is worthless. She cannot stop the sob from rising in her throat and a tear escapes from beneath each closed lid.

'Hey ... you're bound to feel low ... but it won't last for ever.'

Even the nurse's breath is fresh and minty. Maggie feels as though she could shrivel in its path, like Dracula at first light. 'Feel low' – what a strange, insignificant little phrase that is to describe this bleak space she currently inhabits. More fitting for a fat schoolgirl on the sofa with a cold. Again her body begins to shake but now it is with great releasing waves of ... she is not sure what. There are tears racing down her cheeks so this must be grief, but again her body has taken charge. It is convulsed with sobbing, mourning its loss but her mind is small and cold, staying at a distance and observing the carry-on. A tissue begins to mop at her face. For a second she wonders if it is her own hand that is patting gently at her cheeks.

'Listen, Maggie, you're bound to feel this way. It's perfectly normal. Would you care for a little water?' Maggie realises that she does care for a little water, but her cords are strangled with gunk and her tongue won't do her bidding. She opens her eyes and tries to catch hold of her voice.

'Y . . . y . . . ye . . . yes.' It is the voice of a monster in a children's film. She sees the tanned face and the cornflower-blue eyes and the dazzling teeth. How much more wholesome can this woman get?

'There . . . this'll make you feel a little better. Your mouth must be pretty dry.' The water flows over her tongue, like a river over parched ground, making little contact, just careering to its destination. A second sip brings a bitter, poisonous taste to the back of her throat.

'Oh God . . .' Again her voice bubbles with mucus.

'I guess you could do with a mouthwash, huh?' And the nurse disappears, wafting her spring flowers smell as she goes. And the chair by the wall is empty! The man has gone! Michael has gone! Her sobbing stops short with a hiccough and the nurse returns with a paper cup filled with a girl-pink liquid, and Maggie doubts whether the man had ever been there at all.

The Castaway

ℰ∂

'hhhh ... looks like Boileau's disappeared as well ... Oh
no, I spy a familiar underpant on the floor of the closet.
Oh well, a girl can dream, can't she? ... Put the kettle on, Ciss
... let's have a cuppa.' Cissie is sitting on the old brown sofa, her
numb fingers struggling with the bucklers of her biker boots.

'Yeah, a nice cup of tea, vicar. Nothing like a cuppa in a crisis,
and then I think I might have to go to bed shortly.' She stares at
the coffee table. In the middle of it there is a small lake of brown
liquid with a pair of nail clippers sitting in it, like a tiny motor
craft moored at its edge and it looks as though another newspaper
will be indelibly printed on the shabby veneer. She thinks of the
bright morning sunlight filling the pale yellow kitchen back in
London and for the first time she is afraid to think of it as home.

'God, this place needs mucking out. Luke's usually been round
in his pinny by now . . . Soooo ... Cecelia O'Brien, you only
came out here to escape the vermin hacks ... did you?' Helena
is lounging against the jamb of the bedroom door, one eyebrow
raised in a perfect arch.

'No, I just popped over for a carton of milk and a packet of
tea bags! I was always coming! I just came a few days earlier,
that's all.'

'Well, before you do anything you should call Jenny ... So
what if the fucking press know you're a les. You're happy with
Jenny aren't you? What's the big deal?'

Cissie puts her head in her hands but the stench of stale

cigarette butts overflowing from the thick white teacup, its handle lost in some long-forgotten incident, makes her stomach heave and she gets up and goes into the tiny kitchen, just off the hallway.

Helena continues. 'You've got nothing to hide. You love each other. You've got a good relationship. Proclaim it to the world! Shame the fucking devil!' Cissie feels suddenly weak and holds on to the small stainless-steel sink for support.

'I mean for Christ's sake you've got nothing to be ashamed of. Brazen it out, darling.'

Cissie fills the kettle. She can hear Helena, chuntering, clanging cups and glasses together and cursing her own untidiness. She reaches up to the cupboard above the sink and finds it completely devoid of crockery, just a lonely glass lemon-squeezer sits on its bottom shelf, dusty and unused. More puffing and clanking from the living room.

'I think just about every cup we possess is in here, Cis. Perhaps a little washing up might be appropriate at this moment.'

Cissie stares down at the sink, its brilliant sheen long since replaced by a brown, ingrained stain. It is choked with plates and cutlery and glasses, half submerged in a cold, greasy consommé of toast and crumbs and goodness knows what else. Suddenly Marvin Gaye's 'Heard it through the Grapevine' blasts out from the other room at a preposterous pitch. It is quickly adjusted to a more bearable level.

'Sorreeee ... You know, Ciss ... I hate to admit it but I am worried about Maggie. Twenty-four hours would be nothing in England, I mean she's been gone for days on end there and nobody turns a hair ... but here in New York ... it really is a different ballgame. I think perhaps we should check in with old blue eyes Lorenzetti. I mean ... you know, where on earth did she spend last night? ... I go cold just thinking about it ... in every sense of the word!' Helena is now lolling against the kitchen door, each hand clutching a motley bunch of mugs and glasses. She looks at Cissie's back, strangely immobile, the hunched shoulders, still clad in the big rough leather coat, redolent of old footballs and school satchels; her head hung low, the fine dark waves of hair in need of a wash, and Helena feels a small spasm of irritation.

'Oh for Christ's sake, Cissie, don't crawl into a dark little hole, you're worse than Luke! What on earth is wrong with everyone? Just leave all this and go and phone Jenny now, if not least to tell the poor girl where the fuck you are ... There's no point in going on about going home, the airports are going to be shut for days at this rate. Just phone her ... just phone her before she goes to ... I mean what's the worst thing that can happen?'

Cissie's weight sags down onto one leg and she lets go a dry little laugh. She does not turn round and she talks directly into the washing up.

'Oh Jenny might tell me not to come back at all ... that my mother has committed suicide on reading the newspapers ... that Jessica "cockroach" Harvey of the Daily Arsehole is on her way over here to feed off my miserable reaction to all of this! But apart from that? ... No ... I think it'll be a nice girlie chat, packed with fun, fashion ideas and just oozing with juicy gossip!'

'... O.K. Get your point ... but one little phone call could clear most of that up and you could just find that absolutely none of those things are true. So why don't you just shift your diminutive little arse, dial her bloody number and let me get at the washing up.'

Cissie turns; Helena is still standing in the doorway of the tiny cramped kitchen. She suddenly seems enormously tall and imposing, one dark curtain of hair almost covering her left eye. She is chewing the inside of one cheek, pushing her lips out into a cat's arse of a pout. Cissie drops her gaze and looks down at her own feet. They seem smaller than usual in the flecked woolly walking socks. She looks over at Helena's bare feet, long and white with their blood-red nails, and feels a chill prickle across her back. Without looking up she watches her feet join Helena's and putting her arms around Helena's waist she rests her head on the firm high bosom. She can hear Helena's heartbeat, steady and strong. Helena shifts her balance and Cissie can hear the heartbeat quicken. She cannot let go of her. A small oasis in a cold wasteland. She moves her hands slowly up and down the long, high back, the cashmere sweater making the movement easy and sensual. She had not expected the latter and she feels her face go hot. She had been looking for the hard ridge of her mother's spine, or perhaps the comforting plump roll that lies just above Jenny's waist. She wonders if Helena's mouth is still puckered into its unconscious pout or if her eyebrow, half hidden by the dark swathe of hair, is arched with impatience or in irony; or if the large grey eyes are turned towards the ceiling with that familiar look of bored intolerance. Nothing in the soft, perfumed bosom gives a clue as to what Helena's features might be doing. All there is is warmth and a heartbeat and for the moment that is enough.

Helena is in fact looking down into the crowded sink and wondering if there's space to dump the mugs and glasses she still holds. At the same time she is holding her body incredibly still, making her breath shallow and imperceptible, drawing in her stomach muscles and shrinking into herself so that there is nothing of her on the surface of her body, at least nothing that matters; the essential Helena having retreated inwards into a small, tight ball at her centre. It is a technique she had perfected as a child and now when necessary it comes without thought, as second nature. For a moment she thinks of repelling Cissie quickly and efficiently, perhaps using the cups and glasses clasped in her hands, but she continues to hold them, her arms stiff and stick-like, held away from her own body as if she were being fitted for a dress; and she thinks of the small Italian restaurant on the corner of a street in Little Italy somewhere, 79th Street? What is its name? A spaghetti vongole would be nice, with garlic bread and a bottle of Chianti Classico.

She can hear the lift on some other floor. For once she would have welcomed the sound of Luke lumbering in through the door, dragging himself into the living room and collapsing into the armchair as if he had just scaled Everest. It is how he entered every room. She had once commissioned a cartoonist friend to do an affectionate drawing of Luke for his birthday. The result is an ink sketch of the man as a snail. He is lying on a bed with a beautiful girl massaging his shell, another two beauties are standing close by adoringly fanning him with palm leaves. In the background a tranquil sea and coconut palms complete the scene. Luke's face is the picture of hangdog misery, crimson and sweating, his huge eyes myopic and watery and pained. Out of his mouth, sagging open in speech, comes a bubble containing the words: 'Oh this really is intolerable!'

Helena was almost sick with laughter on first seeing it. Luke had sulked for a week or more and had then accused Helena of talking to the artist behind his back about their sex life. 'Nothing to tell sweetheart!' and she had hooted with laughter again. Luke has never allowed her to hang it. Whenever she finds him particularly pompous or self-righteous, Helena brings this drawing to mind; but it is not Luke's face, with its martyred and burdened expression, made more pathetic and ludicrous by two antennae adorning his forehead that causes her hysterics, so much as the sight of his pale, diminutive little legs coming out from underneath the outsized shell, a smattering of cartoon hairs protruding from the slimy flesh; and it is the large feet with their perfectly spaced worm-like toes, bedecked in those loathsome and rotting Birkenstock sandals that she had only recently per-suaded him to get rid of. It is these details complete with another, of Luke's glasses knocked askew and hanging from one ear, both lenses steamed up, that can be guaranteed to lift her spirits on the worst of days; and today is no exception.

Cissie shifts her head. She thinks she can hear something, a distant tinkling sound. On opening her eyes she can see that Helena's right arm is shaking, causing the cups and glasses she holds to clink together. She can feel Helena's tight abdomen begin to twitch and jump against her own and small involuntary pants of breath disturb the air above her head. The breath has the familiar odour of long-smoked cigarettes and she can detect the smell of the coffee, thick with sugar, that they had bought at the famous Carnegie Deli on their way home from the theatre. The subway was not in operation so they were forced to walk, and Cissie had talked for the entire way home: she could not stop it coming; confusion and anger, paranoia and shame; the question of love and pain and Jenny.

For thirty odd blocks, through freezing air and on snow that was now treacherously icy, she had allowed things to tumble forth at will. Thoughts and feelings had come steaming out into that cold, cold afternoon, and now instead of feeling closer to Helena she felt strangely cut off, cut loose and set adrift. Helena had said little until they had got back to the apartment, and then she had tackled the domestic chaos with unusual relish, while spouting her usual cavalier solutions to things, leaving Cissie isolated and somehow ashamed.

Now something is happening, the nature of which Cissie is unsure. The panting is more pronounced and every so often it catches snatches of Helena's voice, high and exhilarated. Cissie slides her arms tighter around the slender waist, not to still whatever it is that is reverberating there but to be closer to it, to be part of it.

'Oh . . . God . . . ha . . . oh . . .' a high-pitched jumble of tiny words ping the air while waves of something – relief? – shudder through Helena's body. Cissie can feel her own body begin to tremble in response.

'Oh Helly . . .' she knows this is going to be a moment of some kind of truth, a defining moment in their relationship. She releases her arms from around Helena's waist and rising onto tiptoe she launches them around her neck. For a second there she thinks she can smell her mother's hair, brittle and neglected, but Helena's essence, made heavy with a mix of Chanel, cigarettes and the stage make-up she still wears from the show that never happened, is instantly all-pervading. She finds Helena's burning cheek with her own and traps a sluggish tear that had been making a meandering river bed through the thick, pale foundation.

The last and only time Cissie had ever seen Helena cry was when, some years before, Helena had lost out on a part to another actress. She had been inconsolable for hours, raging around the Lettice Street flat.

'I AM the Queen of France!' Luke had been appalled at her behaviour and had sat in red-faced silence, whereas Maggie had joined Helena in a vitriolic attack on the poor actress, citing her distinct lack of talent and her great wobbly legs as the two main reasons why she should not be allowed onto a stage, let alone play the Queen of France. The two had eventually dissolved into riotous hysterics as they breathlessly competed for the worst and most accurate denigration of the unfortunate woman: 'the lumpen overgrown Barbie ... pushing forty ... whose poor, lonely little brain cell could never cope with both the text and the minute-to-minute struggle with her ever inflating body.'

Cissie had simply observed, excited and taken aback by Helena's rare display of emotion, and now as Helena's ribcage batters against her own and another hot tear finds its way between their respective cheeks, Cissie can sense that she is party yet again to something rare in Helena: an expression of feeling, unadorned by campery, something pure and straight from source, not having been through Helena's filter of cynicism. It must be something exceptional and probably painful for Helena. A rare moment of genuine intimacy; a wonderful beginning, perhaps. Cissie winds her arms tighter around Helena's neck and squeezes their heads together, her own tears beginning to well.

'... oh ... ha ... for ... Christ's sake, Cissie, you're ... strangling me!'

'Oh Helly, I'm so sorry ... I'm ...' Cissie jerks her head back like someone waking from a dream to discover they are kissing a stranger. Her arms uncoil as if held by a powerful spring and she steps back banging into the sink. Helena, still holding on to the mugs and glasses, throws back her head. Her face is purple, the veins in her neck shockingly engorged, her mouth wide open in the shape of a scream, and her body contorted and shaking. She slides her back down the jamb of the door, her bottom landing with a silent bounce on the grubby linoleum tiles. She is laughing! ... SHE IS LAUGHING.

Cissie watches herself from somewhere else as she claps a hand over her own mouth and tears flood unfettered down her cheeks. She looks down at Helena, whose head is now between her knees, as if she were about to faint. Her shoulders are jumping up and down and vulgar peals of laughter are bursting forth. She lets go of the mugs and glasses and they clink into disarray on either side of her as she rolls helplessly from buttock to buttock, clutching her stomach in painful ecstasy.

'Ooooh ... oh ... oh ... Cissie ... I'm ... so ... sorry ...' She lifts her hand as if to repel an attack. 'I was thinking ... of ...' and again she is helpless.

'Of your bloody self ... as per bloody usual!' And Helena's cackling rises several octaves into hysterical squeaks and squeals.

'No ... no ... you don't ... understand ... I was thinking ... about ... about ...' And Cissie's hands land on her head like the talons of a giant bird, stretched white with fury. Pulling two huge handfuls of the luxuriant hair into a parody of little girl's bunches, she drags Helena's head from side to side. 'Let's get it on,' Marvin Gaye suggests from next door and, digging her nails into Helena's scalp, she hisses into the top of her head.

'I don't give a fuck about what you were thinking about! You stupid, stupid woman! You're not worth the fucking bother!' And with one last jerk bouncing Helena's head against the thin partition wall, she is out, across the living room and into the bathroom, where she lets out a long, guttural roar, causing her head to vibrate and a great gob of foaming saliva to fly across the room and land like a jewel on a pair of leopard skin panties drying above the bath.

Helena is on her side on the kitchen floor. She has stopped

laughing and is rubbing her head, Stan Laurel bemused by Oliver Hardy's wrath. She hears the bedroom door bang shut with an almighty boom. She tries to reconstruct the last couple of minutes in her mind so that she might assess what actually happened, but all it serves to do is bring to mind the image of Luke as the snail and a flurry of giggles comes tittering out, gathering momentum until it is a river in full flood and she is helpless once more.

Cissie is sitting on the bathroom floor, her back against the bath. She has not turned the light on, not wanting to face the sickening brightness of its cold white glare, but the door is securely locked and she sits, empty and spent in a distant cottonwool limbo. She notices her right cheek is twitching and she recalls Maggie in the taxi on their way into Manhattan, her breath sharp with ketones, her eyes large and black with fatigue.

'What am I to you? What happens now?'

Cissie tries to get up, but thinks better of it, her body heavy and immobile. She rests her head back on the bath, feeling the cold comfort of its enamel rim on the base of her skull as Helena's loud, gulping guffaws filter through from the kitchen. Somehow their effect is greatly diminished. This little dark cell with its tightly locked door and overpowering smell of damp washing could be somewhere else entirely, floating deep into outer space, in another disconnected time. She thinks of the warm bosom of just a few moments ago and the subsequent shock horror of her humiliating misinterpretation of events, and it is as a dot on the horizon, something left long ago, too distant to focus on in any detail. Helena's guffaws have subsided now into titters, silly and comical, and Cissie herself feels a trickle of mirth down in her gut and begins to laugh, to laugh at the laughter and bask in its relief. 'She's leavin'', Marvin Gaye continues from next door. She begins to remove the heavy leather coat, and as she does so, she places her palm down heavily on something sharp. Examining it in the dark, she recognises it as a fragment of the little plastic whistle that she'd broken the night before in her fall, and she cannot wait to speak to Jenny.

'Jenny . . . I am so, so sorry . . . please forgive me . . . I want to come home.' She knows that there will then be a silence, and then something a bit harsh and rather cold, but it will be straight.

Cissie is now sitting on Helena's bed, her hand resting on the receiver, her throat dry. On the floor she spies a small black and white photograph, slightly crumpled and curled at the corners. On picking it up she instantly recognises the much younger Helena, stretched out and triumphant, smug in the knowledge that she has what people want, and there is Luke, slightly removed from everyone, at odds with the group; always on the fringe of things, always in the wings looking on, never on the stage. Even as an actor when his character was forced to stand centre stage, he still managed to look peripheral, his face pink with discomfort, his body weirdly stiff and awkward, his eyes darting nervously at the audience. Helena is looking across at him and Cissie is shocked to witness another unguarded millisecond of Helena's life. A look of sympathy? Of empathy? Of compassion? Of love maybe? It is something like that.

'That must have made her face ache,' she says, her voice rough from roaring and exhaustion. 'Those muscles aren't used to that configuration.' But that is a special look rarely seen on anyone's face, never on Helena's.

Cissie looks at her watch: it is ten past six, ten past eleven in Putney. Jenny will just be winding down for the night and as Cissie looks towards the phone it rings, long and urgent, its sharp trill zipping straight through the centre of her chest. Before it can ring a second time she has it at her ear.

'. . . Hello? . . .'

'Hello? . . . who's that? . . . Is that you, Cissie?' It is a man. She can't bring to mind one single man who is likely to ring her from England.

'. . . Yes . . .' Her throat is paper dry. She suspects this could be a reporter. She should not have admitted to her name.

'At last I've found you! . . . I . . . You must have turned your mobile off . . .'

'Look, you arsehole, you've found nothing, now get off my back! You bloody parasite!' She slams the phone down and swallows hard. She can see the man now, small and shambling with a blotched, discoloured face and badly stained teeth. When he'd first approached, outside her house, jumping out at her apparently from nowhere, smelling faintly of a mixture of fish and booze, she had expected him to ask for money and she had reeled back, her chest tightening when he had asked her to comment on her relationship with Jenny. She had rushed into the house, unable to speak. Now she is almost certain that the voice on the phone just now was one and the same. It had the same sadistic flavour of the school sneak.

She picks up the receiver and with a sharp intake of breath she dials her home in London. She can see the familiar green frog phone, sitting snugly on the little blue dresser, next to the huge wooden fruit bowl and surrounded by letters and bills and comforting scraps of domestic detritus, its determined chirrup, persistent and optimistic. 'Please ... please ... Jenny, please!' Another sharp intake of breath: it is Jenny.

'Not available. Please leave a message.' It is Jenny's voice right enough, but coated in a cold, shiny veneer, closed off and uncontactable.

'What?' It is like opening a door into a familiar room and finding instead that it opens out onto the side of a building hundreds of feet up. One step and you're gone. '... I ... it ... SHIT!' She teeters on the threshold, thinking 'why not?' and then bangs the receiver back onto its cradle.

She can hear the clunk of crockery and cutlery coming from the kitchen. It sounds petulant and aggressive and she wants to weep but her energy won't stretch to that. She falls back onto the rumpled bed and her eyes bang shut, the lids heavy and hot. Where could Jenny be? At the theatre perhaps? At her sister's? Or maybe standing right next to the phone? Barefoot, in her pyjamas, silently listening, hands on hips, staring down at the answerphone, her huge eyes dark with disappointment.

'Oh God!' It rings again, startling and shrill. She sits up, but the deep sag of the bed throws her back down again. She scrambles back up against the force of the springs.

'Please, Jenny!' and knocking an empty glass off the night-stand, she whisks the phone to her ear.

'Hello . . .?' It is the same man's voice but in the millisecond between breathing in and uttering her reply another voice, a high, sharp, expectant voice, darts in, filling the tiny crack of air space before she can even breathe out, leaving her sitting there open-mouthed.

'Hello . . .?' It is Helena's voice, on the extension in the next room, a matter of feet away from her.

'Oh for God's sake, Helena, what on earth is going on?'

Cissie's mind reels as the man's voice mutates shockingly and inexorably into a familiar drone. How could it have been anyone else? Helena's voice has dropped several notes and its tone is threatening. Cissie can picture the fine jaw clenching with impatience.

'You may well ask what is going on! Where the hell are you?'

'I, my dear, am at the Bellevue Hospital and you'll never guess who else is here, in somewhat of a state?'

'Oh my God! You've found her! Well what sort of a state for God's sake?'

'Well it seems she has lost a baby. She was five and a half months pregnant! Did you know anything about this?'

Cissie breathes in, short and sharp.

'My God! You sound like you're accusing me of being the father! No, I did not know anything about it!' Helena is hissing, her voice strangled with distaste.

Cissie begins to tune out.

'. . . only assume . . . Hardy's child . . . sort of irresponsible . . .'

She stares down at the little photograph, still clasped in her hand. Frank Hardy smiles back at her from just behind Helena's right shoulder. He had been the most recent of Maggie's lovers, a sometime actor/musician, glib-tongued and slippery with

Stewart Granger looks. Maggie had fallen for banter that the rest of the group merely found entertaining. All of them, even Frank himself, realising it was a performance, and no one was more surprised than Frank at Maggie's ravenous absorption of it. Frank's cool patter and constant impersonations of American film stars she had never heard of had always irritated Cissie. Even now, looking at his slightly blurred image, she feels distinctly uncomfortable.

'... brought in by some stranger ... picked her up in a bar. Quite honestly I think the best course ...' She watches as the little snap, now moist with perspiration, slips from her hand onto the floor. A blood-red sliver of toenail lies next to it on the thin brown carpet.

'... can't think what possessed Cissie to bring her out here in that state.' She covers the photograph lightly with her foot.

'... possessed is certainly the right word!'

'... What's happening? ... phoned up about ten minutes ago ... a torrent of abuse.'

'She made a pass at me, I didn't respond, and so she attacked me.' Cissie places the phone carefully back in its cradle and at the same time she presses the ball of her foot down hard onto the photograph. She can just detect its slippery surface through the thick rough sock; and then something else, something small and sharp painfully pierces the sole of her foot. Swinging the foot up onto her knee she can see the tiny red crescent dangling from the sock like a miniature sickle and she breathes out a long, rushing roar of a breath.

The Identity

𝓟𝓪

Luke hears the sound of skis, their smooth surface skimming across the snow, and the previous night's dream is broken. He sees the blurred image of Helena's dancing body and hears her throat choke with laughter. He pivots to see where the sound is coming from and a figure clad in black except for a scarlet balaclava, a comic-book hero, skis effortlessly by, his great muscular thighs pushing the skis on with superb grace. Luke watches for a moment as the figure breezes his way directly down the centre of Park Avenue, into the gloom ahead, large puffs of steam clouding the air around his head as he goes. Luke makes an attempt at apeing the skier's elegance and pushes off, unsteadily on his right foot like a child at an ice rink. The sidewalk is icy and he sails forward for several seconds on that foot, an image in his head of the black-clad figure and the sidewalk is suddenly whipped out from beneath him, causing him to crash down, bashing his coccyx with a painful jolt.

'Hey, BooWoo boy, you done took a tumble.' A round, dark brown face, wearing a black woolly hat pulled down to eyebrow level, presents itself in front of him. The hat has the word 'Menace' emblazoned on it in red. 'What ya doin' down there, BooWoo boy?' There is a screech of high-pitched laughter somewhere to his right. 'What was you doin' there, BooWoo ... a little piece of ice skatin'?' Two pairs of legs come and stand next to the interrogator. One of them, feet wide apart, one knee springing back and forth, is directly in front of Luke. Luke knows the knee is a sign of impatience, like a horse pawing the ground or the drumming of fingers on a table top, and letting out a small yelp he considers rising up and just bulldozing through them rugby-style and hightailing it to freedom but instead he collapses onto his side. 'Leave me alone! . . . Please!' There is more laughter.

'Hey, what's wrong wit ya, BooWoo? Ya gonna get mighty cold down there, boy.'

Luke can feel the blood pummelling through the veins in his head and he brings his arms up to protect it.

'It's O.K., Boo, we ain't gonna steal your bobble hat . . . you can keep that.'

'Hey, help the man up.' This is a different voice, this is dredged up from a deep, dark cavern. 'I said help the man up.' The brown face disappears and rough fingers grab at Luke, digging into his ribcage; other fingers, in another time, might have been initiating a childish tickling session. Luke had always hated that kind of ridiculous horse-play. Now he longs for old friends to find his funny bone and pull his trousers down amid hoots of laughter. Instead these strangers are heaving his rigid body upright.

'Now come on, BooWoo, you ain't making this too easy for us.' Luke's knees are still drawn up and his chin is pushed hard into his chest.

'*Pleeeease* . . . just let me go and I'll give you everything I've got.' They yank him up off the sidewalk and with his knees still tucked up under him he swings between the two men like an amputee.

'I say, I say, I say, do I hear an incey wincey hint of a British accent there? Do we have ourselves a limey here?' Luke has his eyes tight shut and his teeth clenched. 'I say, sir, are you a friend of dear old Prince Charles?' To his left, the brown-faced 'menace' cackles into his ear, damp puffs of his breath, hot on Luke's cheek, the odour of garlic and cigarettes invading his nostrils.

'No! I'll tell you who you are!' This is from the knee-jerk on his right. Both men are holding Luke painfully tight under each arm. 'You are Waldo! Hey, man, remember Waldo? Where's

Waldo? Well he is here! Waldo . . . I bin looking for you all my life!'

'Who the hell is Waldo? This is my BooWoo.'

'No this is Waldo. Remember the teeny little cartoon dweeb ya had to find in a great messa stuff? Well this is him. He got the hat, the glasses, everything.' There is more laughter.

'Nah I don't know no Waldo. This here is BooWoo. I'd know dear old BooWoo anywhere.' Both men, with one arm holding on to Luke, are now alternately slapping one another's free palm. Luke opens his eyes a fraction and can see them, facing one another across him, inches from the tip of his nose. He can smell their unwashed faces. Their mouths are stretched wide with laughter, their eyes shiny and popping with glee. The clamour of their laughter rushing through his head is causing Luke to have one of his headaches. He can feel the muscles at the back of his neck beginning to seize as the sinews tighten and twist. He closes his eyes for a moment and considers his demise at the hands of these men and on reopening them he sees it is not laughter and joy he is witnessing but what looks like a battle-cry. The mouths are still stretched but with shouting not laughter, the eyes still agog and shining, but with incitement not glee and something else is blaring out above everything.

The two men stop and turn towards Luke, their faces stupid with surprise. It is Luke's own voice that he can hear roaring out into the night. His own voice, thick and guttural and at the end of its tether, roaring into the faces of these men. He sees 'Knee-jerk' for the first time; a child with baby-blond hair, his pretty blue eyes wide and blank, not even reaching Luke's shoulder in height, his mouth is frozen open and 'Menace' in his cretin's hat, even shorter than his comrade, his face jolted into deadpan by the sheer volume of Luke's own voice and a slightly taller, dark figure, backing off some yards away, he of the cavernous voice, 'Shines! . . . Mamba! . . . leave the man alone . . . you got nothin' we want, Waldo.' Luke hears his own voice tailing away into a hiss of steam and he lets his feet down onto the sidewalk, at the same time the two boys let go of his arms with a little shove which sends him off balance and he staggers backwards falling back down onto the sidewalk.

'Say . . . where's Waldo? Why he's right here on his ass, man!'

'Go home to dear old England, BooWoo boy, before the bogeyman come get ya.' And bouncing and swaggering the three boys move off.

Luke watches their walk. There is something offensive about it, straight from the genitals, crude and aggressive. He wants to scream after them, 'Assholes!' but instead he speaks the word quietly. They are laughing and one of them is barking like a dog, he cannot see which. Then 'Menace' jumps up on 'Knee-jerk's' back simulating intercourse and making more barking-type sounds amid gales of laughter from the other two.

'Boowoo . . . boowoo . . . boowoo boy, boowoowoowoo boy.' Luke continues to watch them jostling and sliding on the treacherous sidewalk. In their baggy pants and army boots they are clowns, little clowns, out on the town. Luke scrambles onto his feet and catches sight of his reflection in a shop window. He is standing statue still, his head cocked round at a quizzical angle, his bobble hat shoved over onto one side. To his right is a huge male mannequin, dressed in a silver suit. He is holding on to three pure white huskies as they strain forward on silver leashes. To his left, a willowy female figure swathed in white fur is pulling a sledge carrying two children, packed into tiny white ski suits. He stares at the odd tableau he has inadvertently become part of.

He removes the bobble hat and looks at it. He notices that his hands are shaking. He looks back at his reflection and smoothes his hair back into place. He had worn a bobble hat in winter for as long as he could remember. Even Helena had not been able to persuade him to do otherwise, as she had with his beloved Birkenstock sandals. 'You look like they've let you out for the day!' But he had held on to the bobble hat through years of ridicule. The tortuous daily ritual of having it grabbed from his head on the school bus and passed around a jeering crowd of boys, eventually finding it muddied and squashed, having been trampled underfoot: it became a kind of trademark, something he simply could not let go of for fear of losing ... what? He stuffs the hat into the pocket of his duffle coat and stares again at the reflection. After a matter of seconds he retrieves it, and placing it firmly on his head, he turns and leaves the tableau.

Once back at the hotel he decides not to take the lift, and begins to mount the stairs to the twelfth floor.

The Ocean

ﾑ

Michael is peering at her, wide-eyed and unblinking. Is he hoping that in doing so he will destroy the image? That beneath his powerful gaze reality will simply give up and present him with what he wishes to see? In any respect she stubbornly remains, and the now familiar smell of blood is unmistakable. Hers is different though, it smells of salt and the sea, not sweet and metallic like Maggie's, and she doesn't have Maggie's beauty. She has a plain face but there is something sensual about the mouth, something luscious. Michael is stirred by the set of it and by the abandoned tangle of her body.

Was it the same bar? The same set of circumstances? Or had she been vital and wholesome and available: out for an adventure? Was there a taxi ride home in the snow? Both of them charged with anticipation? Had her friends warned her not to go? Was there a father who had ordered her home by midnight and who was now sick with worry?

'OOOh . . .' His lips freeze around the word as it careers into oblivion. So much blood! The floor is awash and his old moleskin trousers are splattered and stained, on each thigh a perfect hand-print, like you might see decorating an elementary school wall, with a child's name and age beneath, only these were done in blood, still damp. She must have held on to him, pleading for her life. What had she done to cause such a dearth of mercy in him, to cause such butchery?

'What did she do, Michael, to deserve this? . . . Find you

attractive? Kind? Did she ask you for this?' Officer Crowley is standing behind him. He has brought the cold New York night into the apartment to swirl around and cause the hairs on the back of Michael's neck to rise and prickle.

'I don't know ... Sweet Jesus ... I don't know!'

'I smell something ... what is that?' Officer Boyle has just edged into Michael's vision, a dark blot on an already darkened landscape. Michael turns his head to take him in fully but his eyes will not follow. They are trained upon the girl, upon her face. It is not as he had perceived it. It is the eyes; only partly visible beneath her half-closed lids, they have the glacial stare of the dead but they are definitely brown not grey as he had first thought. The mouth remains the same but the hair ... Under a heavy slick of blood, not quite congealed, it is dark and thick and unmistakable. The legs, long and shapely, tossed away from her at painful angles are unmistakable too.

'Oooh nno ... Elizabeth ... Lizzie ... pl ... no!' He falls down onto his knees.

'This is my wife. My Liz ... OOOh no!'

'Oh Michael, how you disappoint.' Michael is seized by that old combination of shame and panic. He turns round clumsily on his knees and looking up, notes that Officer Crowley is nowhere to be seen. Instead another figure stands there, towering. The pale, creased face with its heavy jowls and watery grey eyes, looking down with a kind of sad contempt. It could have been Officer Crowley, had the hair been redder and the man younger. It almost could have been.

'Dad ... dy ... I ... I ...' His mind is a cold, empty room. No helpful friends there. No energy, no AMBITION to create the words he might need. Just an overwhelming sense of pointlessness.

'... I ... I ...'

'We have to take him away, Michael. Your mother and I cannot allow this.'

'Dad ... no!' Michael's father is carrying a child, wrapped in a coarse blue blanket. Michael cannot see its face for his father has the small, limp body flopped over his shoulder in a fireman's lift, but he knows it is Dominic.

'You are simply not able.' With that he turns and leaves, Dominic swaying back and forth against the great broad back, with its inappropriate garb; the bright, short-sleeved Hawaiian shirt – an embarrassment on every vacation and summer outing. Just before they disappear through the apartment door, Dominic strains to lift his head, the warm brown eyes filled with desperate tears, and they are gone.

'Daaaad!! . . . Pleeeeease!!' Michael tries but he cannot lift his knees up as the quagmire of thick, dark blood sucks them to the floor. His voice too is now stuck within his chest, weak and impotent. He begins to take in a deep breath to let out a final plea and finds that he is drowning. Some smothering thing is across his face and everything is black. He realises that somehow he has fallen onto the girl, her corpse squashed beneath him. Revulsion propels him back up and he can breathe once more but everywhere is dark. For a moment he is bewildered, then his fingers find the soft folds of his duvet. Good God he is in his own bed! The bloody, twisted body is in his own bed!

'*No!*' and bounding from the bed, he slams into the tall window that overlooks the snowswept passage. He spins round, staring back through the gloom at the large double bed, and sure enough there is a dark mass on the right-hand side. He cannot make out whether it is the body or not but he can see what looks like an arm and, yes, a leg and there is a head; and a little voice says,

'. . . Please someone . . . help me!' He rushes at the light switch, the little voice following at his ear.

'Oh God . . . oh God . . . oh God . . . oh God . . . oh God . . . oh God . . . oh God . . . oh God . . .!' And after several snatches at the wall beside his bed, he locates the small bank of switches. One quick chop from the side of his hand and all the lights are on. And there it is, lying there spread out, in the inviting golden light of his bedroom, almost as if waving. He goes to touch it, not trusting his own eyes. For it is his long navy dressing gown. He grabs it roughly from the bed.

'For pity's sake!' and screwing it tightly into a ball he hurls it into the far corner of the room where it disappears softly behind the low velvet chair. Elizabeth's chair. She has not forgiven him for removing it from their old place in McDougall Street. She still has the footstool belonging to it. Then banging off the lights with the heel of his hand he collapses onto the bed. The clammy film of sweat covering his body turns icy and within an instant has chilled him to the marrow. He burrows back under the duvet, and as exhaustion begins to drag his body down into sleep, he sees her again, Elizabeth, as clear and sharp as day. Lying on the floor of the downstairs bathroom, ungainly and bloodied. Her long fine limbs flopping and lolling, almost brazen, lying there in a way she could never have done in life.

'Oh no . . .!' He pushes the duvet back and the shock of cool air on his damp body gets him up and scurrying over to the chair to retrieve his dressing gown.

Making his way to the staircase, bashing on lights every which way with the side of his fist, he cannot resist a detour into the study. He does not put the lights on here, but creeps stealthily over to the rail that runs along the edge of the mezzanine and peers down into the living room below. Even through the semi-darkness he can make out a great dark stain on the big sofa and another on his pale cotton rug where he had tried to scrub away Maggie's blood on arriving back from the hospital. The rug would have to go, he would throw it in a dumpster somewhere. Maybe the sofa too, who knows?

He holds his breath to listen . . . Nothing . . . The beat of his heart, a little frenzied maybe, and now a muffled police siren, a long way off, in another part of the city, and the ceaseless tick of the big brown clock. A sound that should be comforting, steady and predictable but instead fills the whole place with an alarming sense of time running out. He darts out and down the spiral staircase, slipping painfully on his heels down the last three steps, and letting out a small, pathetic yelp he stands before the bathroom door. Again he holds his breath to listen ... tick ... tock ... tick ... tock. He can hear the wind moan as it blasts into the passage to whisper around his door and the familiar squeaks and creaks of his lungs; but not a sound from within. He lets out a rasping breath and longs for Dominic to lace his cold little fingers through his own, but Dominic is far away, he would not come within a universe of this. He says her name.

'Lizzie? ...' and as if summoned, Cape Cod is in his nostrils, but not as it was before, dry and salty. This is huge and grey and tidal.

'Oh Lizzie ...' He touches the door with the tips of his fingers. It is shut.

'No ... no Lizzie ...' He takes hold of the handle and, expecting the weight of a body to be against it, he pushes the door open with some force. It flies back easily and he jams on the light with the palm of his hand. He lifts a foot, almost expecting it to be stuck in the blood, but there is nothing. Everywhere is pristine: not a sign, not a speck, everything in its place. He falls down onto his haunches and then forward onto his knees.

'Oh you asshole ... you asshole ... you asshole ... you asshole.' He lies down on his stomach, the top of his head just touching the base of the toilet bowl, his cheek on the smooth warm boards of the bathroom floor. The smell of the Atlantic replaced by the astringent scent of Dettol, redolent of unpleasant little accidents and minor physical mishaps. He marvels at the pink, work-a-day quality of his hand, lying just inches from his face like some marine creature, beached and lifeless. He had done a good job: even at this close range he could not detect a single spot of Maggie's blood. But, my, had he scrubbed! In the wee small hours to the strains of Nina Simone declaring that she had got her heart and her liver, he had screamed along with her that he had got *his* and he had washed and scrubbed and scratched away at the blood with his own fingernails until his head was empty and numb. Only the rug and the sofa had defeated him before he fell onto his bed, asleep even before he had experienced its warm dark sanctuary. Now with the brilliant white skirting board directly in his eyeline, he scans it again for any stray spot that might have escaped his diligence, and a rivulet of sweat scurries down his forehead and slips into his eye before he can close his lid against its salty sting. He squeezes his eye shut in an exaggerated wink and wipes the palm of his hand across his forehead. He is surprised at how cool and wet it is. He allows his hand to drop back down in front of his face, causing a fresh waft of disinfectant to rise into his nostrils. And there at the edge of his thumbnail he can see it. He is bewildered and brings his thumb a little closer. Tucked in next to the cuticle is a tiny black dot, barely visible to the naked eye. Michael continues to stare at it, incredulous that he had missed it, then he touches it with the tip of his tongue. He knows it is another tiny dried fragment of Maggie's blood, a microscopic dot from her most intimate centre. He tries to remove it by dragging his top teeth across it, as he had done before, but this one clings on; a minute part of her lost child, stuck fast to his fingernail.

Michael had not liked the fact that her name was Maggie Salt and not Helena Cassidy. She was not a Maggie at all, and as for Salt: together they made a stolid, unromantic identity. Someone simple, honest and predictable. The absolute opposite of the wild, stormy creature he had found in that bar, the remains of whose unborn child he had mopped from this very floor a short few hours ago. Salt? Whoever heard of such a name! She was and would always be Helena Cassidy. He had not taken to the man either. The bobble-hatted nerd who had stormed angrily up to her bedside and announced with a red face and steamed-up glasses that this was, most definitely, not Helena Cassidy and that it was, in fact, a certain Maggie Salt. The girl, Helena/Maggie, had almost immediately gone into some sort of fit, as if the very sound of this man's voice had set her body quaking. It brought doctors and nurses scurrying from all directions, the nerd making everything worse with his stressed-out questioning and that fey British accent.

And then when the thing had finally subsided, Michael could hear him from behind the curtains hissing abuse at her, lambasting her with a vicious tirade. Michael had hovered nearby, pretending to be waiting for someone, and had thought once or twice of dragging back the curtains and intervening. Finally the jerk had slipped out to go to the phone and Michael had caught sight of Maggie for a second, a flash of her face as the curtains parted, and he felt pretty sure that their eyes had met and that hers were filled with something that had made him reach for his inhaler. He had then followed the angry, striding figure of the man to a telephone booth and eavesdropped. He had caught little of the conversation but from his attitude and demeanour Michael had concluded that the man was a condescending asshole and he had said as much under his breath. A petty, smug individual that he himself would have no time for and who certainly should not be concerned with anyone of 'Maggie's' fragility. She had simply lain there in silence, pinned to the bed by his invective.

Michael tries to picture her sitting on his big sofa, relaxed and at ease; herself and the sofa restored to normality. She has her knees drawn up to her chin and she is smiling, her eyes bright and shining, but he cannot get rid of the shocking lipstick cross on her forehead and she has not removed her boots! The black workman's boots are innocently planted on the pale calico cover. They suddenly seem minuscule, no bigger than a toddler's boot. Her hands too are tiny and chubby like a baby's and now they are waving and jerking erratically in front of her face, but the face has the same delicate perfection and the eyes are of a softer green. Michael longs for her to speak and she does.

'I am so cold, Michael, so very cold.'

The Ache

&

'I'm so c ... c ... cold.' Maggie's teeth are beginning to chatter.
'O.K., we're gonna have you back in bed in seconds flat.'
A towel hangs between Maggie's legs, heavy and sticky with
blood. She had put her head beneath the covers to take in the
latter's rich, meaty odour. She had thought that it might comfort
her but it had made her sick to her stomach and she had
reached out for her glass of water which sat on the edge of the
locker at her bedside. In doing so she had caught sight of her
hand in the dull glow of the night light. The nails, ragged
and misshapen as always, appeared to be clogged with dirt, a
gardener's hand, fresh from the potting shed. As she stared at it
suspended in mid-action, she had tried to imagine how the dirt
had arrived there.

'Ya fuckin' bastard! ... Ya fuckin' bastard! ... Ya fuckin' bastard!' A man was bellowing somewhere down a long echoing
corridor.

'Ya fuckin' bastard!' At the top of his voice. A stylus stuck in
a groove.

'Ya fuckin' bastard! ...' She had continued to stare at the hand
and without thinking had brought it to her nostrils and there it
was.

'Ya fuckin' bastard! ...' The stench from beneath the covers,
sweet and putrid.

'Ya fuckin' bastard! ...' The hand must have gone fumbling
there without her knowledge.

'Ya fuckin' bastard! ...' Curious as to what the discomfort might be.

'Ya fuckin' bastard!'

'Oh God! Nurse ... please ... somebody pleeease!' Maggie could hear someone running; the squeak of rubber soles as they thud onto polished lino, the chafing together of hefty knees, clad in nylon tights, the jingling of keys and chains and then a pair of strong arms and she was up on unsteady legs.

'What is it you need, dear ... the bathroom?'

'I need to get this shit off my hands!'

'Ohhhh I see, it's just a little blood.' Her breath smelt of tobacco and peppermint, and Maggie had clung on to the large soft arm that seemed to fill the sleeve of the woman's dress to bursting point.

Now Maggie's teeth are chattering but her hands are scrubbed and pink. She moves her cold cheek and places it against the warm, solid shoulder of the nurse as they walk back towards the ward. A fair aroma of eau de Cologne mingled with sweat overwhelms her with sadness and she burrows her head right under the woman's arm, where the odour is hot and over-powering, and there begins an unstoppable lament. From deep, deep inside her comes a high, keening cry; a long plaintive note of pure sadness. The nurse stops and enfolds Maggie in her plump, sure arms and the note continues for longer than either woman can believe possible. And then the sobbing; and when that finally stops, no one speaks; neither one being capable.

Maggie can hear a heartbeat, strong and rapid. Or it could be the fob watch that jingled on the nurse's chest when she ran; or there again the soft, frantic flutter of distant wings. Or ... well, whatever. The nurse gently extricates Maggie from her armpit and without a word guides her back to her bed where she flops heavily down onto the pillows and pulling the covers up around her she draws her knees into the foetal position.

'Now, can I get you a drink of something?' For the first time

Maggie takes a proper look at the woman into whose armpit she has been spilling her grief.

'Hi . . . I'm Sadie Maclachlan,' she whispers with a big broad smile and Maggie notices her pretty blue eyes and even teeth.

'I'm in charge of you folks tonight.' She is a thickset woman with apple cheeks and a mop of unruly grey curls, pure white at the temples. Maggie wonders whether her being 'in charge' means that it was she who had put a stop to the 'fuckin' bastard'. She could well imagine one of those short powerful arms with some poor devil's head in an armlock.

'You got any pain?'

'Oh, plenty of that,' Maggie replies in a tiny voice she hardly recognises.

'Pardon me?' the woman is tidying the bedclothes with quick, efficient tugs, smoothing the counterpane here and there with the palm of her hand. Maggie looks at the scrubbed, wrinkled hands, their short, smooth nails as white as snow, a wedding ring embedded deeply into the third finger of the left one, and her throat contracts with pity she does not understand.

'Did you speak with Sam Consadine today? Or should I say yesterday?' She looks down at her fob watch. 'Oh my! Do you know it was just gone two a.m.?' Maggie cannot speak.

'He's a nice fellow isn't he . . . Sam?' Maggie didn't think so but she had played her cards close to her chest, she had given nothing away as Sam Consadine sat patiently at her bedside, knees together and arms folded; waiting. She had seen all the trip wires and booby traps way ahead of time. Sam Consadine was no match for her. She knew full well he was just waiting for her madness to bubble up and leak out somewhere, and he knew just where to push and prod, but she had been ready for him and she was an old hand at this.

Still she does not speak.

'He's new here. Our old psychy left to have a baby . . .'

Suddenly the round farmer's-wife face bobs down beside the bed, the blue eyes with their dark lashes looking directly into Maggie's.

'I'm sorry . . . that was what you might call tactless. Heavens . . . you'd think I'd know better wouldn't you . . . at my age? Please forgive me.'

A dull, heavy ache begins in Maggie's lower abdomen and in the small of her back and a trickle of warm blood goes cold as it runs across the back of her thigh.

'Can I get you something to help you sleep?' Maggie had woken with a jolt some time earlier feeling cold and clammy with images flashing on and off in her mind at sickening speed: the man, Michael, he was a persistent one, and then of course Helena and Frank and Cissie and Luke and, inevitably, her parents. And then the thoughts would take over, crashing into her mind and out again into the ether before she could catch hold of them. Each one making her heart beat faster. Each one leaving her drenched in anxiety, all of them angry and frightening and jumbled.

'Oh God yes! Put me to sleep!' The nurse stays on her haunches and runs a cool hand over Maggie's brow.

'See if I can't get you a couple of pills.' And with a little strain she's up and bouncing off, tights rubbings and watch jingling.

Another warm rivulet makes its way down onto the sheet. Maggie lets out a small, soft moan as it does so.

'Here, these'll help you sleep.' Sadie Maclachlan is back with two pills in a tiny plastic cup, Maggie grabs them, and anticipating oblivion she rears up on one elbow and knocks them back with a sudden jerk of the head.

'Now you settle down and before you know it, it will be tomorrow and your friends will be here to pick you up and whisk you home . . . and won't that be nice?'

Maggie closes her eyes. She cannot bear to look at this bright-cheeked optimism a minute longer. She thinks of the grey corridor and the simple seeping away of survival, and she slides down into the dark, humid space beneath the bed cover but she does not think of tomorrow and she cannot contemplate 'nice'.

The Celebration

❧

'At considerable risk to my own personal safety I'm asking
you to get out of my bedroom and preferably out of my
sight. Now!' Helena has opened the door to the bedroom with a
loud, rattling jerk of the handle and marching towards the bathroom with furious po-faced determination she slams its door
behind her like a kick in the teeth. Cissie winces at her ferocity
but does not move. Sitting in the same position on the crumpled
quilt she stares at the bathroom door and without thinking she
removes Helena's painful little toe-clipping from the end of her
sock. She hears a deep, semi-vocal sigh from within and the ping
of the cord as the light is yanked into awful being.

'God . . .' she says with her own little sigh. She tries to think
of an aggressive little jibe by way of a reply but the moment is
gone. 'Can't be fucked . . .' She lets out a little humourless snort
instead.

She gets up and as she does so she hears the rude, slurping
suction of the bath water as it drains from the tub. Helena is
removing the sopping knickers. Cissie can see in her mind's eye
the long, painted nails dipping into the icy water, its soapy
tension broken into jagged little islands. She can hear her muffled
chuntering and can make out 'shit!' and 'sick and tired!' and
possibly 'Jesus H. Christ!' She goes back into the sitting room
and is about to close the door but thinks better of it and leaves
it ajar.

She stands by the door for an immeasurable length of time,

her eyes staring at but not seeing the faded pink telephone that sits across the room on the dark cupboard by the door. Her mind, defocused and nowhere, is forced to stay in this woolly limbo where it can do no harm. There is no sound save the ever-present hum of the building, but it's somehow different now: louder, more invasive, vibrating inside her, making her stomach queasy.

'Did you know she was pregnant?!' Cissie is shoved forward by the door swinging open from an angry push. She falls onto the back of the sofa having stumbled over Maggie's huge unopened carpetbag.

'What . . .?' her voice feels rough and hoarse, like it sometimes did when she was tired or when she had been smoking too much blow. It was a quality she normally liked, it gave her voice an edge of earthiness and warmth, of sexiness even. Now it just feels sore, a mark of her exhaustion.

'Luke has found her. She is in a hospital downtown. Telling everyone she is me. She has just lost a baby. I asked you, did you know that she was pregnant?'

Leaning forward onto the back of the sofa, Cissie looks down at her feet where Maggie's big soft bag stubbornly sits and momentarily loses herself in its bright, dancing patterns. Another follows and another. She lowers herself slowly down onto her haunches and fingers the metal clasp. Maggie had packed God knows what into this bag. Cissie can see it now, on the day of their departure, placed in readiness on the homely rag rug beside Maggie's bed, and next to it Maggie's polished black boots, with Maggie herself sitting on the bed stock-still in the sunlight, her knees together, her hands clasped on her lap, her blue velvet cloak hanging perfectly around her shoulders: a Victorian heroine; Paddington Bear with a label that reads 'The Loneliest Place on Earth please'.

Helena has moved into the centre of the room, facing Cissie across the brown corduroy sofa, her voice taut and steely. She is standing, hand on hip, her jaw thrust forward, her mouth set and angry, a yob in a brawl. The heavy curtain of hair, usually a seductive veil over her left eye, is dragged roughly back behind her ear, causing it to protrude at right-angles to her head. Behind them a hot gush of bathwater fills the tub and damp clouds of Helena's amber and lavender bath oil begin to drift through the open door.

'I . . . didn't . . . kn . . .' Cissie, now standing, is trying to defend herself, her voice an urgent whisper.

'What? . . . For crying out loud look at me! . . . You'd do well to practise some eye contact . . . not something you've ever really developed, is it? If you *had*, you might not have made that bloody ridiculous mistake you made earlier this evening and I might not be on the verge of ripping your fucking head off your shoulders!'

'I didn't *know*!' Cissie bangs her fists several times on the back of the sofa, her face hot and crimson, teardrops flying this way and that.

'No! I bet you didn't because you never looked into *Maggie's* eyes either, did you?' Helena has taken a couple of steps forward.

'I knew . . . she . . . was in a . . . strange . . . state . . . But I thought . . . this trip . . . might bring her . . . out of it.' Cissie is now looking at the floor by Helena's feet, her voice bursting out in little hissing spasms.

'You know, it's a funny thing, Cissie, but I don't believe a fucking word of it. I think you knew only too well what you were doing. It's too much of a bloody coincidence. I'm at a . . . I'm at a pinnacle now . . . no it's . . . it's . . . it's probably *the* pinnacle of my fucking career, this is probably the best it's going to get . . . And I *deserve* it! I deserve to be the bloody sodding toast of Broadway! I deserve that frigging Tony . . . And you come here . . . purely to escape that fucking mess you call a life . . . for Christ's sake all I've seen is the top of your fucking head for the last two days! And to top it all you drag Maggie along in the throes of a serious nervous breakdown and about to lose a baby! Well thank you very fucking much for making this oh so special visit! I obviously mean a hell of a lot to you!'

The hum of the building rushes into Cissie's head and spins ferociously around inside it, sucking her energy into its furious whirl. She lifts her head to see if Helena is still speaking and fully expects to see her mouth contorting its way around angry soundless words, her invective made impotent by the smothering roar of the building. Instead the mouth is still, the lips sitting in a neutral pout, poised for something, and the curtain of hair has swung back, partially covering her left eye. The set of her features is indecipherable, unreadable things are going on. The face is stunned or blank or neither but Cissie won't be fooled again and sure enough there it is: the tell-tale sign; the mocking judder of the shoulders, the repetitive, careless shrug that always occurs in the face of another's impossible stupidity. She waits for the face to flush with unexpressed mirth, for the mouth to gape for breath and the eyes to squeeze into laughing slits. She waits; the shoulders moving faster now and beneath what remains of her make-up the face is red but the eyes are frozen. The right one is huge and staring with its brow a perfect arch of surprise, the left lying dark now and secretive behind the thick drape of hair, and the mouth has left its pout, its corners turned down in a perfect expression of childish tragedy. The hum of the building leaves Cissie's head and retreats beyond the walls of the room.

She mentally checks her own face and finds her mouth hanging open. At the same time Helena's face creases painfully into a bright red grimace and her fine long hands are there in seconds to protect it from the other's gawping curiosity. Cissie shuts her mouth instantly and notes the dryness of her tongue as it sticks to the roof. Helena collapses into the armchair and lets out an anguished howl of pain. Immediately jumping up, she retrieves a fork from amongst the crumpled newspapers lying there and, slinging it across the room so that it ricochets off the wooden arm of the saggy green chair with a ping, she bumps back down amongst the crackling newspapers.

'Oh fucking hell.' The words are squashed and muffled behind the palms of both hands.

Cissie feels her own hands lift up and reach out to Helena across the back of the sofa, almost of their own accord. Then, tripping over Maggie's carpetbag, she pads around the sofa to place a tentative hand of comfort on Helena's back. No sooner do Cissie's fingertips make contact than Helena's hands shoot up as if a gun has been thrust between her shoulderblades and immediately in turn Cissie's hands spring back with the same gesture. As if both women are being held up by an invisible intruder.

'Da! . . . don't! If you must do something, get me a drink.' Helena's hands clap down over her ears and her elbows drop onto her knees. Cissie stares at the broad shoulders and the bent head and for several seconds sees a stranger sitting there. A stranger in a strange room. In some cut-off place. Perhaps a product of her own imagination; the fleeting moments of a dream. She sees Jenny by her bedside with a big red steaming mug and she turns and pads quickly to the kitchen.

The fridge smells faintly of fish and of rotting vegetables and yet it is empty bar a small piece of hard cracked cheese and a bottle of champagne.

'I can only find this. I don't expec—'

'Open it!' It sounds like a threat and Cissie scuttles back to the kitchen for glasses.

The bottle has 'Darling "H" be wonderful xxx' scrawled all over the label with thick black marker pen. Now the cork makes a bright, hollow pop before disappearing into the bedroom and the telephone rings.

The Slippers

❧

'Answer that, somebody.'
   'Yeah ... O.K.'
  'Is Caroline Hooley in yet?'
  '... he should have looked at the chart ... why is he ...'
  'I'm dyin' here! ... she stuck somethin' in me! ... oh God ...'
  'Dana, go get your coffee.'
  'Will somebody please get that?'
  'Suzie, can you get that?'
  'Where is Caroline Hooley?'
  '... are the x-rays back? ...'
  'She stuck a fuckin' needle in my ass! ... please ... somebody! ...'
  'Dana, go put your feet up for ten minutes.'
  'Suzieeeee .... the phone!'
  'Where the hell is Caroline?'
  '... he was here six months back ... same thing.'
  'Aaaargh!!!'
  'Is Dana on a coffee break?'
  'Will somebody go see Mr Mackalenski, *please*?'
  'Maggie? You didn't touch your breakfast.'
  'Oh Jesus, I'll get it!'
  'Caroline called in sick.'
  '... no, in the cerebro-spinal fluid ...'
  'Please somebody ... help me ... I'm dyin' here!'
  'Where's Dana?'

'Mr Mackalenski, you are not dying. Just give the shot time to work.'

'Maggie ... you're dressed already! You know your friends aren't picking you up till around noon.'

'Suzie? Lonnie Spears needs to talk to you.'

'Where is Caroline?'

'... that's why you need to look at the x-rays.'

'Please, my ass is burnin' up!'

'Can Laura go on coffee break now or has Dana gone?'

'If you sit in that cloak all morning, Maggie, you won't appreciate it when you get outside, it's real cold out there.'

'Suzie?! Will you take this call?'

'Is Caroline in yet?'

'Well ... Campion did it ... and what a mess.'

'He's right, his ass is burnin' up.'

'Where's Dana?'

'Sam Consadine will be stopping by this morning to speak with you, Maggie, and so will Stella, Stella Galbraith, she did your D and E yesterday.'

'Suzie? Call Lonnie Spears asap.'

'Is Caroline sick?'

'... he should have been seen two weeks ago, this is ridiculous.'

'Please, Mr Mackalenski, you're not helping yourself by doing that.'

'I think Laura's due a coffee break. Laura? I think you're due a coffee break.'

'Hi Maggie ... it's me ... Michael.'

Michael had not had a good start to his day. He had woken with his right arm a sickening mass of pins and needles and the side of his face stuck to the floor of the downstairs bathroom. The first thing he had done whilst lying there was to bring his left thumbnail into view to check out the tiny stubborn speck of Maggie's blood and on finding it gone a sharp dart of panic had shot through his chest. He could not remember having successfully removed it and then could not work out if it had been an image left over from an exhausting night of hellish dreams or a reality. Having unpeeled his face from the polished boards like a piece of raw chicken, he had stumbled downstairs to the kitchen and had been stopped short by its ransacked state. He had expected to find its normal pleasing orderliness, having momentarily forgotten the chaos wrought by Maggie's visit. He had been too tired the night before to clear it up and anyway he had had other priorities. Bending down to pick up the overturned drawer his attention had been drawn to a tea towel. It is one that Elizabeth had put in his Christmas stocking a few years back. It had the warning 'Watch out, there's a Chef about!' in bold red lettering next to a line drawing of a little man in a chef's hat sneaking around what was obviously meant to be a kitchen door with his forefinger pressed to his lips. Right across the figure of the little chef was a big clear bootprint, about size twelve Michael had calculated.

'Boyle!' Michael had spat the word out through rigid, disgusted lips, and then he had vowed to himself in a voice he reserved only for reasoning with Dominic that he would shower, have a nice cup of coffee and call Elizabeth. Then he might venture out in search of a newspaper and provisions and a dumpster into which he could dispose of both the rug and the cover of his large sofa and that would mark an end to this whole sad business.

Now he is standing before her, a large brown paper bag containing bread, milk and apples, bacon, cheese and pasta tucked under his arm, and the *New York Times* in his overcoat pocket. She does not look up and he sees that her hair has been washed. It is fine and fluffy and the curl has lost its definition. She has on her blue velvet cloak, dragged around her as if to protect her from a gale, and he is not sure but Michael thinks she might be shaking.

'Maggie?' He looks down at the white face, the eyes bruised and baggy, and realises with a little churn in his stomach that he has not thought of Dominic today, at least not properly, at least not heart-achingly, gut-wrenchingly properly, but now he can feel the little arms clinging on around his neck and he takes her face in his hands.

'Maggie . . .?' She has a clean, fresh, soapy smell and the skin of her face feels dry and papery. He tilts her chin up, towards him. Those eyes; he looks for recognition in them but finds that same unsettling inscrutability. They are looking back at him, yet not seeing and then again seeing it all; the wise eyes of a child.

'Maggie? . . . How are you?' Maggie does not know.

With some difficulty Maggie extricates her tongue from the roof of her mouth and leaves it suspended there. She is waiting to see if anything will happen. To see if another part of her, a part that perhaps lies dormant within her, will revive and speak up.

Maggie stands. She is inches from him and he still has hold of her face. He has an urge to kiss her on the mouth, a rough, all-consuming, mouth-watering kiss and he moves his face towards her but the bag of provisions is slipping out from under his arm.

Michael takes one hand away from her face to save the bag from falling and as he does so Maggie catches hold of the hand in hers.

The hand is ice-cold. Michael looks at it with its familiar ragged nails now scrubbed clean and observes its white-knuckled grip. Lifting it briefly to his mouth, half comfort, half kiss, he turns and makes a move to leave. Without looking back at her and not knowing whether she will follow, he steps forward, her hand now beginning to pinch his fingers with its grip. He feels his chest tighten as he senses her resistance. His arm is now stretched out behind him. Without yanking her forward he cannot move on. He dare not look back for fear of her eyes and what, in their ancient wisdom, they might say.

'Daddy . . .' Michael can feel the pressure of Dominic's cold soft cheek on his own and he turns his head in the hopes of kissing the boy's delicate skin, of touching it with his tongue, tasting him, taking in his sweet fresh fragrance. As he turns she is at his side with her own new scent of harsh shampoo and hospital soap. Her profile perfect, patrician, her hair a light, tangled fuzz somehow filled with light. She does not return his gaze, but head held high walks on, and with her strong grip pulls him along in her wake.

Once in the corridor they move on apace, gathering speed with every step until they break into a little scurrying run. Up high above the echoing metallic sounds of the corridor, someone laughs a screeching hoot of a laugh and Michael feels his face opening, creeping open into a smile. It is as if the physical sensation of his muscles stretching releases his own laughter and brings it chuckling out into the air, and there within it he is sure he can hear the echo of Dominic's childish glee urging him on. And so faster they go, each stride longer than the last until they are running flat out.

Michael, still laughing, turns to look across at Maggie, sure that she must be sharing this exhilaration but her eyes are huge and her mouth agape, her face is death-white and sparkling with sweat. She is not joining in; she is running for her life. Suddenly she is gone; wrenching his arm painfully in its socket she pulls him down unceremoniously onto his back. For a brief moment they both lie there, in the middle of the corridor, side by side, strangers in a double bed. Michael sits up, his laughter turning to coughing, and reaches for his inhaler. Two women in leather trousers and big puffer jackets edge nervously around them as if trying not to disturb them, and a black man swathed like a Sherpa in a multi-coloured scarf bends down and hands Michael two apples that have rolled out of his bag. He lets go of Maggie's hand and at the same time notices her feet. They are wet and bare, her toes curled over as if gripping onto something for dear life. At first Michael thinks she might have lost her shoes whilst running, but he instantly remembers the little black boots; not the sort of footwear one easily loses; or forgets. An elderly gentleman wearing a bright paisley bow-tie is approaching them, obviously with the intention of helping them up, and Michael springs to his feet.

'Is she alright? Can I be of some assistance?' Michael raises his arm in a 'halt who goes there?' kind of gesture.

'No! How kind ... but we're fine thank you. She just slipped on the wet floor. We're fine thank you.' And with that he bends down to drag Maggie up onto her feet.

'Yes ... but ... she has no shoes on. She must be freezing.' Michael is still struggling with Maggie who has gone quite rigid, her arms crossed tightly in front of her chest. She is trying to get into a foetal position on her side.

'Yes, I see that. Thank you, sir. I see that.'

'Do you want me to get some help?' Michael now has her sitting up.

'No ... we're fine ... Maggie, come on now ... it's O.K. ... you're going to be fine.'

'Well she doesn't look too fine to me. Does she have any shoes?'

Michael, now purple with the effort of getting Maggie to her feet, wheels round on the old gentleman.

'Look! Would you just mind going away and minding your own business? I've told you ... she is fine! Now just ... get gone, will you!'

'Alright ... take it easy, fella,' and the old man backs away, staring at them, muttering something about it being unwise to take her outside without any shoes. Michael feels like letting Maggie fall back down so that he can pursue the fellow and kick his interfering old ass. Instead he drags the rigid Maggie, her toes still curled under her, to the seating area at the end of the corridor and dumps her unsteadily, like a doll, on one of the plastic chairs. Again he takes her face in his hands.

'Now where are your boots?' He sees that her eyes are softened with tears but still she does not speak.

'Oh Maggie ... you are crying ... I'm sorry ... Oh no ...' He takes out his handkerchief and dabs at her eyes, noticing that her expression does not alter. Then he gets down on his haunches and dries her feet, rubbing and patting them and hugging them to his chest, until the tight curled toes relax. As he is doing this he sees that the feet, like her hands, are somehow ill fitting. In the boots they had looked quite small and almost childlike, but here they are surprisingly large and rough-looking.

'You never grew into these, huh?' He smiles up at her. 'Probably a good job ...' He winks at her and kisses the ball of each foot in turn as if bidding them both goodbye. 'I'm going to go back to the ward to see if I can't find your boots ... O.K.?' She does not answer of course and again he sees she is shivering. He whips off his coat, and with a matador's swirl he places it over her, tucking it in around her like a blanket. 'Now Maggie ... everything is fine ... I'll be right back real quick ... O.K.?'

As he turns to go back down the corridor, he sees that the old man is standing at the other end, still staring at him. Michael can just pick out the frowning, quizzical set of his features but as he begins to jog in the old man's direction the latter rushes off into the ward. When Michael reaches the ward entrance, the old man is nowhere to be seen and so, hovering there for a moment, he gets down on one knee in the hopes that he might be able to see across the ward and under Maggie's bed, without going in and perhaps attracting unwanted attention.

'Can I help you?' The attention is there in seconds, in the form of a pair of legs sporting crisp white trousers. They are standing directly in Michael's eyeline. He looks up to meet the puzzled gaze of a diminutive woman carrying a disposable kidney bowl in one hand, with what looks like the barrel of a plastic syringe sticking out of it and a mucky-looking paper towel in the other.

'No ... no, no, no ... not at all ... I ... I was just looking for something.'

'Oh. What?' The woman is not giving up. Her beetle-browed, dark-eyed gaze is unwaveringly suspicious. Michael gets up feeling his face redden and towers over her.

'I ... dropped something ... Please don't let me keep you from your work.'

'You're not. What did you drop?' The woman continues to stare unblinkingly up at him and Michael can smell something unpleasant coming from the bowl she is carrying, but as he flicks his eyes down to see what it might be, she whisks the bowl away, half hiding it behind her back. As if it was a surprise dessert to be sampled later.

'It ... it ... it was my lens ... my contact lens.' Michael rubs his right eye and laughs foolishly. The woman whose name badge proclaims her to be Suzanne Bateman looks at him coolly and he swears that she has yet to blink.

'Suzie? ... Come quick, I need you!'

'Sure! I'm there! ... Well, I hope you find it and nobody's stamped their great hoof on it.' And she is gone, leaving the mystery pong of the kidney dish hanging in the air. Michael heads straight for Maggie's bed and drops down beside it to see if the boots are underneath.

'Are you looking for Maggie?' Michael shoots back up and comes face to face with a bespectacled red-haired man in a white coat. 'Our patients usually sit on top of the bed.' The man laughs with a smug twist to his mouth. 'She was here a minute ago. She probably just went to the bathroom. Anything I can do?'

'Wither and die?' Michael suggests in his head, but then says, 'No, thank you, I'll just wait.' He sits on the side of the bed and strikes an awkward 'I am waiting for someone' pose, tapping his fingers lightly on his knee, and watches the man's cocky walk as he leaves the ward.

'Jimmy? ... Jim? Is that you?' The voice is thin and wavery and floats, light, on the thick hospital air. Michael turns and there in the bed next to Maggie's is a frail and ancient woman. She is peering at Michael through milky cataracts, a yellow, vein-riddled hand reaching out to him. He instinctively goes to her side, taking the hand in his.

'Jim? ... Is Marsha here?'

'Erm . . . w . . .'

'Tell her I'm sorry . . . will you?'

'Er . . .' On top of the bed, hooked over her other hand, is a transparent plastic carrier bag containing a pair of pink fur-trimmed slippers, a crêpe bandage pushed into one of them, and what looks like a pair of thick tights or possibly stockings pushed into the other.

'Please tell her I'm sorry . . . we'll go dancin' next time.' Michael squeezes her hand and as if in response she closes her eyes. The crinkly dry lids flicker and twitch for a moment and then the stubby white lashes fan out and relax and the lids are still.

A big-bosomed nurse in a dress stretched to capacity bounces by and flashes Michael a white toothy smile and he notices that the old woman has loosened her grip. He lets go of the hand and sets it gently down on the counterpane. For a moment he looks at it, lying there in repose, with its loose mottled skin and thick yellow nails, and then back at her face. It is framed with thin white hair, through which a baby-pink scalp can easily be seen. Michael is touched by its vulnerability and makes to smooth the hair back from her forehead. As he does so she lets out a long, soft sigh. There is what looks like a smile on her face and immediately around her there is a sudden stillness. A cold, inert stillness. He recognises it.

'Oh . . . oh.' He quickly withdraws his hand and holds it to his chest, covering it protectively with the other one, as if it had been bitten or burnt. Now there is a scuffle behind the curtains of a bed on the opposite side of the ward. Six or seven people are behind there. He can see their shapes billowing out; elbows, shoulders and bottoms pushing and pulling the curtains this way and that, their shoes squeaking like squashed rodents.

'Get her flat! . . . Get her flat!' There is a clanking of metal and something plastic falls to the floor with a dull clunk. Michael looks back at the old woman and hears a familiar voice.

'Can I help here?' It is the old gentleman. He has his back to Michael and is poking his head through the curtains where the emergency is going on. People are telling him in no uncertain terms that he is not needed but he is stubbornly staying put. Michael can hear the smug tones of the red-haired man suggesting that if the old gentleman doesn't move he might end up in a similar position to the patient, and Michael makes a grab for the polythene bag around the old woman's wrist. It seems to be stuck. He wrenches at it causing her head to flop over onto one side and her mouth to loll open.

'Oh God!' He sees that it is stuck on the plastic name tag secured around her wrist and that her name is Katya Erhardt.

'Oh Katya, please ... let me have them ... you don't need them any more.' The bag slips free. As he goes to leave he notices that the top set of her dentures has slipped down and is hanging bizarrely between her open lips like a set of novelty bucked teeth.

'No I don't need those ... but thanks.'

As he crosses the ward on his way to the door he sees the old gentleman come out from between the curtains and as Michael quickens his pace he hears him yell. 'Katya ... Oh my God! ... Katya!'

Michael sprints down the corridor, avoiding the black puddle of melted snow where Maggie had slipped, and comes to a screeching halt at the entrance to the waiting area. His coat is lying splayed out, half on the chair where she had been sitting, half off. The bag of groceries is lying on its side, on the floor. The two runaway apples, having made a second bid for freedom, are lying some feet away. And she is gone. Maggie is gone.

The Writing

❧

'Maggie's gone missing. I can't just up and go. I can't just leave her here,' says Cissie. There is a silence.

'Pardon?'

'I can't talk any louder. Helena's asleep. Maggie needs me.' A longer silence. 'She needs you ... and you can't leave her. Do you mean by that, that you can't leave a dear friend in a bad situation to cope on her own?'

'Well ... yes.'

'Have you any idea what the last forty-eight hours have been like here? I have a suspicion that you do and that is why you left *me*, your more than "dear friend", here to cope; very much on my own.'

'Oh Jenny ...'

'Cissie, I need you. I needed you here so that we could face this together. Maggie is a gaping wound that no amount of dressing will ever fill. She'll suck any poor sucker into this destructive whirlpool that she's created. Whoever happens to be standing by. But I need YOU ... specifically YOU ... Cissie.'

'I don't know what to do ...' This is a pathetic wail. A globule of snot falls from Cissie's nose and makes a swinging descent on a thin string of mucus, splatting onto her sweater like an unfortunate bungee jumper.

'Your sister came to the house yesterday.'

'Oh shit, no! Frances?' She drags the sleeve of her sweater

roughly across her nose, making a thick gurgling sniff as she does so. 'What did she want?'

'Well, they're all in shock. They tried to keep it from your mother but of course that was impossible.'

Cissie stands stock-still for some seconds. Her arm still frozen in front of her face, post-sniff. 'Wh … w … what? … She knows? … My mother knows?'

'Cissie … they were on her doorstep for at least twenty-four hours. And even if they hadn't been, it was all over the papers yesterday and again this morning. The story today being that you have left me behind to take the flak and to deal with your family's "pain and confusion" while you swan off with "beautiful but troubled actress Maggie Salt"; and this, accompanied by an extremely unflattering photograph of me on the doorstep in my 'jamas, looking like a bad mix of Pooh Bear and Rosemary West, next to one of Maggie looking glamorous and of course beautiful at some film première. That was the *Daily Mail* … and pretty bloody accurate actually!'

'What did Frances say? What did my mum …? What did they say? Jesus!' Cissie slides down the wall into a crouch, one arm curled protectively over her head.

'I think your mother has pretty much taken to her bed as far as I can make out. As for your sister, she thought that the papers had made the whole thing up.'

'Oh … so she didn't believe it then?' Cissie slides back up the wall.

'No she didn't … but then I put her right, Cissie.'

Cissie slides back down the wall, the knuckles of her left hand pressed to her lips, a cliché of angst.

'Cissie, your priority is not Maggie. Helena and Luke can take care of her.'

'But it's like I've dumped her on them.' Cissie takes her hand away from her mouth just long enough to say this and instantly replaces it as if preventing an unstoppable avalanche of anxiety from pouring out and smothering her.

'Cissie, they're your friends . . . if you explain the situation . . .'

'We've had a row.' Cissie looks across at the bedroom door and holds her head in her hand.

'What sort of row?' Cissie now has her forehead on her knees and speaks into the warm space above her thighs.

'Oh, it was just a misunderstanding over something but I don't feel I can ask for Helena's help at the moment . . . and anyway the whole city is at a standstill . . . we've had this terrible snow . . . I wouldn't be able to get a flight out.'

'Cissie, I think it's time we put things into perspective here. The situation is this: overcoming your misunderstanding with Helena and asking for her help, versus the demise of your mother's mental health and your relationship with me.'

Cissie lifts her head up sharply. 'But that's . . .'

'Ring British Airways.' The light, jolly trill of the dialling tone is there before Cissie can speak. She puts the phone down and collapses into the jaws of the brown corduroy sofa. A waft of stale tobacco rising up as she does so. It seems the sofa has spat something up from its innards and it is now sticking into Cissie's back. Pulling it out from underneath her she finds it to be Maggie's spiral notepad.

'Oh no.' She tosses it to the end of the sofa out of arm's reach and then immediately retrieves it. She stares at the cover. There is a biro doodle in the top right-hand corner. It is of a pair of feathery disembodied wings, and where they join in the middle a huge nail has been driven in with big dark drops of blood spurting out.

'Oh God.' There is another of a horse's head, slumped over onto one side, its eyes bulging from their sockets, its huge tongue flopping out and a noose, pulled tight around its powerful neck. Then in the centre, at the bottom, is a drawing of two women's heads on the same torso. They appear to be shouting at one another. The head of one of them is lunging forward, screaming angrily at the other; her teeth are bared, her eyes wild, her cheeks coloured but under closer scrutiny the other head is trying to retreat, the eyes are wild and tear-filled, the mouth wide, but with terror, the hair standing cartoonishly on end with droplets of sweat springing from the forehead.

Maggie's artistry. It only seemed to find form during these manic periods of insanity. Once on an even keel Maggie professed that she hadn't an artistic bone in her body. It was as if she disowned the weird and often quite wonderful drawings that emerged during these lost times. Cissie had caught her once staring at one such effort. Unusually it was a painting, and Maggie was goggling at it in complete astonishment. It was a self-portrait, with the eyes missing, and in their place was a flaming inferno and tiny tormented souls spilling out onto her cheeks, looks of agony and horror on their faces. When Cissie commented upon its brilliance Maggie had seemed both bewildered and embarrassed, as if taking the praise for someone else's incomprehensible work.

Cissie leafs through the notepad; more frantic sketches and squiggles and wild erratic writing whipping and swirling across the page at breakneck speed, the letters of words veering from one precarious angle to the other making the reader seasick in an effort to decipher it. Cissie is looking for the section that had referred to her.

'Who is Cissie?' she reminds herself with a snort, 'Who indeed!' The page flips into view and in the middle of a paragraph, in which Cissie's name seems to be the only legible word, is a small, vivid sketch that she had not taken in before. She instantly recognises the face with its soft double chin and full mouth but it is the eyes that grab her attention. Maggie has pressed so hard with the biro whilst colouring them in that she has made a hole where each iris should be. Cissie stares for a second and then sees that a crown of thorns is placed in amongst the thick dark curls with dribbles of blood beginning to trickle down the forehead. It is Jenny; as clear as day. It is her Jenny.

'Jenny . . .' she whispers with a surprise that suggests that Jenny has just entered that room. Maggie has even caught Jenny's very personal pain in the turn of the mouth, and she has done it with a few casually wicked strokes of a smudgy old biro. Underneath in tiny block capitals, for anyone to see, is written: THE SAVIOUR FINALLY GETS HERS! FORGIVE THEM O JENNY FOR THEY KNOW NOT WHAT THEY DO!

'Oh my ...' Cissie turns the page over with a violent flick of her thumb, almost ripping it off the spiral. On the next page are several lines of completely illegible scrawl but for a couple of words that look like 'mother' and 'cunt' and underneath is a Madonna-type drawing of a woman in a veil, holding a bundle lovingly in her arms, except that the face nestling amongst the swaddling clothes and looking equally lovingly back up at its mother is that of a monstrous-looking gargoyle creature with huge ears and vicious pointed teeth. Cissie turns several pages over in quick succession until the writing stops and she comes upon a blank page.

She runs the tips of her fingers easily over its silky, smooth surface, lifting it to her nose to take in its dry school-desk smell and tucks the other discarded pages underneath out of view. She stares at the empty page: it seems vast. Then from the corner of her eye she spies a pencil on the coffee table; its metal end, where once there was a rubber, is chewed and mangled.

'Dear Helena ...' she finds herself saying, '... and Luke.' The pencil is sticky in her hand and she puts the squashed metal tip to her lips before thinking better of it. Then she writes the words that she has just spoken carefully and neatly at the top of the page. On the opposite side she writes: 'Monday morning, 7.50 a.m.' Then she flips the pencil back and forth between her thumb and forefinger like a wobbly metronome.

Cissie hates letters like this, 'farewell' letters, the cowardly slipping away. 'Dear Brendan and my lovely girls, by the time you get this letter I will be ...' while others lie innocently sleeping. '... for your sakes, my angels ...' 'unaware of what the morning will bring', '... not worthy of your love ...' breaking childish hearts with their brutal shite, '... you will be better off . . .', then creeping back, unctuous with self-pity and guilt, '. . . why didn't you let me . . .?'

'Why indeed, mother! . . . Oh fuck you, mother . . . fuck you,' she whispers and begins to write.

The Door

♊

'FUCK YOU, MOTHER-FUCKER!!!' The door screams at her in sticky red lettering. Maggie is bleeding. In one great stomach-lurching cramp the remains of that other life are draining from her. The toilet seat is cold and a small split in one side of it is painfully pinching her right buttock.

'SHIT STINKS' shouts the door in thin, colourless scratches.

'Yes,' says Maggie, and drops her elbows down onto her knees, the toilet seat nipping harder at her buttock as she does so. She regards her feet, squelches of filthy black water squeezing up between her toes. They are red and swollen, burning up from their sojourn in the snow. Someone had shouted 'Jesus, Lady, get something on your feet! You'll catch your death!' and Maggie had stopped mid-stride to realise the intolerable pain that was just beginning down there. So far away, in the ends of her toes.

'Catch my death ...' she had said quietly to herself and now she repeats the words, 'Catch ... my ... death.'

'DONNIE GAVE ME CRABS!' replies the door. Maggie lifts her feet up off the floor and hugs her knees to her chest. The seat lets go its grip of her bottom and a warm ache ripples slowly through her belly, releasing more of that life. More of that death.

'BIG BLACK BITCH WANTS BIG BEAUTIFUL WASP CALL JEZ 631-4712' invites the door in squishy pink lipstick.

A kindly woman in a sheepskin hat pulled down around her

ears had taken Maggie by the arm, 'Why don't you come inside dear?' and Maggie had obeyed her, and as she was allowing herself to be guided along by this stranger back into the hospital, she had considered that her own will had been lost, along with the child inside her. Now she opens her knees to inspect the towel, suspended there. It is saturated with a thick cake of reddish-brown blood. Her head aches and there is a banging inside it, and a tapping begins on the door, a thin, tinny tapping like that of fingernails on a window pane. She looks up at the door.

'JESUS LOVES YOU,' it tells her with concern, and she is surprised to find that the tapping is the tapping of her own teeth. They are chattering and now her knees are bashing together. They look very white and childlike; bashing out a rhythm with her teeth, a one-woman percussion band.

She thinks of the man and the gallant swirl of his coat as he had draped it over her. She remembers his feet as they had come into view, that morning in the ward. Gone were the warm, polished brogues that she had seen and touched with such pleasure back in that other place; before; in the madness. These new shoes were black, featureless, boot-like things and not new at all. They were dull and stained and uncared for. She had had no desire to get down on her haunches and touch them; but still, without looking up, she knew it was him. When he had taken her face in his hands it had dawned on her that perhaps it was him she had been waiting for. She had felt no fear as she looked at him, that had all seeped away, discarded somewhere along the ragged trail of the last God knows how many days. 'I STAMP ON BALLS!' confesses the door.

'Oh . . . my boots,' answers Maggie in a small, weak voice and letting her feet back down onto the floor she stands gingerly, steadying herself with both hands on the walls of the cubicle. Then, realising her towel is down around her knees, she bends to pull up the elasticated belt, and a rushing in her head dumps her heavily back down, the seat biting her nastily in response.

'Oooooh . . .' It is the hoarse, throaty sigh of an unused voice. 'Where the hell am I?' She slumps back against the cistern, her head flopping backwards onto the wall with a little dizzying bump. She cannot quite piece together the jumbled fragments of time that make up the space since the man left her, tucked up like a child under his coat, and this freezing, inhospitable place with its angry door and aggressive seat and its all-pervading smell of some corrosive disinfectant.

'A WOMAN NEEDS A MAN LIKE A FISH NEEDS A BICYCLE,' informs the door and she recalls the discomfort that she had felt in her belly as she had sat there, back in the waiting area. She remembers the need to get up and move around, and that two women were having an argument somewhere nearby which quickly progressed to pushing and shoving and the furious screaming of insults. Maggie had been seized by a breathtaking panic as the growing rage of the two women seemed to be reaching a climax. Making a move to get away, she had collided with one of them – a beefy, striking-looking woman with black hair and flaring nostrils. The woman had completely ignored her and had returned to the fray like a fighter bouncing back off the ropes. Maggie cannot recollect leaving the hospital, only her experience out in the snow culminating in the kindly woman directing her into some warm bustling building and into this toilet. She again draws her knees up to her chin.

'*A**I* **L* IS A FUCKWIT,' the door mumbles in a very small, childish hand and Maggie hears the outer door to the toilet being bashed open. She listens as a conversation ensues:

'Do you want to go or not?'

'I don't know.'

'Well make up your mind.'

'Just give me a minute will you? I don't know if I'm comin' or goin'.'

'Oh Lord . . . give me strength . . . you said you wanted to go, back there.' The door to the next cubicle is banged open.

'Floor's wet.'

157

'Yes, yes, come on.' There is a rustling of clothes and a pinging of elastic and finally the sound of a huge and weighty bottom being lowered down with much huffing and puffing and landing with a crack onto the thin plastic seat.

'It's cold.'

'Well hurry up.'

'Shut the door.'

'No! I am not shutting the door.'

'I want some privacy. Anyone could walk in.'

'I am not shutting the door. Not after what happened last time.' Silence.

'What happened last time?'

'You know full well what happened last time. Are you going to go or not?'

'My life is not my own.'

'Yeah, yeah, yeah. Neither is mine, Mother.'

'You're punishing me.'

'Look, do you want me to go and leave you here?'

'Yes ... but I'd better come with you.'

'Yes, what would you think of me if I walked out and left you here?' A long trumpeting fart rends the air.

'Oh mother! ... Couldn't you have waited until you got outside? I'm getting out of here. I'll see you outside. Don't close the door!'

The outer door bangs shut and the old woman mutters, 'What would I think of you? Huh! I'd think you were a bitch and I'd be right ... oh Lord ... why hast thou forsaken me?' Another fart, on a different note, short and succinct, like a quacking duck, adds to the already sulphurous air. '... That's better.'

And Maggie wobbles again to her feet, the toilet seat grabbing at her buttock for one last painful goose.

'A GOOD MAN IS HARD TO FIND!' warns the door and Maggie opens it to leave.

The Draw

༄

The door gives a thin high squeal as she opens it. The room is in darkness and to her right Helena can just make out the long soft hump of Cissie's body, still sleeping, the quilt pulled around her like a great caterpillar. Behind her, in the bedroom, Luke lies sleeping on his front, spreadeagled across the bed, his left arm outstretched as if trying to pinion a reluctant sleeper. The door emits another shocked little squeak as she closes it on the slight snore of his breathing and she picks her way across the darkened living room.

'Shit!' Her right foot finds the full ashtray on the floor next to the armchair and sends it somersaulting ahead of her, depositing a trail of dog-ends in its wake. Last night's mucking out had barely begun when the baffling episode with Cissie had occurred. Helena holds her breath for several seconds, listening for any sign of her stirring, but the silence is untroubled and the quilted form inordinately still.

Once in the kitchen, having closed the living-room door in relative silence, she takes in a huge breath and savours its long, slow release. She closes her eyes momentarily against the lurid harshness of the strip light and reaches for the packet of Marlboros in the breast pocket of her pyjamas. The first drag of this cigarette is what has drawn her from her bed and into the dismal little space.

Something had woken her from a fitful, angry sleep and she had woken with a plan. It was all she could do not to speak it out loud. Cissie must go. Helena didn't much care where, just out of her domain, and she, Helena, would make sure that it happened. Distance was needed, maybe permanent distance and plain talking. She had reached out to the nightstand, as she did every morning, for her cigarettes and lighter. Finding only the cigarettes, an image of the lighter popped into her mind. It was sitting on the draining board, next to a heap of unwashed bowls and plates, and she had wanted to kick Luke's sleeping form away from her with full force. She had wanted to send him rolling off the bed and crashing onto the floor and away and away and away, off into the darkness.

Instead she is in the kitchen, taking a second ecstatic drag on the Marlboro. She regards the lighter now placed in the palm of her hand and she moves it gently from side to side, so that its gold veneer catches the light.

'Oh Lukey.' She sees Luke's unsure smile as he hands her the small, badly wrapped package in a crowded, smoke-filled pub, a little over a decade ago. She had hoped to lose the cheap, brash-looking thing pretty quickly but no; it had stuck close to her, down the years, through thick and thin, its sharp corners now a dull grey metallic colour where the gold paint had given up the ghost.

Once she had left it on the train and had remembered doing so just as she had stepped off it. She had walked down the platform, planning a trip to the jewellers and a throwaway lighter for the interim when a young man had called out to her, 'Excuse me! You left this on the seat.'

'. . . Oh . . .' She tosses the lighter back onto the draining board with a clang and surveys the squalor. It is much the same as it had been the previous evening, Cissie's attempt at washing up only being at the planning stage before the fateful fracas had taken place.

'Jesus.' A carpet of sodden mangled newspapers and magazines is squelching and oozing beneath her bare feet, the delicate scent of amber and lavender bath oil floating incongruously in the air around them. The fat neighbour from downstairs had alerted them to the deluge by screaming down the phone and then galumphing up the stairs to hammer on the door and scream some more. She had stood in the doorway sweating and wheezing, her face blotched and shiny with effort.

'Your damn bath is going to be sitting right on top of my bath any second!'

Luke had arrived back from the hospital just minutes before, a face red with spite and spitting sarcasm, and the three of them had simply stood and stared in response to the woman and then had simultaneously scooted to the bathroom to find water cascading over the side of the bath, carrying clouds of foam with it as it spread its way across the bathroom floor and into the bedroom. Helena recalls Luke's face again, as he set about masterminding the clean-up operation. It was flushed with something that looked like exasperation but bordered on something else. She feels sure that she had detected an air of exhilaration in him as he tossed down his bobble hat and rolled up his sleeves, high-handed orders coming thick and fast, and then later in bed he had been intolerable. Her usual tactics of repelling all boarders hadn't worked: he had scaled the steep slope of sagging mattress, at the top of which she had marooned herself, but as usual was not quite able to plant his flag. Helena had sent him rolling back down again into the dip with a curt, 'It's late, Luke.'

'Huh!' She snorts, and notes that her feet are getting cold from standing on the damp newspaper. She lifts one foot up and places the sole against the warm flannelette of her pyjama leg and is comforted by the sound of the kettle rising to the boil. With thumb and forefinger she fishes a greasy cup out of the crowded washing-up bowl, and after a cursory rub with a wet tea towel she pours coffee straight into it from the jar.

As she adds the boiling water from the kettle she sees for the first time a thin red scratch running from knuckle to wrist on the back of her right hand. The memory of Cissie's ferocious attack sends her hands straight up to her head and she riffles through the thick hair to find the sore marks where the vicious little talons had dug shockingly into her scalp. She swaps her feet, so that her left one throbs with warmth against the right pyjama leg. Then, breathing in the kick-up-the-arse aroma of the instant coffee, she hastily wipes a perfect lipstick print off another cup and makes a second coffee.

It takes several seconds of pitch-black before Cissie's sleeping form takes dim shape, still in the same position on the fold-down bed in the corner. Helena does not switch the lights on but she can see that just the top of her head is sticking out above the quilt, and that she must have burrowed down protectively in its warm folds. Helena stands there for a moment, the light from the kitchen casting a shadowy gloom into the darkness. She peers at her friend, the smoke from the cigarette gripped between her teeth stinging her eyes and the hot cups beginning to burn her fingers.

'Cissie? ...' Helena pads around the armchair, and now urgently needing to put the cups down she misjudges the height of the coffee table and smashes them down with a bang, burning her hands in the process.

'Oww! ... Oh Christ!' Sitting down and wiping her wet hands on the arms of the chair she continues to peer at Cissie, at the dark little bit of her that lies on the pillow. 'Cissie? ...' It is a theatrical whisper, and as it hits the air her throat closes with a sudden sense of loss.

'Oh for God's sake! ... Come on, you little dykelet ... wake up.' Cissie does not move. 'Look ... it's alright ... there's nothing a little straight talking, excuse the pun, can't sort out. I know you're awake ... I'm not going to throw you out ... I'm not going to staple your tongue to your arse and roll you down the freeway ...' Cissie still does not move. Helena snatches a slurp at the scalding coffee and despite its heat she suddenly feels a chill around her. She holds her breath, there is the distant blare of a car horn somewhere, and in the kitchen the muffled hiss of plumbing, but in the room there is no sound. She catches her breath.

'Cissie? . . . Cissie . . .?' Nothing. 'Cissie . . .? . . . Oh my G . . . Cissie please . . .!' She feels a familiar sense of elation, first in her chest, rising quickly to her neck and head and then moving south through her gut and out through her limbs, until her whole body is whirring with a light, fizzy energy.

She is not aware of any movement until she sees the top of her own head coming into view. It had first happened when she was twelve and she had thought that God had given her special powers. That He had answered her prayers and on certain nights He surely had. Once she had confided in her mother as to the new powers invested in her, and although her mother had stood silently staring, Helena saw in her face what she believed to be instant recognition. Now the dark shape of the light shade sways gently at eye-level. She stares down at the two women. Her own hunched figure in men's pyjamas staring wide-eyed at the dark shape that has spilled on the pillow of the fold-down bed; she is amazed by the breadth of her own shoulders and touched by the slight curve of her back and by the broad crown of her head. She knows that she could now let go and soar; leaving this room, this hotel, but that she might also lose herself, up above in the blackness.

Looking down, the only movement beneath her is the lazy ribbon of smoke from the cigarette, and she knows too that this soft grey column will be her deliverance. From the top of the room, she sucks it into her, and after hitting the back of her throat she feels the harsh pleasure of it spreading down through her lungs. She drags it in again, and with the sweet taste of the smoke in her mouth and her eyes beginning to stream from its sting she fixes them on the neon tip of the cigarette: it draws her back down, the whirling energy leaving her inch by inch, until she is sitting, heavy in the armchair, with its familiar smell of people long gone. She drops the cigarette into Cissie's undrunk coffee and it makes a sharp little hiss. Now nothing moves but the gentle rise and fall of her own ribcage. Not a sound but that of her own breathing.

'Oh God, Cissie . . . you . . . no . . . don't you do this to me . . .' she rises stiffly to her feet. 'Luke!!'

The Lost One

✺

In amongst the echoing clamour of the hospital, Michael is sure he can make out the old man's voice, keening his wife's name, over and over again: high falsetto whoops isolated by grief. He stares down at Katya Erhardt's slippers and then at the place on his coat where Maggie had sat. Two women are having some sort of row nearby, screaming what must be obscenities at each other in streams of fast-flowing strongly accented babble. One seems to have the upper hand, the younger of the two. She is gesticulating angrily, bright-red talons flashing on the end of long, dark fingers. The other, plainer woman, her face red and wet from crying, seems to be backing off. Which appears to make the other worse. She moves in on her, pushing her shoulder roughly and screeching right into her face. Michael can hear 'bitch' and 'whore' and the ubiquitous 'fuck', peppered in between strings of totally unintelligible, guttural sounds. For a moment he is both scared of the woman and attracted by her. Then a nervous man with a rather timid-looking woman who is hovering behind him try to intervene and the younger woman pushes them aside with some force, sending the two of them crashing backwards in tandem like a pantomime horse into some nearby chairs, the man ending up sitting on the timid woman's lap. The aggressive young woman then turns her back on the plain one with a dismissive gesture of the arm, and as she swaggers away from her, a triumphant prize fighter leaving the ring, Michael is alarmed to find her staring right at him, her nostrils still flared from the fray. She has full red lips curled into a defiant snarl and black eyes, shining with anger.

'You want some too, Jackass? Why you put your face in my business? ... Keep your big ass out of my face!' Michael can make out every word of this only too well and lifts his hands in supplication.

'Sure ... sure ... I ... I didn't mean t-to intrude.'

'You bet yer sweet motherfucker ... Jackass!' Michael quickly turns away, hoping the woman will turn her attention elsewhere. He picks up the abandoned coat, and plunging his hand into the pocket for his inhaler he is sure he can detect the faint residue of Maggie's body heat. On a second blast from the inhaler he takes a surreptitious sideways glance in the direction of the woman. She is standing some way off, sniffing and muttering, the bright bee-sting mouth now in a pantomime pout of self-pity. She still has her back to her weeping opponent, who is sitting being comforted by the timid woman, and she is examining one of her huge red nails, a casualty of the run-in with her friend. Michael is transfixed for a moment by the sulking childish pose of this big voluptuous woman, when apparently from nowhere Maggie appears beside her like a ghost. She stands there, her shoulders slumped under the blue velvet cloak, looking into the middle distance with unfocused eyes, as if she had been planted there by a great unseen hand, and a brief spasm of mirth erupts in Michael's gut. He feels his face redden as he prevents it from issuing forth into uncontrollable laughter. Something in the contrast of these two: one burgeoning with life and sexuality and colour, the other zombie-like and moribund, the faded husk of something once beautiful, tickles him mercilessly and he longs to spin around and to give it vent. Then Maggie's eyes are upon him and his heart turns on a sixpence. He moves towards her and the other woman's head shoots up, her pout twisting with disgust. She mutters something long and garbled, punctuated with 'fucks' and ending in 'motherfucking jackass!' Then she swivels on a red stilettoed ankle boot and marches off to the end seat of the row of chairs where her friend still sits being comforted by the timid woman.

Michael takes Maggie's face in his hands. Her cheeks feel cold to the touch and she is shivering.

'Where did you go? I was worried.' She opens her mouth as if to speak but nothing comes. A deep frown splays her eyebrows into a wide, mousey valley and once again her eyes are wet with tears. Michael holds her to him.

'It's O.K. . . . I'm here now . . .'

'Ahh . . .' From a cobwebbed throat, a creaking sound, like something being dragged with difficulty across a hard, rough surface.

'I know . . . I know . . . I should never have left you on your own like that . . . but . . .'

'Ahhh . . .' Her face is frozen, a snapshot of torment.

'Shhhhh . . . I'm here now . . . I have to get you something to put on your feet . . . you couldn't . . .'

'You . . . ahh . . .'

'What? . . . What did you say, sweetheart?'

'. . . my ffffffff . . .'

'Your feet? . . . I know . . . they must be freezing, but I have got you some nice soft slippers to put on and . . .'

'You're standing on my foot!'

'Oh my . . .' Michael stumbles backwards, managing to tread on her other foot as he does so and Maggie lets out a yelp of both pain and relief. Michael stares down with horror at the two feet, both of them a blotched, purplish colour, with little muddy tidemarks between each toe and the clear stripes of his bootprint across her right instep.

'Oh my darling . . . how could I be so clumsy? I am so sorry.' With that he steers her to a nearby chair and sits her down.

'Look what I have for you.' He produces Katya Erhardt's pink slippers from out of the polythene bag with the flourish of a magician but Maggie's eyes are on his face, on the simple, mechanical workings of his mouth. Discarding the crêpe bandage, he pulls the pair of thick lisle stockings out of the other slipper and finds, shoved into its toe, two home-made elastic garters, stretched and grey with age.

'Now . . . we're going to have these feet *so* nice and toasty . . .' He is down on this haunches, rubbing each foot in turn and blowing hot breath through the spaces between her toes. Dominic is giggling somewhere and Michael lifts his head to listen for a moment. A smile warms the muscles of his face and as always something in the soft squeal of the boy's laugh sets Michael tittering. He plunges Maggie's feet into the stockings and hoiks them up with the practised ease of a hands-on father. He tries securing them above her knees but finds the garters too big. For a moment he stares at the swell of her legs as the thigh disappears up into the darkness beneath her skirt and at the long dark cleavage where the two legs touch, and he quickly rolls the stockings down around her ankles. He looks at the rough white knees, an identical patch of pale gold hairs just below each kneecap, and Dominic has gone. He takes a deep breath in and his lungs whine with complaint.

'O.K. let's get out of here.'

Pulling her to her feet he pushes her cloak off her shoulders so that it hangs down her back like a curtain. He then stuffs each limp arm into a sleeve of his overcoat, and picking up the bag of provisions he moves her towards the door. As they approach it, a big man is being pushed through in a wheelchair, one leg elevated in a splint like a battering ram. He is dressed in a black ski suit and is wearing a red balaclava. Across his knees are a pair of skis with ski poles.

'Look, Spiderman has hurt his leg.' Michael breathes hot and moist into Maggie's ear and Dominic appreciates the joke.

'. . . yeah? Well skiing is for the Rockies, not Fifth Avenue, sir.'

Michael recognises the tone of bored cynicism. The black eyes are looking straight at him with not even a hint of acknowledgement. It is the Hispanic-looking paramedic who had helped take Maggie's stretchered body to the hospital just twenty-four hours ago. A languorous contempt hanging from every feature, she roughly manoeuvres the wheelchair around an old woman who appears to be lost. The latter is turning round and round, gazing with fearful confusion on her surroundings as if she had just been dropped in from another age, another world. As she turns they see that the hem of her skirt is tucked up into the waistband of her tights, exposing the huge expanse of her backside, over which the thick tights are stretched to transparency; beneath them a crumpled pair of pink bloomers can easily be seen. Michael quickly twists Maggie round, pointing her instead in the direction of the main entrance and away from the scornful gaze of the paramedic.

'... er ... I think we'll go this way,' but Maggie pushes him away.

'Wait ...' She approaches the old woman, narrowly missing the protruding foot of the wheelchair-bound skier.

'Whoa!' The paramedic raises her eyes to heaven and Michael giggles stupidly at her before she whips past him leaving an icy draught in her wake. Maggie pulls the skirt out of the top of the old woman's tights and she wheels round with unexpected speed.

'Ellen? ... w ... where's Ellen?' Maggie touches the woman's arm, only the tips of her fingers showing below the sleeve of the overcoat.

'She's coming back.'

With that she guides her to the nearest chair and sits her down, the old woman looking up at her, a frightened child.

'What? ... She's my daughter ... Ellen. I made her angry.'

Maggie wants to cry. She doesn't want to hear about anyone making anyone angry, but especially this lost woman, sitting neatly on the chair.

'Maggie ... we really have to go.' Michael is at her side, pulling gently at her elbow.

Maggie yanks it out of his grasp and sits resolutely down next to the old woman then speaks hoarsely through clenched teeth.

'No! We can't leave her!' She does not look at Michael but stares fixedly at the floor in front of her, a faint pinkness beginning to show in her cheeks.

'Oh! There you are, Mother. I thought I told you to wait over there.'

A large woman dragging swollen feet ballooning out of flat, sensible shoes is waddling over to them.

'Ellen . . . I couldn't see you anywhere.'

'Oh my, I can't leave you for two minutes.' Again Michael takes hold of Maggie's elbow.

'There you are, dear . . . your daughter's here . . . come, Maggie.' Maggie reluctantly rises from the chair.

'Oh I'm sorry. Was my mother bothering you? She gets . . .'

'*No!*' Maggie has spun round and is glaring at the newcomer.

'Oh . . . oh . . . I . . . it's . . . it's just that she gets confused and . . . and . . .' The woman is wide-eyed and open-mouthed.

'Sure, we understand . . . O.K. . . . we really have to go . . .' Michael pulls Maggie away. She keeps her eyes on the woman for some time before turning.

'Good luck to you!' Michael calls over his shoulder. The woman is still standing there, staring at them. When they are some way away, they hear her world-weary tones.

'Come on, let's get ya home,' and Maggie turns.

'Oh pl . . .' An elbow is thrust with force into Michael's gut, causing him to jackknife over and Maggie rushes at the two women. From the back she is a strange sight. Her cloak has gathered into a Quasimodo hump beneath Michael's big black coat and with her legs flying out at all angles and her arms doing the same inside the great flapping sleeves, she looks prehistoric and predatory, the lead player of a childish nightmare. As she nears them, the daughter backs away, the great sausage legs shuddering as she does so.

Both women simply stare, an unavoidable avalanche coming down upon them. Maggie comes to a stop, almost falling on top of the old woman who is still sitting in the chair, their knees crashing together, and Maggie's face ending up inches from hers.

Then she plants a hard, passionate kiss on the plump, sagging cheek. It lasts for several seconds before she removes her lips with a satisfying smack, and she is back at Michael's side, pulling him towards the main entrance corridor. Her fingernails are digging painfully into his bicep. He considers that he might be making a mistake.

The Departure

'Luke!' Luke watches as Helena's face turns an unfamiliar puce. He notes that it is a long time since he has seen her blush; years probably. Or did she ever blush at all? If anyone had reason to . . .

'Luke!! Pleeease!' The hands around her neck are unfamiliar. The skin is ruddy and cracked and coarse, black hairs sprout unevenly between wrist and knuckle. The fingers are short and powerful, a ring of filth emphasising the edge of each thumbnail.

'Luke!' With the two thumbs now embedded so deeply in the centre of her neck, Luke is amazed that her voice sounds so unimpeded. An actress's voice, resonant and eloquent.

'Luke!! For Jesus' sake!' Not like his voice which had once, in a drama school tutorial, been referred to as like a bucket of dead fish.

'Luke *please*! . . . It's Cissie!'

'Luke, for Christ's sake!' He watches her face expand, losing the fine contours of cheek and jaw and as it fills up with blood, so the large ruddy hands go pale. It is as if the face, now with its monstrous popping eyes, is sucking life from the hands rather than the hands squeezing life from the face. And although still angry and hateful, the hands have taken on a certain grace. It must have been a trick of the light, or an invention of his imagination, but there are no hairs, or at least not to speak of. The black squiggles that he thought he saw spiralling aggressively through the skin any which way they pleased have paled into thin golden wisps lying flat in compliant unison.

'Luke!'

These are not hands that would make his mother giggle and squirm, but hands that slithered with ease across the keys of a piano. Chopin might well have had hands like these.

'Nooo!' He shoots up on one elbow 'Helen!' he stares down at his own hands and examines his fingers, stretching them out and holding them within an inch of the end of his nose. In doing so he lets go of a corner of the duvet; it is hot and crumpled and damp from sweat. His fingers give off an acrid smell. He stares hard at the grimy little oval of nail embedded deeply into each finger. He can hear her quietly chuntering in the other room, and grabbing his glasses from the nightstand he throws back the covers. He is out of bed and making a dash for the living-room door when something light and slippery under his right heel sends him down hard onto his arse.

'Jesus! . . .' He rubs his coccyx, already bruised from his fall on the ice the night before.

'Come quickly!'

'Alright! I'm coming.' Getting to his feet, he finds the little group snapshot he had been looking at the day before is stuck to his heel. Peeling it off, he cannot see its detail in the dim light of the room and so throws it carelessly in the direction of the bed.

'Luke? What the fuck are you doing?' He opens the door to the living room and Helena is sitting in the armchair, her back to the light from the kitchen, her knees drawn up under her chin.

'What on earth is the matter?'

'Please come and see. I think Cissie might be dead!' Her voice is tremulous. He stands there for a moment, a slight draught making him aware that the tee-shirt he is wearing does not cover his nether regions.

'What?'

'PLEASE COME AND SEE IF CISSIE IS DEAD!'

He stumbles around the sofa, his face burning into an

unexpected blush. He stands looking down at the shadowy hump and speaks in a gentle whisper.

'Cissie?'

'Oh for Christ's sake! Shake her! Take her pulse or something! Don't just stand there whispering!'

'Alright! Alright!' Luke cracks down onto his haunches next to her bed and with a tentative hand reaches out and touches the dark ridge of the duvet. Its soft puffs collapse under the weight of his hand until he can feel the firm surface of the mattress beneath. Then with both hands he begins to pat the rest of it down, expecting at any moment to come across Cissie's warm sleeping body. He thrusts both hands underneath the duvet and swishes them from side to side like someone playing Blindman's Bluff, but the bed is cold and there is no Cissie, just the sharp clean smell of patchouli warmed by her own essence of skin and hair.

'She's not here. Is this another bloody joke? What the hell is going on?'

The Mist

⸙

'Maggie?' She tries to remember the warm dull ache and the dark place beneath the sheet where her exhaustion had given her no choice but to sleep. And although it must be there, in her memory, she cannot recreate it, she cannot replace the unbearable nothing.

'Maggie? . . . can I get you . . . What can I get you?'

She looks up at the man, his face framed by the dark garland of curls, the skin corpse-white, save for a sprinkling of freckles that she had not noticed before on his forehead and cheeks. His eyes darkened with a moist, glassy sheen are red-rimmed, each puffy lid clearly defined and seemingly bare of lashes. It is a face that wouldn't look out of place in an Elizabethan painting. Now Maggie can see this clearly, the ruff around his neck, like an oversized Christmas decoration, the unshaven chin extended and transformed into a neat goatee.

'Maggie?' His mouth moves into a smile. He is one of Elizabeth's favourites, off to fight the Spanish and come back a hero.

They are sitting in a room that she cannot quite place but remembers as if it were yesterday. It is a room from another time; another shard of shattered memory. She stares back at the face, the features no longer uncertain and mercurial as they had been when she had known him before. Now, despite the effort of the upturned mouth, they hang in stillness, grief hollowing the cheeks and lining the forehead; and something else, anger perhaps or bewilderment, carving a deep crevice between the brows.

'How're you doin'?'

A thick, grey mist gathers behind her eyes and descends past her throat, down into emptiness.

'How're you doing?' she repeats inside her head. Michael gets off the sofa, each knee thumping softly down onto the polished wooden floor in quick succession and slides himself towards her. He rummages inside the overcoat she still has wrapped around her in search of her hands. He finds them, each one holding on to a sweaty gathered clump of the blue velvet cloak beneath.

'Oh Maggie . . .' He drops his head for a moment and then lifts it with an inhalation of pure optimism which almost makes his head spin.

'How about I fix you a hot chocolate?' The eyebrows lift and the cleft of uncertainty between them disappears. '. . . Or a "nice cup of tea"?' he says with a Dick Van Dyke attempt at Cockney and a cheeky chappie tilt of the head.

She closes her eyes and for several seconds she cannot tell whether she is awake or sleeping but she hears the strain in the man's knees as he gets to his feet and the crackle of brown paper as he picks up the bag of provisions from the coffee table and her hands, now abandoned in her lap, feel chilled and strangely detached from the rest of her. As he moves away from her a cool wave of air brings the sweet scent of apple skin into her nostrils, and she knows that she is in fact awake and that sleep is an alien state, belonging to some other existence, remote and shrinking. A carefree, fresh-faced existence.

'Oh come back here!' The soft pulpy bounce of an apple repeats itself across the wooden floor behind her.

'Oh my . . .' Another joins it and she hears the man's stockinged feet slide across the polished surface, and as he scrabbles to retrieve them he lets out a barrage of little falsetto laughs that pepper the back of Maggie's head, passing through her skull with ease. Once inside they bounce and screech; hooligans in an empty building. They are gone in an instant and the apples are jumping playfully down a set of stairs. She remembers the stairs.

Michael nips down them with well-worn grace. He stops at the bottom and sits down on the penultimate step to listen; firstly to Dominic's squealed enjoyment of the chase and then to the silence above. She had not uttered a single word since the encounter with the old woman in the hospital waiting room. Heading north through the icy wastes of lower Manhattan, she had dragged Katya Erhardt's slippers with a strange, stiff-legged gait and they had walked at least two blocks of Seventh Avenue before Michael went skidding off the treacherous sidewalk and through a mini-alpine mountain range of piled-up snow to stop a yellow cab on the street. The driver, a blond hulk of a man, with what looked like an earring tattooed on his left earlobe, had looked suspiciously at Maggie as Michael had dragged her through the huge heap of snow and had manhandled her near rigid form into the back of his taxi.

'What is this? You gotta be back home by midnight?'

Michael, already ensconced, blowing his nails and rubbing his arms, could not think for a moment what time of day it was and had looked at his watch.

'Cinderella's left her slipper,' the driver had said, a nod of his huge head to emphasise each word.

Michael had stared at him and considered that again he had attracted a lunatic. The man nodded out of his window towards the sidewalk and following his gaze Michael had spotted a lone pink slipper, Katya Erhardt's slipper, perched precariously on top of the dirty ridge of snow at the side of the road.

'Oh she . . . she has sor . . . s . . . ba . . . her feet are bad.' A tiny chuckle had died in Michael's throat.

'Well, she ain't gonna get her prince without her other slipper.' Michael had smiled at the man, hoping that he would oblige, for the thought of getting back out into the bitter morning air was almost more than he could bear.

'Well hurry up! I got a long day ahead of me. I don't want to turn into a pumpkin just yet.'

Michael had looked at the Sumo profile with its fat, tattooed earlobe and its pink, broken-veined jowl and, painting it orange in his mind's eye, he had then added a little green foliage to the top and had got out to retrieve the slipper with a smile. In contrast to their first taxi ride together this one was totally uneventful. Maggie had sat facing forwards the whole way, her face immobile but for a cloudy dewdrop gradually forming on the tip of her nose. Michael, his teeth beginning to chatter, had patted the pockets of his trousers in the vain hope of finding a handkerchief, and on finding nothing had pinched the droplet off with thumb and forefinger just as it had been wobbling itself free. Then he had snuggled up to her for warmth.

Now he gets up to make the hot chocolate and there is a sudden rushing in the top of his head which sends him reeling back down. He drops his head into his hands with a feeling of nausea and notices a certain stiffness in his neck. The little kitchen is hot and he can feel his lungs contracting, a dry squeak accompanying each breath. He looks up to scan the work surface for his inhaler and is distracted by its perfect granite shine, not a smear, not a blemish; God is in His heaven. He lowers his head down level with its sharp, flawless edge just to further appreciate the glistening perfection, and is briefly in awe.

Now he feels Dominic at his elbow as he pours the milk into the pan.

'Oh ... of course!' He reaches up to a cupboard above and brings out a half-empty cellophane packet of pink and white marshmallows: 'Oh please, Dad ... pleeeeease ... just one ... please!' 'Dominic, it will make you sick. No.' Mixing the chocolate powder into the milk he can hear the boy stomp off up the stairs. 'I never get to eat anything I like any more!'

Michael pours the chocolate into a purple mug decorated with a colourful matchstick figure wearing a baseball cap backwards and scooting a skateboard up into the air. 'Cool Dude,' it boasts in jaunty, clashing letters. He pops two marshmallows into the mug and gulps back an avalanche of grief.

'Oh dear God . . . my darling, darling boy.' He turns, mopping at a runaway tear with the heel of his hand. 'Jesus God!'

She is standing on the bottom step, still wearing his overcoat. Her face without a trace of colour; her skin geisha-white, her eyes as black as jet. The mouth, although it cannot help but smile, has lost its colour beneath a pale shell of dried skin and dark scab. She speaks as if the dryness does not stop at the lips but extends inside, along her tongue and down across her throat.

'I need a towel.'

'Oh! . . .' Again Michael sends high-pitched titters to reverberate around her head and slops the scalding drink over one of his stockinged feet. 'Ow!' He tries to wipe it with the sole of the other foot, but just succeeds in losing his balance and spilling more of the stuff onto the same foot. 'Ooooh yaaa!' He hops, lifting the scalded foot into the air. He puts it back down onto a pink marshmallow sitting in a small pool of frothy brown milk whereupon the foot skids from underneath him and he goes over to one side like a skater on a sharp bend with both legs dead straight and falls heavily onto his right hip banging his head with a hollow clunk on a cupboard door.

'Oh . . . I'm so sorry! I didn't realise . . . You gave me such a start. I didn't realise you were there. Oh Je—' He gets up, rubbing his hip and still clutching the mug, now only a third full. Putting it down he reaches for a small kitchen towel which has been placed, neatly folded, on the worktop, and staggers, almost losing his footing again.

'Oh my, I'm a little dizzy today, I don't know why.' He laughs his laugh. 'You wanted a towel?' He hands her the striped linen towel and she stares at him without taking it.

She looks down and he follows her gaze. A small, blood-brown rivulet has sunk into the pink fluffy trim of one of Katya Erhardt's slippers. He looks at it for a moment and all at once he notices

179

the room is not only oven-hot, but seems to be rapidly running out of air.

'Oh m ... er yes ... of course ... you ... you need a ... a ... towel ... Just let ... do you ... you think? ... would it be possible for you to just ... say ... make do with this ... this ... towel ... just for a moment? I think I may have to lie down ... just for a little while ... I ... I seem to be ... feeling ... I feel real sick.'

He pushes past her, the room tilting and turning as he goes. On reaching the top of the stairs he sinks down to sit on the top step in the relative cool of the living area, an image of Maggie's mouth, its corners stretching drily upwards, hovers before his mind's eye. Had his ridiculous display of ineptitude caused her to smile or was it simply the one that nature had pressed so sweetly on her mouth from birth? Dizziness and nausea combine successfully inside his head and bring it crashing down with a distant painless bump onto the floor. As he closes his eyes against the darkening room, the honeyed smell of maple and varnish that he thought had all but disappeared rises comfortingly into his nostrils and he hears the mechanical click of the answerphone.

'Michael? ... It's Elizabeth ... The heating's down here. I would love to come sit in the sauna. Call me. Soon ... before I freeze to death.'

The Reception

છ

'A person could freeze to death. Half the city has no electricity. My heart goes out to the old folks,' says the waiter. The waiter has faded reddish hair, which in his youth was probably called 'strawberry blond'. Several oiled strands of it are raked across his bald pink pate. When he speaks, he addresses Cissie's forehead, his watery grey eyes only meeting her own for a split second before darting several centimetres upwards. 'Can I fix you another coffee? Or how 'bout another doughnut?'

Cissie's heart is racing from the coffee and her stomach distended from the sweet stodge of two hastily eaten doughnuts.

'No thanks, I think I've overdone it as it is.' She can see her own reflection in the dimpled brass top of the bar. Most of it is distorted, the image stretched and smeared beyond recognition; all, that is, except for her left eye, which is perfectly mirrored. She is drawn and enamoured by its blackness: the deep dark shine of the iris contrasting with the bluish white of its surround. It is a child's eye and something in its wary innocence touches her. It is an eye that she has seen in countless family photographs; in the faces of aunts and cousins and sisters – she would know its anxious sheen anywhere. She moves closer to the counter and as she does so the eye melts and mangles, its ludicrously misshapen form somehow exaggerating the moist innocence.

'You here for business or pleasure?' She cannot look up. Somewhere in the reflection of her eye there is a chance to see. Instead of looking back at her, it appears to be looking off at an angle, which gives her the odd sensation that she is catching herself unawares. An older self, peeking slyly from the shadows at a younger more innocent one.

'Oh, I wouldn't look too closely at that. Lost a lot of its sheen over the years. Doesn't gleam like it used to.' It is her mother's eye. She sits bolt upright with a sharp intake of breath.

'You alright, miss? . . . Can I get you something?'

'No . . . erm . . .' She notices that her eyes are hot and itchy. 'I'm just tired . . . I haven't had a lot of sleep.'

'Oh sure, tell me about it!'

'No, I'd rather not . . . Please, put this on my room.' He moves to the end of the counter to get her tab but turns to see her moving towards the exit of the empty bar. He lifts his voice and pitches it out, over the gloom of the long dark room to catch her, before she leaves, 'What room?' Cissie can hear a tenor in his voice.

'The Lincoln Suite!'

'But you need to sign this!'

'Oh Jesus!' She stomps back to the bar, her red face twitching with barely controlled emotion. Snorting back snot, she rapidly signs her name in a wild hand that she does not herself recognise.

'That's fine and if you could print your name just there.' His voice has taken on a becalming tone.

'Jesus Christ! Can't you see me?' Looking at the man Cissie sees that his gaze has now violently swung away from the centre of her forehead to about a foot above her head and to the right. She resists the urge to see if there is someone standing there.

'I know, miss, but these things have to be done.' Cissie prints her name, scratching right through the paper on the last letter and shoves it unceremoniously towards him.

'No! You don't know . . . You don't know fuck all! God save me from . . . th . . . fr . . . from . . . from you!' And she is gone.

The lift, an oblong thing with barely enough room for two people to stand in line, clanks slowly up to the sixth floor. The air is heavy with a mixture of fresh underarm sweat and loud citrus aftershave.

'Huh! "Eau de Businessman"!'

Its walls are lined with thin dark red carpet. On one is a faded advertisement for 'Dino's Deli' encased under glass. It has a mystifying bleached quality, as if it has been in the sun for too long. Cissie can make out two diners – a man with a ridiculously teased hairstyle and a floral shirt, and a woman with too much eye make-up on. The couple are being presented with two plates, each covered with an unidentifiable brown mass. They are smiling up at a smirking waiter, who sports a *Viva Zapata* moustache, presumably the eponymous Dino. Around this, several cigarette burns are peppered into the carpet, like buckshot. Cissie sticks the tip of her forefinger into one of them and twists it round. There is something pleasurable in the rough texture of its melted pile and she is reluctant to remove it. The lift jolts sickeningly to a halt and the outer door is wrenched open by a squat, plump woman carrying a small pile of white towels. She smiles and there is a dark gap where one of her front teeth is missing. One-handed, she pulls back the retractable lift door with ease. Cissie had needed both hands. She removes her finger from the hole in the carpet.

'You want this flo?'

'I . . . oh . . . I . . . I dunno . . . er . . . What . . . is this? . . . what floor is this?'

'What flo you want?'

'Why can't you . . . f . . . th . . . answer my . . . fucking question? Why don't people fucking well respect . . . what am I? Two?!' Cissie takes in a deep, shuddering breath and holds it while the two women stare at each other over a vast expanse of no man's land. The woman's mouth jerks open as if she is about to say something, but it remains a dark quivering hole and nothing comes. She bows her head and backs away from the lift, a subject backing away from the throne, shrinking in size. A much smaller woman says, with a tiny, distant voice, 'Is O.K. . . . I wait.'

The woman stares at the ground in front of her and Cissie is sure she had caught a moistening in her eyes. The deep, shuddering breath comes bursting back out, bringing with it a hot rush of both pity and shame.

'Oh ... I ... I'm so sorry ... I did ... didn't ... mean ... to ... I just ... am ... so ...' The woman looks up; child's eyes in a face weathered by life. 'Please ... please come in ... pleeease.'

The mouth has closed and now it twists into a crooked half-smile, the lips sliding back over the teeth to reveal again the black vacant lot where her front tooth should be. With what looks like a half-curtsey she comes back into the lift and, turning her back, stands in front of Cissie and presses the button for the fifth floor. Again she bows her head and Cissie looks down on the white shiny skin of her thick neck. Just where neck and shoulder meet, directly above the white nylon overall, is an eruption of skin, a wart or cyst. Cissie's mother had had one of these, awkwardly situated halfway down her back, right under her bra strap. It bled regularly and Cissie can see her now standing at the sink, her back to the room, rigid, motionless, a harbinger of inexplicable coldness and neglect. Cissie's stomach tightens as in her mind's eye she sees a small spot spread out into a crimson island, in a sea of white, perfectly pressed rayon.

'Please forgive me.'

'Yes, ma'am.' The woman continues to look down as the lift comes to a dizzying stop on the fifth floor. With one swift practised yank the lift door is pulled back. Once outside she pulls it carefully to, her eyes studiously trained on Cissie's knees. 'Good mownin.' Now all that is left of her is the sweet scent of her freshly washed hair and Cissie can barely breathe.

'The Apollo Ho ... the hotel A ... pollo or something ... some dreary little place in Manhattan.'

'I can't even begin to tell you what I feel about you at this precise moment, Cissie. I am so angry.'

Cissie's stomach gathers and twists, bringing up small belches of bitter wind into her mouth. 'Please . . . Fran, just tell me what they've said.'

'What they have "SAID" is that our mother is in a coma from which she may never recover!' Cissie tries for a moment to recall the scent of the woman's hair in the lift but all she can get is the slightly unpleasant smell of recently vacuumed carpet; old odours exhumed from deep within its pile.

'But . . . where was . . . where did it happen? Did she have a heart attack?'

'Oh! Like you *care*! You know full well how fragile she is. How the hell did you think she was going to cope with all this crap being dumped on her?'

'But I . . .'

'So yes . . . surprise, surprise, she had a heart attack, followed pretty swiftly by a stroke.' Cissie gulps at the air.

'I'm so sorry I didn't . . . I didn't know what the press were going to do. I was going to tell you all . . . th . . .'

'Oh sure you were! Why has it taken you three days to ring? You ran off to New York with some other woman as soon as the story broke. Thinking of your own bloody neck, as usual. Even your bloody girlfriend couldn't get hold of you! How do you think it feels to discover in a filthy tabloid that your "oh so successful" youngest daughter is a bloody lesbian?'

'I can only imagine the pain . . .'

'Yes! Well you're good at imagining, aren't you? Well imagine this . . . you have no longer got an older sister called Frances O'Brien . . . and I imagine, but let's face it I was never as good at it as you, that Catherine and Mari feel the same. They're just too distraught to articulate it at the moment.' The persistent whine of the dialling tone and Frances has gone.

Anxiety ballooning in her chest, Cissie slumps back on the bed, sending the loose headboard crashing against the wall, and she takes in the cheap attempt at Regency of the Apollo Hotel. Its scuffed, tattered edges and the optimism of its cleanliness and

185

of its bright spring colours conspire oddly to inflate her chest to bursting point.

She sits back up to undo her bra strap and whilst doing so she looks down at the little pad next to the phone. She had doodled on it absent-mindedly while her sister was lashing her with the dreadful news from home. 'Mum' is written in strange, faint handwriting, and tightly surrounding it a ring of deeply etched xs. Cissie stares at them, gulping in huge breaths of air. She can see her mother's legs stretched out beneath her grey pencil skirt, one in front of the other on the kitchen floor at home, her toes elegantly pointing downwards, as if for all the world she was delicately tiptoeing somewhere, and she recalls the sense of alarm as her eleven-year-old self spots the ladder in the pale sheer stockings, the sky-blue slipper lying nearby, the other one half on and half off, and the all-pervading, lung-rasping atmosphere.

Now she moves over to the small brown refrigerator and opening it removes several miniatures. Moving back to the bed she opens her mouth and sucks in air, momentarily cooling the panic within. She looks again at the ring of xs and considers from where in her subconscious they might have come; kisses? barbed wire? a crown of thorns?

'Oh Jesus . . .' Clattering the bottles onto the nightstand she dials reception. No one replies.

'Oh come on . . . you . . . fucking dump!' More gulps of air are sucked in. Still no reply. 'Oooh how bloody predictable!'

Cissie had been brought to the Apollo Hotel by taxi, as dawn was breaking blood-red over Manhattan. She had tried to get the driver to take her to the airport. He had refused, saying that it had snowed again in the night and that not all the roads had been cleared and anyway all airports were closed.

'Good morning, Reception, Jana speaking, how can I help you?' The voice sounds pinched as if the speaker has a peg on her nose and an eastern European-sounding accent.

'Oh . . . hello, could you get me some painkillers please?'

'Yes? . . . Sorry? You want . . . wh . . . er Jana speaking, how can I help you?'

'Yes, Jana, I want some painkillers. Can you get some for me?'

'You want pang . . . what? . . . I'm sorry?'

Cissie takes in a mammoth breath and says quietly to the ceiling, 'You will be in a fucking minute.'

'I'm sorry . . . er . . . Mrs O'Brien could you please repeat that please?'

'I WOULD LIKE SOME PAINKILLERS PLEASE. I'VE GOT A HEADACHE!' Then with her teeth Cissie opens a miniature of gin.

'Oh, you have a headache. Can I get you something for that, Mrs O'Brien?

'YES . . . THAT IS WHY I RANG. I WANT SOME PILLS.'

'Could I get you some pills maybe, Mrs O'Brien? We have codeine, Mrs O'Brien?'

'Yes fine, could you bring some up to my room?' She takes a swig from the tiny gin bottle.

'I could send some up to your room, Mrs O'Brien?'

'YES PLEASE! As soon as possible.'

'Would you like them right away, Mrs O'Brien?'

'For crying out loud . . . YES! And for your information, I'm not MRS O'Brien I'm . . . MS O'Brien.'

'. . . I'm sorry? . . . You are not Mrs O'Brien?'

'NO! MRS O'Brien is my mother!'

'. . . I'm sorry M . . . M . . . er what room are you staying in?'

'Oh for Christ's sake! THIS ONE!'

'. . . and your mother? . . . She is staying there too?'

'JESUS GOD! No . . .'

'. . . because this is a single room.'

'Nooo! My mother is in England! I am MS . . . MS . . . MS . . . Ms O'Brien! I'm not married! I'm a bloody lesbian for Christ's sake. Just don't call me Mrs O'Brien!'

'I'm sorry, there has been a mistake. We have you registered as Mrs Cissie O'Brien. This is wrong?'

'I am Miss Cissie O'Brien and you can forget the codeine. I was going to kill myself, but now I'm too depressed.' She slams the phone down with a satisfying plastic clunk and again sees her mother's blue slippers. Her mother's stiff white profile against the grey linoleum with its morning Dettol smell; the small drool of saliva collecting in a sticky pool beneath her half-open mouth.

Cissie reaches for the little bottle of gin and finishes it. There is a hammering at the door. She opens it to a wall of perfume; something sweet and cloying, and a tall blonde woman is standing there.

'Some pills for Mrs O'Brien?' Cissie stares at the eager face with its mask of orange make-up and its huge clear eyes and feels an unwanted smile warm her face.

'I think she prefers gas actually.'

'I am sorry? . . .'

'Are you? . . . So am I . . .' Cissie takes the pills from the woman's outstretched hand. 'Thank you, you've been . . . very helpful.' Closing the door, Cissie sits on the bed and takes the cap off the pill bottle.

'Cheers, Mother.'

The Child

❧

'Cheers, Helen! ... I really needed that.' Luke turns and sits on Cissie's bed. 'If this is another of your childish japes, I swear I'll ...'

'No!' She sniffs with a loud unpleasant snort. 'I dn ... I ... I thought ... oh I don't know what I thought! Where the hell is she?'

'Well ... we seem to have successfully lost our two closest friends within the space of forty-eight hours. That has to be some sort of a record ... Put the bloody light on, she's probably left a note!' Luke is already at the light switch. He snaps it up with an impatient flick of his forefinger, flooding the place with a gloom of dull yellow light. 'Jesus, this place is disgusting. Look at it! No wonder they've both moved out.'

'Well ... it's possible she's just going out to get some air or something ... she is still a bit jet-lagged.'

Luke stares at her, a sneer of almost Elvis proportions curling his upper lip. He speaks quietly to begin with, carefully enunciating each word and building in volume as he continues:

'It is not yet dawn in the middle of freezing February, in the middle of freezing, fucking New York City! I ask you, is that likely? And there is a note for Christ's sake! What's that there; right in front of you?' A sheet of lined paper has been ripped from Maggie's notepad and placed on top of the clutter on the coffee table, a perfect brown circle, the result of a misplaced coffee cup, decorating the bottom right-hand corner and within its circumference is a simple line drawing of a face, its mouth turned down in a little glum arc.

'Oh . . . God.' Her voice is small and high, and full of wonderment: like that of a child being shown a conjuring trick. She reaches forward to pick it up and finds it is stuck to the rim of a wineglass. Luke tuts as she tears it off, leaving a corner still attached.

DEAR HELENA AND LUKE,   *4.45 a.m.*
 HAVING NOT SLEPT FOR MOST OF THE NIGHT AND FEELING BLOODY DESPERATE ABOUT EVERYTHING, I RANG JENNY, ONLY TO DISCOVER THAT THINGS AT HOME HAVE BECOME EPICALLY DREADFUL. THE PAPERS HAVE BEEN DOORSTEPPING MY FAMILY AND IT HAS MADE MY MOTHER ILL. I AM SO SORRY THAT WHAT I INTENDED TO BE A MUCH NEEDED BREAK HAS TURNED OUT TO BE AN UTTER NIGHTMARE AND I HATE THE THOUGHT OF LEAVING YOU TO DEAL WITH MAGGIE, BUT I FEEL I MUST TRY AND GET HOME AND FACE UP TO SOME OF THIS. ANYWAY I THINK WE COULD ALL DO WITH A BIT OF SPACE. I DO LOVE YOU BOTH,
 TIRED AND CONFUSED OF FULHAM
 P.S. PLEASE DON'T HATE ME XXX

'Well? . . . What does it say?' Without looking up, Helena passes the note to Luke.

'Well it seems I've excelled myself in the hostess stakes. Let's see now . . . who else can I invite to stay?'

She flicks back the thick drape of hair with a horse's toss of the head and looks at Luke, who is reading the note, his nose almost tickling the page. Helena inhales audibly as she takes in his appearance. His glasses, roughly shoved up at an odd angle on top of his head, have caused two small clumps of hair to stand up on end, looking for all the world like horns. He is wearing a tee-shirt, once white but now an overwashed, misshapen article of a sad grey hue. On its front is a faded print of a black and white photograph. It is of an old woman photographed from behind in silhouette. She is endeavouring to climb a steep set of stone steps in what looks like a narrow Mediterranean street. Luke is otherwise naked, the uncertain hem of the aforementioned tee-shirt failing miserably to cover his modesty.

Helena breathes out in a series of silent titters as she continues to take him in. She marvels at the almost complete lack of colour in him, a monochrome being; the hair, neither blond nor brown, but an indefinite mousey thatch; the delicate white skin that burns and blisters from just seconds in the sun, and the grey eyes, pale shields protecting ...? She thinks of the boy crying and shivering in her bedsit in Manchester all those years ago, and sorrow rises through her gut to her heart at breakneck speed, catching her breath in a gasp. She avoids looking at his penis and instead drops her gaze downwards to his feet, beached and colourless, then upwards to the legs, long spindles, the knee making more of an impression than the thigh or calf could ever hope to do, and she can hold on to the gasp no longer. It erupts in a squawk, followed by a series of hard flat gulps on a knife-edge of feeling; laughter or tears in equal measure, both vying for an explosion. Luke's head shoots up, causing his glasses to crash back down, landing skewiff on top of his nose, and laughter wins the day.

'Oh God, Lukey! What *do* you look like!' Luke stares back at her, his eyes are like glass, his face immobile, inscrutable except for a small round patch of pink at the centre of each cheek. For a moment they look like the cheeks of a clown inappropriately painted on, and Helena's laughter is cranked up a gear, tears beginning and veins bulging.

'What on earth do you expect ... Armani? You've just got me

out of bed for heaven's sake! But there again that's probably preferable to getting me INTO it!'

Luke knows she cannot hear, her ears full of the sound of her own laughter, and he is surprised at the volcanic rise of his own venom, rushing to his throat, leaving it impotent and aching. He thinks of the boys who had accosted him the previous night, their words ricocheting around inside his head, the bitter garlic smell of breath, the uncouth animal screeches of their laughter. He looks briefly down at his splayed white feet and feels his face begin to burn and that small roar begin to grow again inside his chest, just as it had the night before. He looks back at Helena, the mane of hair now having swung back into place, covering her left eye, her mouth open with laughter, and she is clapping her hands and lifting her knees into the air, rocking back and forth. Now all of a sudden his teeth have collided with hers and he can taste her blood in his mouth. Now they are on the floor, he is not sure how, but the wooden arm of the chair seems to have come adrift and is lying next to Helena's head.

'YAAAAAAAAAArrrrrggggh!! Yerrrrrrr ... aaaaaa ... berrrrrrr!!!!!' the roar is deafening, a bubbling geyser of bile and pain, its sheer force making the formation of words impossible. Helena's eyes are huge and she is speaking, screaming even, but he cannot hear her above the roar. Then from nowhere a hand is at his face, the painful drag of fingernails down across his forehead and onto his nose and cheeks as his glasses are whisked from his eyes. Again his teeth crash onto hers and again he can taste her blood, fresh and sticky in his mouth, and the acrid taste of stale tobacco on her tongue. But the roaring has now diminished, reduced to a vibration at the centre of his chest. Instead he hears a child. It is the urgent cry of an abandoned child. He rears up, and sees mockery in the set of her blurring features and a wantonness in the dark gape of her mouth and stuffs his tongue deep into her throat. More blood, and now he can smell that perfume, sickly and whorish, insidiously enveloping his senses. With a rush of anger and disgust he tears at her pyjama bottoms. He feels her body relax and he plunges himself into her, with an ejaculation he feels will never ever end.

The Human

❦

The child is silent. Maggie stares at the tiny white face and watches its image appear as she breathes in, and then disappear beneath a cloud of condensation as she breathes out again onto the cool glass of the photograph. She lifts her forefinger to touch the large crack which forks viciously down the centre of the glass and veers off to one side, cutting Michael off from the children, except for one of his arms placed proprietorially around this particular child's neck in a playful lock. She does not in fact touch the glass, but stops her finger in mid-air and instead turns it around to find the rough little scab in the centre of her own forehead. She gently fingers it and, finding its dry edge to be raised at one side, she slides her nail underneath and with a degree of relish lifts it almost completely off. All, that is, except for a small corner of congealed blood, softer than the rest, the scab having not fully formed and still attached to the wound beneath.

She looks carefully at the child whose neck Michael pretends to crush; and sees something aged, ancient even, in the sad wilting of its head; and in the perfectly round black circles of its eyes she sees the loneliness of one who knows but cannot say. And then there is Michael: his eyes too are perfectly round, and in this photograph too are black as pitch but oddly younger than the child's, and in him she sees something else, a tenderness, and she sees it also in the hunch of his shoulder and the soft squeeze of his arm around the child's neck. A slow, warm spasm gathers deep in her belly, ending in a rush of blood. She feels its escape down the inside of her leg and looks down to see where it will stop. The pink nylon fluff of Katya Erhardt's slipper stops it in its tracks. It is the colour of henna, the colour of life, yet full of death.

She turns and sits on the bottom step and, lifting her skirt, she bends to examine its thick red flow at close quarters. She can smell the earth in it and dragging her forefinger up the inside of her calf she holds its bloody tip to her nose and inhales deeply: the smell of soil and damp terracotta, the smell of autumn, of leaves kicked up underfoot. She sees her mother's large rough hands scooping compost quickly and efficiently into tiny pots, black crumbs of the stuff, moist and rich as fruit cake, spilling out onto a dusty shelf.

Very slowly she lowers the finger down into the waiting tip of her tongue and instantly her tongue retracts and she pulls her finger away as if each had been burnt by the other. Now for a moment she savours and is intrigued by the piquancy of its strong, salty taste and she places the finger more firmly onto her tongue and sucks at the remainder of the blood and now, her finger wet with spit, she traces the tiny river up to the top of her thigh, stopping every few seconds to suck at it with quick, slurping licks, careful not to spill a drop, until all that is left is a smudged brown stain, already cracking like a river bed in drought. She stares at it for a moment. 'God save you,' she says in the softest of whispers and then from behind she hears a movement.

She looks round to see that the man is sitting above her on the top step but that only his legs are visible, the upper part of his body having flopped down onto the floor of the upstairs room. She watches the gentle ebb and flow of the slight paunch above his belt and notices a large damp patch under his right arm. She gets up to look at the man again in the photograph above her on the wall, the white face with the shadow of a smile cast over its soft, creased features, the playful machismo of the encircling arm and the child fragile and sapped, a snowdrop in a warm fist. A dry little crackle erupts deep in her throat; a strange sound; one that she does not recognise as her own.

'Oh ... oh dear ...' It is the man's voice, Michael's voice. '... oh dear ... I feel so sick ...'

Maggie looks up to see his feet disappearing as he slithers on what appears to be all-fours into the room above. She looks down at her own feet: Katya Erhardt's slippers, stained with dirty melted New York snow and the blood of her lost child. As she stares down at them she notices a warm spot beginning in the small of her back, as if someone had placed a heat pad there. Then with alarming speed and intensity the heat builds and rushes upwards like a fire in a lift shaft, through her chest and neck to her face, where it burns, red-hot, for several seconds and is then released in a cool sweat. As she stands there, her heart battering at her ribs, she spies at the edge of her vision the black rectangle cut into the wooden flooring. She looks at the brass ring-pull for a moment but thinks better of yanking it up to see if Hades really does lie beneath. It can wait.

She wipes away the perspiration from her face and neck with the lining of her blue velvet cloak and a heavy exhaustion overwhelms her. She turns to climb the stairs. 'Oh ... God ...' It is the man in the room above. She can hear him shuffling across the floor. As she turns into the room she sees the man slumped on the large sofa, apparently asleep, his face white and waxy and his hairline wet with perspiration. She can hear the dry rasp of his lungs as she approaches.

'You're only human ...' she whispers, as she stands looking down at him. The puffy pink lids twitch and the pale lashes sweep up to half-mast and beneath them she can see that the dark eyes look dull and unfocused.

'I'm sorry ...' he says, like a drunkard, 'I just felt so sick ... I think I must have 'flu.' The eyes close again and she finds herself touched by the thick fair lashes, and then by the lines and creases of his face, and she sits down next to him to take a closer look.

He is lying on his side stretched out full length. In one hand he is holding his inhaler just a few inches from his mouth like a microphone. She feels she might smile but it doesn't happen. She might say something funny but instead, 'I can look at you without fear ...' And where the flush of heat had begun, in the small of her back, so a fierce chill begins and with the same speed and intensity and taking the same route as the fire it rushes up through her body, causing her to shiver, and goose bumps to prick her arms and legs, and the fine down of her face to rise and stiffen the skin of her cheeks. She gets up, and stepping over the man she slides down behind him into the space between him and the sofa back. Spreading her cloak over the two of them, she nestles into his fevered back, pushing her face into the damp curls at his neck. From behind there is an electronic click and then a laconic voice says, 'Michael? ... Are you there? ...'

Michael groans. 'Pick up if you're there ... O.K. look, I'm coming round ... the heating won't be back on today ... and I am FROZEN! So ... I have a meeting this afternoon, so I'm thinking around six? ... I'll sleep on the sofa. Call me if you need anything.'

Michael lifts his head for a second: 'Oh God!'

The Mrs

&

'**O**h God.' Jenny scratches the back of her neck. 'She doesn't appear to be answering her phone. Has she gone out do you know?'

'Oh . . . Mrs O'Brien, she go to her room.'

'MISS O'Brien . . . Ms . . . Ms O'Brien. Has she . . .'

'Yes! . . . Oh yes . . . er yes of course . . . Miss O'Brien! Not M . . . her mother has not checked in!' The broad, Slavic cheekbones lift and soften into a smile.

'. . . I beg your pardon? . . . Her mother? . . . Her mother is checking in?'

'No, I have already explained to Mrssmzznnn O'Brien that the room is a single room. Her mother cannot stay in there. She must book another room for her mother.'

'. . . I'm sorry, are you telling me Cissie O'Brien's mother . . . is coming to stay here?'

'NO! No I tell her her mother must leave. She can . . .'

'Her mother is here? . . . That's not possible.'

'No it is not possible. The room is for single occupancy only.'

'No, dear, none of this makes any sense whatsoever. Look, I need to see Miss O'Brien. Will you see if she is in her room?'

'She is not answering her phone . . . I . . .'

'No I know that. I have just tried to ring her myself. There are three possibilities here. She may have gone out. She may be asleep or she may be choosing not to answer the phone. But I need to see her urgently.'

'Oh but . . .'

'I have just flown in from England. I am very tired and I want to see her now. It is very important. So can we now go to her room please?' The woman stares at Jenny, her blue eyes blank with incomprehension. Then as Jenny bends to catch the handle of her small suitcase, the woman breathes in sharply.

'No . . . no, no . . . you cannot stay in there!' She expels an impatient sigh. 'This is not a double room!'

'No, dear, I have no intention of moving into Ms O'Brien's room. It seems as though it might be more than a little crowded. I shall be wanting a room all of my own. I tell you what, why don't you just see if you haven't got a nice little single room, close to Ms O'Brien's?' Jenny removes the red beanie hat she had had pulled down over her ears and, shaking off the grey melted snowflakes, she drops it on the dark oak counter of the reception desk. 'In fact why don't you make that a great big fat double.' She then unzips her Michelin Man black puffer jacket and whilst doing so she appraises the demeanour of the blonde Amazon with her swimmer's shoulders and bewildered smile, and notices from a small plastic badge pinned to her sweater, just above her left bosom, that her name is Jana.

'I'm presuming I'm right in thinking your name is pronounced Yana?'

'Oh . . . my name is pronounced Yana . . . not like "J".'

'Precisely. Now . . . Jana, can you help me?' Jana's smile is unwavering.

'Yes . . . Can I help you?' Jenny dumps her anorak on top of her case and proceeds with one hand to yank her brown velour sweat pants up, whilst using the other to hoik her bosoms out of the way. Jana's smile takes on a slight hint of panic.

'Now.' Jenny places both palms on the edge of the counter, then with arms straight, one leg flexed and the other stretched out behind, she leans her full weight on it as if she were about to push the lot into the room next door. 'I would like a room please.' A series of tiny creaks emanate from the desk and Jana looks nervously behind her as if checking to see if the reception desk will in fact fit into the room next door.

'Would you like room?' Jana speaks as though addressing a dangerous lunatic.

'I would like a room, very much indeed. Thank you.' Jenny speaks as though addressing a primary school child, who is showing a great deal of unexpected promise.

A form is produced from beneath the desk and a long, slender hand sporting orange pearl varnish on its nails and an assortment of rings on every finger pushes it across the polished surface towards Jenny. She peruses the slip of paper for several silent seconds before writing her responses to its demands, and as she does so she speaks them, clearly and carefully as if giving dictation to a halfwit. 'Jennifer ... Murdo ... I am a knight in shining armour, Jana, come to rescue a maiden in deep shit.' For the 'deep shit' she lifts her head and stares directly into Jana's eyes. The words are enunciated with much stretching and pushing out of lips as if the girl were stone-deaf and needed to lip-read. Jana's smile remains intact, complete with its hint of panic.

'Yes ...' She wants to say more but at a loss she broadens the smile to grimace proportions. Meanwhile, a middle-aged couple have entered and are stamping the snow off their boots. Jenny continues to fill out the form.

'Forty-three ... Fortuna ... Road ... Ms O'Brien is my lover, Jana.' Again she looks up into the girl's worried eyes, and widening her own she uses the same lip technique to say, 'She is in much distress.'

'Yes ... erm ... thank you ...'

'No need to thank me, Jana, I have had very little to do with it ... South West nineteen ...' She stands up straight and takes a huge breath in. 'Now, have you got a nice, quiet room for a very tired old lesbian?'

There is silence. Jana stares at Jenny, still smiling. The middle-aged couple stare at Jenny; they are not smiling. Jenny then pulls her brown velour sweatshirt up, to rest on top of her massive bosoms, causing the middle-aged woman to gasp, clapping a hand to her mouth like a bad actress, and the man to say 'Dear God' under his breath. Underneath the sweatshirt is what appears to be a rather bobbly greyish thermal vest, stretched across the aforesaid bosom. She then pulls out the elasticated waistband of the pants with one hand whilst tucking in the thermal vest vigorously with the other. Then putting her clothes back in order she places both hands on her hips and beams at Jana. Jana is indeed about to speak but Jenny gets there first.

'You look very pretty when you blush, Jana.'

'. . . Yes . . . we have room . . .'

'Good! There's no need to worry, dear, I don't fancy you. You're quite safe on that score. You're far too obviously heterosexual for my tastes.'

'. . . Yes . . .' Jana's cheek muscles are beginning to twitch. '. . . Would you like *New York Times*?'

'. . . I trust the room has a bathroom?'

'. . . Yes . . . has bathroom.'

'Good. And that bathroom will have toilet paper?'

'. . . Toilet paper? . . . Yes of course.'

'Then I shan't be requiring the *New York Times*, thank you very much.' The smile is still twitching on Jana's face, though her eyes have given up and a frown is now trying to do battle with it.

'Would you like a wake-up call?'

'I think I've already had a rather rude one of those, so no, I'll forgo that facility thank you, Jana.'

'. . . You have . . . w . . .'

'What, dear?'

'. . . I . . . I . . . I . . . Welcome to the Hotel Apollo, Mrs . . . Murdo.'

The Beating

☙

Luke can feel the beating of her heart through the large artery in her neck, booming through his temples and flushing his cheeks. He feels the gradual shrinking of his penis.

'Oh my dear, sweet Helen ... how long have we waited?' He lets go of a long, pent-up sigh, punctuated by two high-pitched little sobs. 'We should have guessed that it would take an eruption of rage and passion to get us to this point I suppose.' He stares down at the brown and orange swirls of the carpet, just inches from his face, and feels he might cry. He can smell lives past and trodden underfoot, mingling with the carpet's coarse cheap fibres and his own 'horse's arse' breath fighting for recognition with her perfume. That perfume: he tries to single out its scent from the other odours. In fact it was little more than an odour itself. The preferred choice of cheap Lotharios and cheaper whores. It had enraged and enticed him only moments before but now the disgust had slipped away leaving nothing but a scent almost indecipherable from an old cheap carpet. He nuzzles his face into her hair.

'Oh ... Helly ...' He begins to cry with a long, reedy moan, which builds in volume and seems unstoppable, his mouth opening wider and wider until at top volume he is suddenly stopped by a crack to the back of his head so severe that the swirls on the carpet begin to lose colour and to weave independently around one another. Huge, swishing feathers, humming like wind in a chimney. Gradually the swirls disappear and the place is showered by millions of little diamante-like dancing stars.

'Get the fuck off meee!' Letting the broken chair arm fall to the floor, Helena uses both hands to heave Luke's unconscious body from on top of her. 'You fucking, fucking ... fucker!' She leaps to her feet, surprised by her own agility and stands over him. 'I hope I've fucking well killed you! You dumb, dumb, DUMB fucker you!'

Helena touches her lip and checks her fingertips. Finding them to be covered in blood she steadies herself, a footballer about to take a crucial penalty, all her weight on her left foot, her arms out in mid air for perfect balance and then, the tip of her tongue pushing firmly on her painful upper lip for concentration, she gives a magnificent 'Roy of the Rovers' goal kick to Luke's left buttock, almost flipping him back over onto his front. 'NO!' She rushes through to the bathroom, kicking her Filofax and one of her boots across the bedroom floor as she goes. Once inside the bathroom she yanks the light cord, snapping the small plastic pull off the end and sending it flying back into the darkness of the bedroom behind. She then slams the door with a wood-splitting crack and wheels round to look at herself in the mirror.

'Shit! ... Oh shit! ... I will never *ever* forgive you.' Her top lip is twice its normal size and has taken on a dark purplish hue. The bottom one is raw and bloodied, and growing too in size. It strikes her that it no longer looks like a mouth, but more like the rampant, enlarged genitalia of some wild beast on heat. She moves in closer to the glass and touches the lip lightly with the middle finger of her left hand, whilst her right hand goes down to her crotch and cups it gently. She continues to watch the travesty of her mouth as its massive bloated sneer opens into an angry gash, the white teeth bared and behind them the dark chasm, its heat unbearable. 'You fucking arsehooole!' ... and then silence.

The Space

❧

Elizabeth Spence stands before the heavy dark green door of Michael's loft. It is five months, ten days and some hours she does not care to count since she was last here and she is biting the inside of her right cheek. When at last she realises she is doing this, she stops with an abrupt sucking noise. With an impatient huff she shoves the key into the lock and simultaneously there is a small muscular twinge on the right side of her chest which makes her let go of the key and drop her hand down by her side.

'For God's sake ... come on.'

She had, that morning, sat down wearing her full-length sheepskin coat in the freezing basement kitchen of her house on McDougall Street and had drunk three and a half fairly large mugs of her favourite lotus flower green tea before deciding that she would call Michael. It had been just over two and a half weeks since she had last spoken to him. She had simply wanted to know if he knew where the tiny key to the upstairs bookcase was as its door kept swinging open. She hadn't seen the key since – she couldn't remember when. She had made an innocent enough comment about how odd it was that she had never actually seen the door open by itself, but that she would close it and then irritatingly discover it to be open when she went by later, as if some unseen prankster was having fun at her expense. Michael had then begun to babble and giggle excitedly about Dominic never being far away and that this was just the sort of jape that would send him into paroxysms of laughter.

Elizabeth had been irritated by this. In fact she was becoming increasingly impatient with the absurdity of this sort of talk. It was, she thought, bordering on the lunatic and she had as much as told him so. He, in turn, had angered her by questioning whether she had actually begun to mourn her son's death at all or whether in fact she had even accepted it. And then his confident assertion that Dominic was 'still very much with us', whether she liked it or not, had caused her to slam the phone down in a fury.

Elizabeth had thought long and hard about coming here today. She had never felt comfortable in Michael's loft, even before he left the house and moved into it, when it was simply his photographic studio. It was in a part of town she didn't much care for and it had a hard, linear, masculine edge which made it feel somehow exclusive. And then once he had moved in, everything in it seemed to be an expression of a Michael she didn't really know. A Michael she didn't really have access to. His study, with its sixties-style black leather and chrome furnishings, incongruously mixed with that ugly great mahogany desk that had apparently belonged to some cousin or other and all presided over by his father's huge, plain-faced clock with its punishing tick. The clock had caused the very first argument of their married life. No! She was not having it on any wall of any building that she inhabited! And so off it went to the lumber room at the top of the house, along with his old school trunk, a Victorian watercolour of the Pyramids and a plaster cast of his own erect penis, which had been made by a girl called Wanda Finche, back in high school. This last item had disgusted Elizabeth, especially the sight of several of Michael's pubic hairs still trapped in the plaster. Then Michael bought the loft and so all these precious things found a home and his father's clock had been given pride of place, its tick now heard in every room: lovingly tended once a week, when Michael got out its brass key, wound it up and dusted its big old face with a soft clean duster.

There had been days when she felt that there was something vaguely mutinous about it all, and during one hellish row just before he left she had screamed, 'Well I suppose the worm has finally turned!'

And then there was Dominic's room! Well, Dominic's room simply confirmed what Elizabeth had always suspected; and that is that despite being a photographer Michael had no practical spatial awareness. He had put Dominic's bed in the middle of the room! Such a ludicrous waste of space! And so ugly! It had made the little room look completely cluttered.

But Dominic had loved the loft and he had especially loved the bed in the middle of the room. He was captain of a ship, surveying a safe, rolling sea of his very own stuff. Toys left out on the floor would remain there, discarded in mid-play, so that games never really came to an end; instead they had a chance to grow and develop over days and even weeks, each one into something new and different. It was such a change from the way things were handled at home where his mother would put an abrupt stop to proceedings at certain times of the day and toys and books would have to be put away to make way for supper or bathtime or homework. Here at the loft on the other hand, Dominic and his father would sometimes grab a snack from the kitchen and eat it whilst continuing to play! Elizabeth had heard the child talking to his father on the phone. 'Mom would never let me do that!' It had quite shocked her that she could be marginalised, however temporarily, by the two of them; she could never recall it happening before Michael's move to the loft and she had felt hurt and angry by this new exclusive twist to their relationship. The loft was a place where Mom had no jurisdiction. Later she had often joked with Dominic, when she left him at the loft to be with his father, that she was dropping him off at the boys' club. He had said on several occasions, during the weeks leading up to his death, 'I need to go to the Boys' Club, Mom' and on one of these occasions, when she was feeling particularly isolated and overwrought, she had snapped back,

'Well you know where the phone is, call your damn father yourself! It's not my fault he's abandoned us!' The incident now flags itself up in her mind and before the memory of Dominic's voice has a chance to click in, with its poignant request, she says, 'Right!' and opens the door.

The Rock

❧

'Right!' Jenny closes the door and stands in front of it, hands on hips, feet apart. 'I'm here for a little under twenty-four hours.'

Cissie flops onto the bed with a huge clatter from the loose headboard that reverberates painfully inside her head and looks back at the familiar stance and the expectant face with its eyebrows raised and head cocked and feels an overwhelming desire to run at Jenny and ram her head up under the voluminous velour top and hold on to the sizeable ring of warm flesh that surrounds her waist, no matter how much exercise she does or how little she eats. 'It's in case I fall into hostile waters and can't keep up. It's my very own built-in rubber ring,' she had explained the first time they made love.

'Well, Mrs O'Brien? What on earth are we going to do now?' Jenny switches the overhead light on and its dim glow is enough to cause a dull ache to tighten the muscles of Cissie's forehead and a faint feeling of nausea at the back of her throat. Lying on her back she hurls both arms up into the air and lets them fall down, the forearms protecting her eyes.

'I want to die.' Cissie's voice is rough and frayed at the edges.

'Well if you think I've travelled three thousand miles across the Atlantic Ocean just to see you expire right in front of me you have another think . . . etceterarse etceterarse.'

Cissie squints out from beneath the soft arch of her arms, the effort making her head swim.

'How on earth did you get here? I feel like we've only just spoken on the phone ... I couldn't even get a cab out of Manhattan.'

'Ah the old broomstick never fails, sweetheart. Directly after I spoke to you I rang up and got myself on a 2 p.m. United standby to Newark, went straight to Heathrow and basically got on it. It couldn't have been easier. Landed here at four o'clock this afternoon ... it was the first flight in after they'd opened the airport. There was a chance of it being diverted to some godforsaken backwater in Canada, but my need was too great to worry about that. So here I am! Just in the nick of time I'd say ... for both of us.'

Cissie has retreated back under her arms but Jenny can see that what is visible of her face has flushed deep crimson.

'Oh angel.' Flicking off the main switch, Cissie is partly lit by a block of dull yellow light from the half-open bathroom door, and with a very loud double clatter from the headboard Jenny sits down on the edge of the bed, in semi-darkness, and gently extricates Cissie's arms from her face. 'Look at me.'

Cissie's eyes remain tightly shut.

'Look at me,' Jenny says, with a softer but more insistent tone. Cissie screws her eyes up even more tightly. Jenny lets go of her wrists and takes the hot face in her hands, wiping away the tears with her thumbs. 'Now listen to me.' She continues to hold Cissie's face as she speaks. 'All of this is copeable with. All of this is very easily sorted out.' A great 'boo' explodes from Cissie's mouth followed by a barrage of ragged sobs. Still holding her face, Jenny plants several loud firm kisses, which sound like a large bird cheeping, on each cheek, ending with a very long-drawn-out one in the centre of her forehead. As she draws back, Cissie flings her arms around Jenny's neck and pushes her face into the soft dark curls at the side of her head. More 'boos' blow Jenny's hair into hot, damp, stand-up waves and she reciprocates with a bear-hug that causes Cissie's back to crack. The two of them sit there, in this position, for some minutes rocking back and forth, Cissie continuing to 'boohoo' and Jenny at first laughing at the almighty crack from Cissie's back and then her laughter seguing into tears of overwhelming relief at holding and being held. Back and forth they rock, the headboard joining in with a dull clunk each time Cissie leans forward and Jenny back. The women don't hear it, but as the feelings begin to subside so the headboard begins to make itself heard, its silly intrusion drawing them back down to the practicalities of where they are and why. Cissie begins to titter first and Jenny holds her breath for a few moments, in case what she is hearing is a fresh onslaught of sobbing, but then she knows this titter, she can feel its familiar rhythm, and as if by chemical reaction its soulmate sparks into life in her own solar plexus, and they are off, laughing in that old comfortable unison. They exaggerate the rocking, like a pair of racing rowers, sending the headboard into a frenzy of battering. They can hear bits of plaster coming loose and falling onto the floor and their laughter reaches new levels of screeching, breathless hysteria. Then, in between the wheezing whoops of laughter, they simultaneously hear a high-pitched, agitated voice, accompanied by a muffled but urgent knocking on the wall behind the bed. They both stop at once and scissoring apart like a pair of Siamese twins pleasantly surprised at their separation, stare at one another their eyes frozen wide in shocked glee.

'... YOU DOING? ... FOR PETE'S SAKE! WILL YOU KEEP IT DOWN?! THIS IS NOT A FREAKIN' CAT HOUSE!' They both continue to stare at one another. Stray little chuckles cluck sporadically from each of them, gradually fading away into soft, silent smiles, and now, eventually, it is Cissie who wipes away Jenny's tears, with the cuff of her sweater.

'How did you find me? I don't remember saying ...'

'Your big sister obliged. Or should I say your ex-big sister!'

'... Oh.'

'Yes "Oh" indeed!' She disentangles herself from Cissie and with a big sigh, takes time to give her a big-sister look. 'Right! Now is there any alcoholic beverage you *haven't* tried since you booked into this excellent hostelry?' Jenny has now shifted her gaze to the array of tiny bottles on the nightstand. 'It looks as if the Borrowers have been holding a rather sumptuous reception on the top of your bedside cabinet.'

'Yeah . . . desperate measures.'

'Yes aren't they?!! And talking of desperate measures . . .' With that she picks up the phone, knocking over two of the empty miniatures, one of Southern Comfort and the other of Campari. She sniffs at the latter with a grimace.

'Oh! It smells like . . . Hello? To whom am I speaking please? I thought so . . . Hello, lovely Jana, I am the very tired middle-aged lesbian you showed into the Edith Wharton suite a little while ago . . . yes I know your name is Jana and I know this is the Apollo Hotel, thank you . . . Yes, this is Miss Jenny Murdo speaking and I wish to order a pot of coffee for two and four large bottles of your finest still mineral water . . . Yes, Jana, that is correct, I do wish to place an order.' She takes a deep breath.

The Scent

Elizabeth takes a deep breath and quietly closes the door behind her. She decides not to put the light on but stands, her feet numb with cold, resulting in the strange sensation that she is suspended in the darkness. She takes in the cluttered familiar scents of the apartment. The citrus freshness of Michael's aftershave and shower gel from the bathroom to her left, the woolly, faintly animal whiff of the old Afghan rug beneath her feet, coffee and spices drifting up from the kitchen below and Michael's own woody uncomplicated maleness touching everything. The first scent though that she recognised as soon as she entered the apartment but the last that she acknowledges is something light and dancing: sandalwood and strawberry with an inkling of sweet milk and marshmallow. It makes her head spin and her heart lurch. It is of course the inimitable scent of Dominic, but it is not stale, it is not of the past, it has a present thriving energy which suggests he might be standing right next to her. She has an urge to say his name but cannot. There is no such vivid reminder of her beloved son back in the house on McDougall Street. His bedroom is the only room where his scent remains, but not like this, there, it is just that: the remainder of him, a reminder of him, a relic. She has not been able to go into the room for weeks.

Suddenly it is gone, sucked out of the atmosphere without a trace, like a cruel joke. She casts about in the darkness with lots of tiny, frantic sniffs, sifting through the other smells to no avail, and then she comes upon it. Not Dominic at all but something new, something other. It is just a suggestion at first, in front and to the right of her. It is a scent that does not belong here that is for sure; harsh, antiseptic, yet not quite clean. And now it asserts itself, a hint of ammonia, of sickness maybe? Holding her breath and gently gnawing at the inside of her right cheek she turns towards the sitting area, now lit only by the three tall rectangles of muted light coming from the windows, and she hears a tiny scraping sound, like metal on metal. It could be coming from the street outside, she cannot tell, its perspective dulled and fuzzed by the cottonwool silence of the city. Then someone shouts and laughs out in the street and instantly the strange little sound zooms back to its rightful perspective; to within a couple of feet of where Elizabeth is standing. Now with new-found clarity it takes on another note, another rhythm, not metallic at all but living, human and visceral. It is the breathing of one in difficulty, of a system half closed down, clogged with shit – half-snore, half-gasp.

She moves blindly forward on tiptoe, sucking madly at her inner cheek, arms outstretched in front of her until she reaches the back of the big sofa, bumping it softly with her thighs. She drops her arms and touches the dry rough calico with her fingertips. No sooner has she done this than the three dim blocks of light illuminating the room are suddenly cranked up by several notches to a bright silver, as the street lamps outside come on in unison. Elizabeth finds herself perfectly lit in the cold white spotlight of the right-hand window, as is the sofa in front of her. The breathing is now so close that she can smell its sweet gluey smell. Before she looks down she sees Dominic's little face, angelic in sleep, his mouth ajar, his hair stuck in damp little curls behind his ears, his breathing laboured . . . Don't be ridiculous!

She looks down at the sofa with a sharp, purposeful downward tilt of the head. It is Michael! She had always known it was Michael! It is his bloody asthma and another bloody winter cold! They are his damp curls and his gluey breath that she had had to turn away from so often in bed! ... But there is someone else on the sofa! Lying in the dark gap behind Michael. A small figure, snuggled up to his back, the light from the street lamp only catching tangled blonde curls. Stop this! Slowly she lowers her face towards the sleeping pair. The shape of the head is right. Stop it! The jawline, though it's only a shadow. Stop iiit! She considers for the briefest second that Dominic may not be dead at all. That the 'Boys' Club' was a far more sinister set-up than she had ever imagined. Then moving right in close she spots the full pink mouth, with the tiny upward twist at each corner, the bottle-blonde hair with its black roots. And in a gap between the fluffy over-bleached tendrils partly strewn across the woman's face, Elizabeth sees an eye, wide and shining! A tiny shard of light from the street lamp captured dead in the centre of its bright green iris, it is looking right back at her. She makes a little gasp and the cold inrush of air causes the inside of her cheek to sting. It feels fleshy and ragged and Elizabeth can taste blood.

The Distance

His head pumping with pain Luke had stood outside the bathroom door for some immeasurable amount of time, in the almost complete darkness of the bedroom, his fist raised to knock, his mouth just open, ready to speak, but he had done neither. Instead he had flopped onto the bed and lain there, his head filled with nothing but the dull, thumping ache.

He must have slept on and off throughout the day for now he can see through the bedroom door that night has fallen; the sitting room being lit only by the overhead light, casting its depressing yellow gloom. For a brief elating moment he considers that he may have dreamt the encounter with Helena. After all it would not be the first time he had dreamt of a passionate sexual clash with her, but then a warm throbbing sensation in his upper lip causes him to touch it with the tips of his fingers.

'Ow … God.' He looks towards the bathroom door, and notices that it is now ajar; at the same time he touches the back of his head to feel the hot egg-sized lump that has formed there. It is sore and tacky to the touch and he wonders what on earth could have fallen on his head during the clinch to make him see stars and lose consciousness like that. Helena's face, purple and grotesque with laughter, flicks into his mind and putting on his glasses, he springs up from the bed and tiptoes over to the bathroom. It is in darkness and he gently pushes the door open. It creaks like an old ship. Inside the air is warm and damp and heavy with the amber and lavender scent of Helena's new bath oil. Breathing it in, his head begins to spin and he feels a little nauseous. Like the perfume it is alarming and heady. It had slipped in between them like an invisible gauze, throwing feelings and instincts into chaos. Then debasing and soiling its way through his sensibilities.

He turns and moves towards the sitting room, each creak of the floorboards making him stop and hold his breath. Now he can smell cigarette smoke. He has never cared for the mixture of heavy perfume and smoke. There is something cloying, even suffocating, about it. He stands in the doorway and she is sitting with her back to him in the middle of the brown corduroy sofa, a perfect column of thin blue smoke dividing the space in front of her. Her head is slightly bowed, her hair wet and uncharacteristically scraped back into an untidy, tangled ponytail, and as he stares at the wide crown he touches the back of his own head again and winces at the sharp twinge of pain.

'Helly . . .?'

'. . . Oh . . . I think you had better leave me alone.' She does not move, even the column of smoke is only slightly disturbed.

'. . . I'm in need of a cuddle . . . from my Helly . . .' He is standing stock-still, a foot or so back from the back of the sofa, but directly behind her, staring down at the top of her head.

'I don't think so . . . please go away.' The line of smoke does a little squiggle of a detour before resuming its inexorable upward stream to the ceiling, where it breaks into a slow cloud and hovers for a moment, depositing another coat of nicotine.

'We have to talk.'

She takes a drag of the cigarette but does not reply. For a moment he hesitates and then walks carefully round to the front of her chair, remembering as he goes that he is still only dressed in his tee-shirt and nothing else. He pulls it down at the front to cover his modesty, causing it to shoot up at the back and reveal his arse. He momentarily places a protective hand, palm outwards, over his buttocks as if someone were threatening to kick him, and gasps as he takes in her face with its bloody, bloated lips and its eyes pink and puffed. He notices a small black clot of dried blood beneath her left nostril and brings his hand up to feel his own mouth again. She does not look at him. She takes another careful drag on her cigarette and holds on to the wooden arm of the chair with her left hand, her knuckles taut and white. Luke can detect a slight tremor in the hand that holds the cigarette.

'Helly? ...' This is barely more than a whisper. 'Can I just hold you?' She makes a strangled little sound in the back of her throat and he cannot make out whether it is a snort or a sob or a cough, or whether she is agreeing with his request. She drops her head; the heavy curtain of hair would normally fall from behind her ear and almost cover her face, instead she lets go of the arm of the chair and brings her hand up to shield her face, as if from a bright light. 'Help me here ... Helly?' He moves tentatively towards her and drops down onto his haunches. 'Helly?' She slowly turns her head to look at him.

'What makes you think ... ?' Putting equal emphasis on each word, she stops mid-question, her hand still shading her eyes as if she were staring out at the horizon on a bright, sunny day. He sees the blue of her eyes is dull and the surrounding white, bloodshot.

'What? ... Oh Helly ... What's happening? ... What has happened?' She continues to stare at him.

'My God ...' She turns away and, closing her eyes, lets her head fall with an exhausted flop onto the back of her chair.

She had planned a violent, vehement assault the minute he walked through the door. It would be 'shock and awe'. She would destroy him. She had all the weapons to hand. She knew his fragility. It ran seamlessly into her own. It would be a matter of seconds. Now he crouches, semi-naked, next to her and the small space between them stretches out for light years; cold, inhospitable, the surface of Mars, needing the energy and commitment of an exploring astronaut. She allows the thrum from the building to stop her ears and ripple through her body with its delicate vibration. In it she can hear the Universe: distant music she cannot quite grasp; a vast choir, coming and going on the wind; rivers in full flood, rushing and dashing across rocks and down mountainsides; a baby crying, a mother humming and shushing; a long, high moan of grief; an axe through a skull; the eternal babbling and chattering of humanity. The great dull drone and incessant hissing of the building, splintered into a thousand fragments like a prism splitting white light into a rainbow. She sinks gratefully into its warm, all-enveloping throat.

The Light

✂

As the door clicks gently to, a small cloud of sadness rises up in Maggie. She had wanted to hold on to the woman's gaze, to her scent, of roses and hair and wool. The dark hollows of the woman's eyes had suddenly been charged with light, a shocking flash of grief and loss and disappointment. Maggie had wanted to speak, to utter something, to say ... yes... I know ... yes, yes I see ... I SEE YOU! But her voice was this tiny, tiny little thing, way down deep in the darkness, too minuscule to be heard by any living soul, and there wasn't the power or the mechanism to get it out.

She had lain there for what felt like hours, in the warm, humid space between the man and the sofa back, eluded by the deep, dreamless sleep she craved to be smothered by. Instead, anxiety had lapped gently around her like an untroubled lake and any drift towards sleep would be brought back to cold, heart-racing consciousness by the slightest shift in the man's febrile body.

Somewhere above her a big heavy clock ticks, and next to her the man's congested lungs heave in and out with a sound like a rusty saw. She can feel the damp heat of his body steaming through her grey velveteen top and her own neck is wet with perspiration. Every so often there is a great moist glug of mucus on soft palate and he appears to stop breathing altogether for several seconds. When this happens Maggie finds herself taking huge gulps of air and then, when he continues to breathe, she breathes along with him, sucking in as much air as possible with each inhalation and willing it into his ailing lungs. Then after one huge wheezing and stuttering intake of breath, he stops again. She too holds her breath, topping up her lungs with a frantic flurry of little gulps as if this were the last air ever to be had. She waits; there is nothing, just the tiniest high-pitched squeak, the last-ditch effort of a minute creature stranded deep within the man's chest.

It continues, desperate and plaintive, until she feels her own chest will burst. She nudges the man in the back and the creature's cry ends abruptly with a little upward yelp. But still the man does not breathe out. It must be at least a minute, maybe two … or more! The air in her lungs turns to exasperation and explodes out of her, a delicious, unstoppable blast. 'Arrggh!!!' At the same time she gives the man another almighty shove in the back, whilst kicking him in the back of the legs, shifting him clean off the sofa into a dark heap on the floor. Then there is silence, but she can still feel the rasping boom of her voice, echoing through her body and up around her head.

She gets up from the sofa, stepping over the man, into the middle of the room. She can feel her feet through Katya Erhardt's stockings, standing firmly on a thick soft rug and a sensation very close to elation or freedom or something sits for a moment at the base of her gut. She listens to her own breathing; clear, free, deep breaths; strong, muscular ribs, rising and falling, supporting her life, and she laughs: a crystal Tinkerbell laugh. She looks down at the man. She cannot see him clearly in the gloom but she can hear the rusty scrapings of his lungs.

'Good,' she says. Then he twists as he takes in another dry, grating breath which seems as if it may never end. 'Oh no!' Maggie moves towards him and as she does so he begins to cough the air back out in painful little spasms. She heaves a small involuntary sigh, blowing her own breath gently out between pursed lips. Then she sees herself.

She is standing in the middle of a warm dark space, somewhere in New York City. At her feet a man writhes and twists in an increasingly laboured attempt to get air in and out of his body. She does not know this man. She knows his name is Michael. She knows he is part of something she herself does not wish to be a part of. Something dark and shameful and labyrinthine; but she is through the labyrinth and does not wish to return.

'I'm going home.' She looks about in the semi-darkness for her boots, and remembers Katya Erhardt's slippers.

The Need

ꝏ

'I'm going home on the 4.55 out of Newark.'

  'Oh ... God ... *no*. I'm coming with you.'

  'Even if we could get you a seat, which I doubt, I think you should stay and sort the Maggie business out. I have to go, I can't afford to leave the office for any length of time ... not at the moment. Things are pretty hectic and with mummy away people will be getting out of their prams and goodness only knows what chaos will ensue. Anyway, you'll be home in a week's time. It may be better that you stay. It'll give things a chance to blow over a bit.'

  'Oh Christ! What am I going to do here without you? Jesus, I don't even know what you're doing at the moment. I feel like ...' For a moment she turns her face round and presses it into the smooth forgiving velour of Jenny's bosom as if taking the vital sustenance she needs to continue. Breathing in, she lets its earthy mix of sweat and skin and Wright's coaltar soap fill her head. Then, breathing out, she turns her head back and stares up at the ceiling, concentrating on the ornate twists and turns of the circular moulding from which a fake tatty crystal chandelier hangs, a layer of dust obscuring its plastic sparkle. 'I feel like I've been on one of those journeys for the past few months, that you know, that ... it's like it's a journey that you do all the time, you know, like the trip to the supermarket or something and you know that you've done it but ... you can't really recall making any of the steps ... and there are these great vast wedges of time that are silent and empty of ... of ... of anything and you think, you know ... that it's down to just familiarity or stress or something. But ... actually it's about not being here ... it's about not being present in your own life ... and just running and running and running and running and running and running and fucking running!' Her right fist is raised as if it holds a sharp implement and each time she says the word 'running' she jabs it at the air as if chipping away at something. 'I don't even know what day it is ... what day is it?' With this Cissie sits bolt upright and twists round to look Jenny directly in the eye.

'It's Monday and we are doing exactly what we were doing when you buggered off on Friday.'

'... Oh ... what? ... were you doing?' She drags the heel of her hand up under her nose with a sniff. Jenny lightly touches her cheek and clucks.

'It's alright, darling, you're not going to fail G.C.S.E. Jenny-ology if you don't know. We're still shooting *The Face in the Jar*, but the D.P. and the director are at loggerheads with one another; it's handbags at dawn, so that hasn't been an easy ride. The second series of *Lucky Bastard* starts shooting in two weeks and we've just lost our prime location. And there's all the other stuff at varying levels of development and crisis; but hey! What's new?'

Cissie's face lifts into a smile and she crashes her head back down onto Jenny's bosom. Her eyes closed, she rubs her cheek back and forth in search of that warm, safe spot like the blind nuzzling of an infant in search of its mother's milk.

'You are exhausted and, from the look of you, in need of a good meal. So that is what we shall do next.'

Cissie can feel the mellow no-nonsense tones of Jenny's voice resonating through the soft cushion of her chest, its fuzzy, gentle vibration warming her cheek and a little girl's laugh springs from her chest and another follows in surprise and delight at the first.

'Yes.' And in the word, she hears her mother. 'Yes' – her mother looking joyous when her father suggests a trip out to the seaside.

'Yes', her mother's eyes shining in anticipation of a trip to see her sister in Ireland.

'I need to see my mum.' She notices that the same little girl that she had heard in her own laughter, moments before, is still there in her voice but that she is somehow older and sadder. Jenny places a hand on Cissie's cheek pressing her face against her own heart and firmly kisses the top of her head.

'I know you do, my darling, and of course … you shall. But first things first. I'm beginning to feel a bit lagged, so I think if we're going to go out and eat, we should think about making a move … Or of course we could always eat here … but are we ready to sample the many delights that the kitchen at the Hotel Apollo has to offer?'

Cissie laughs and the little girl's lilt is gone.

'And can the lovely Jana cope with an order at eight o'clock in the evening that isn't for breakfast?'

Cissie jumps up off the bed. 'I'll get my coat.'

The Timing

❦

Helena can feel the cigarette scorching her fingers as it burns down into its tip and with a sudden jerk she lifts her head to watch it, as the perfect blue column falters into a grey, uncertain squiggle, its tobacco aroma turning to the unsatisfying smell of burning paper and saltpetre as it begins to die. She leans forward and thrusts it into the filthy ashtray, squashing and twisting it with her forefinger long after it has gone out, and when she has finished she gives the ashtray a petulant shove, sending it over the edge of the coffee table and sailing through the air until it lands upside down next to the skirting board. She glares at it hard and screams, 'CUNT!'

'Pardon?'

She does not look at Luke. She does not wish to see the down-turned features, pulling the doughy flesh of his face into an expression of bemused distaste. She does not wish to see this because she is fearful of how she might herself respond. Instead she resumes her position; her head flopped back on the sofa and stares up at the ceiling. She wants to light another cigarette but a sick feeling, centred in her head or her stomach, she cannot decide which, prevents her. Luke sits in silence, opposite her, in the one remaining armchair.

She had felt the usual fizz of energy in her limbs and abdomen, the gathering of the stuff that lifts her up there, out of the shit and darkness, out of the paralysing dread ... but nothing! For the first time ever she has not achieved lift-off. From the very outset the blue column of cigarette smoke had been part of the ritual; its gentle ascent from the bedside table of her childhood room, upon the edge of which it balanced precariously, a point of focus; a stairway to heaven or at least limbo; a key to the exit. And there she would stay, high up above it all, like a party balloon, looking down on the scene from a corner of the ceiling; a cool, uninvolved observer, when necessary soaring way up into the atmosphere: where only the prospect of permanent endless space would coax her down. Then the red tip of the cigarette would become her landing light. It had always begun with a new cigarette and it was always over before it had burnt down to the tip. On several occasions as a child she had stolen one of her mother's cigarettes and let it burn on the side of the little table next to her bed, timing it with her Snow White watch with its bright-red leather strap. One of the seven dwarfs (Happy? Grumpy? Dopey? She had never been able to tell which one it was meant to be) jerked his head like a nervous twitch with each second that passed. Then she would comfort herself with the thought that it was what ... five minutes? But of course several drags would have been taken before the cigarette was set down in the first place. So naturally several other timings had to take place, each with a different number of drags and with drags of different lengths, before it was placed on the edge of the table to burn away.

Now the internal vibrations are all but gone, leaving the hollowness of an unachieved orgasm and a rising sense of panic. She can see the watch, her first watch, given to her on her eighth birthday: Snow White's gentle, rosy-cheeked innocence, bluebirds dancing attendance around her head with its dark lustrous hair.

'Fuck me.'

She closes her eyes tightly and Snow White disappears, taking the panic with her and leaving a landscape of bright incandescent red.

The Beseeching

M ichael can hear the girl, Maggie, moving about the apartment, and notes how heavy she is on her feet, the maple
cracking and complaining beneath them. He covets her energy
and her breezy will but he also wants to tell her to slow down, her
movements are exhausting and becoming scattered and urgent as
if she were looking for something and he is afraid that her
stockinged feet will slip on the polished veneer of the wood; both
of them ending up prostrate on the floor, both of them helpless.
He makes an attempt at her name but only gets halfway through,
sounding like an unfussed goat.

'Maaa ...' He can smell the sweat on his upper lip, sour, like
milk on the turn. It is familiar in that he knows it to be his own,
and unfamiliar in that he knows it has never smelt this way
before. He begins to feel cold as a shot of ice goes through his
kidneys.

'Ple ... Mag ...' is all he can manage. He reaches for his
inhaler and remembers that it is now empty and anyway his head
is so heavy with pain that he feels one more puff might just blast
it to oblivion.

She had tucked herself in behind him, moulding herself into
his back and legs, the heat of her body causing his to reach
furnace proportions. At several points during his stupor, for it
could hardly be called sleep, he had felt certain that it was
Dominic whose breath he could feel on the back of his neck,
that it was Dominic's bony little legs that had folded themselves

227

in behind his own. Then at other moments the alien scent of the girl's hair and skin and clothes, an odd mixture of acid clean and uncared for mustiness, would slam shockingly into his senses and he would consider that it might be good to simply slip away. Then just as he had sensed that perhaps he was doing just that, a violent combination of shove and kick had sent him rolling unceremoniously onto the floor. His landing had caused a sickening jolt to judder through his joints and limbs, giving way to a dull ache. Now the ice is spreading, blowing round to his stomach and up under his ribs; he can feel it hardening his gut and frosting his lungs.

'Oh ... G ... God ...' Gingerly, he rolls over onto his front, which makes him instantly nauseous, and up onto all fours, where he stays for a moment, to try and still the dizziness inside his head.

Maggie is at the window now, eyes fixed on the brownstone house directly opposite. On the sidewalk, at the foot of the steps leading up to the front door, someone has made a snowman: a big misshapen fellow, like something a child might have drawn on a home-made Christmas card. He has what looks like a clown's red nose stuck in the middle of his roughly slapped-together face, a couple of coins or buttons for eyes and something orange (peel?) cut into a crescent shape for his mouth. On top of his outsized head, at a rakish angle, is a small petrol-blue woollen hat, the sort with flaps designed to fold down over a person's ears.

She had gone to that window, holding something close to her centre. It is something tiny, a barely felt stirring. It had made her swallow hard. It had made her clasp her hands together and press her thumbs to her lips, which were closed tight shut. Now the sight of this malformed effort, standing beneath the street lamp, with its lopsided features, its two battered stumps where an attempt at a pair of arms had run out of steam and its unbearable innocent optimism was threatening the Tinkerbell flutter in her chest with a deluge. She could feel it gathering beneath her ribs,

228

a tonnage of grey ready to choke everything in its path, to leaden her limbs and deaden her mind. She doesn't wish to turn round. The man's whimpers are clearly a device designed to make her do just that. Their needy timbre, the little sob cleverly hidden inside each utterance. She spins round on the ball of one foot and feels a little flurry of heat blossoming on her face.

'Oh ... fuck ... wit ... what? ... What? What is it?' She is amazed by her speech, by the skill and competence of it. Even the man, Michael, turns his head unsteadily towards her and there in the pale moon of his face she can see that he is surprised, impressed even. She does not wish to look into his face and chooses instead to focus on her blue velvet cloak, lying crumpled in the darkness, on the floor between the man and the sofa. She wants to be swaddled in it, to feel its soft pile on her cheek, to be warm and secret inside its dark circle, to take in its scent, the old familiar scent of her life, of way back when ... She wants to be ... somewhere ...

'Oh ...' The man's voice, weak and scuffed with pain. There is a begging in it that makes her want to stamp her foot.

'Don't ...' But her voice mimics his, the same weakness, the same beseeching.

His lungs let out a high, whistling rasp as at the edge of her vision she sees the dark shape of his body move slowly into a ball. She feels her own might collapse and fold up into nothing and the vast greyness sits poised at bursting point.

'Come ... see ...' This is now a whisper and the cool smoothness of its tone draws her face around to look. A discordant keening comes from his lungs.

'Seeeee ...' But this is a soft hiss of a sound and without choice she moves towards him. She can see even in the near darkness of the room that he is shaking and she looks again at the cloak. It is partly caught up in the man's boots. She untangles it, tutting like her mother as she does so. She touches one of the boots and can just make out in the street-lamp gloom the salty white tidemark left there after the snow had melted and traces her forefinger along it.

'You have small feet.'

'Oh Maggie ... mm ... mm ...' Now his voice is fearful and wanting, his lungs screaming for relief. She yanks his boot up quickly and unzipping it she whips it off and sitting up onto the sofa she plunges her own foot into its sweaty warmth. It is somewhat tight but the pressure is soothing and its heat causes her to let out a little moan which almost ends in a smile.

'Ohh ...' She grabs at the other boot and soon both feet are encased in the hot, damp leather and she shoots up into a standing position with a little totter forward and she is tall, so tall!

'Give me the shoes and I'll play the part.'

The man groans, a laboured weedy sound and then comes the whisper again, cutting through the air like a laser, making her temperature plummet and a shudder to slither up her backbone and over the top of her scalp.

'Nooo ... see me.' She bends down and scoops up the cloak, having to pull some of it from beneath the man's body. As she does so she sees his head twist round. He says something pleading and unintelligible and his head drops back.

'Look ... I'm sorry ... I just ... I can't ... I am in no fit ... please just don't ...!' She remains bent over him, staring at a face she cannot see. There is a strangled little snort. It might be an attempt at speech and she waits frozen for a moment. There is nothing; no sound at all. She peers down, straining to see a sign of his breathing. She is holding her own breath just as she had when they had lain together and still nothing, until it explodes from her lungs:

'STOP IT! For Christ's sake!' She clasps hold of his shoulder and roughly shakes it back and forth, but does not wait to see if it has had the desired effect. She is up and clomping round the back of the sofa towards the door.

The Switch

With a practised flick of her wrists the cloak twirls through the air and as it lands with a soft swish about her shoulders every light in the place comes on! There is a snapshot, now emblazoned on her retina, of an airy golden space. An instant imprint before her lids banged shut with a little yelp of shock.

'What ...? ... Who ...?' She must have touched an extra sensitive light switch with the tip of the cloak. She does not wish to see the room and both hands are now up, covering her eyes as the memory of a dark place so very close to here threatens to break the camel's back. She spins round to face the door and with her back to the scene she does not want to witness she opens her eyes to find the latch. And as her hand is raised to open the door, the tiniest breeze of a whisper blows at her ear like a kiss.

'Stop ... please.' Her fingers do not reach the latch, but remain suspended above it. Through the gap between the two big double doors an ice-cold draught of air blows straight through her chest.

'Ahh ...' What she hears is like the highest note on a violin, stretched out on a thin, quivering breath. It is ageless and gen-derless. It reaches her womb with a sharp little spasm and her chest with a quick involuntary intake of breath. She turns and takes in the room for the first time and briefly marks its beauty. Then on urgent solid feet she makes her way back to Michael.

She sees him. He is a small man. His dark curly hair is soaked with sweat, his face as white as a clown's. His body is shaking and his breathing ebbs and flows unevenly in tight little voiceless squeaks. He must have sensed her return, because he draws his eyelids up to full mast and casts a sideways look at her. After several seconds of focusing, a funny lopsided smile warms his face and she is helpless to stop a reciprocal one of her own. She pulls off her cloak and bends down to cover him with it. She pats it in around him and begins to rub his back with quick round movements, a mother winding her infant before sleep. He closes his eyes for a moment, the smile still pulling at his mouth, and when he opens them again they are shining and wet.

'Thank you . . . Dominic . . .'

'What? . . . Oh no, I'm Maggie . . . The flaming nutter you probably wish you had never met.'

'You . . .'

'Yes . . . do you remember? Or perhaps . . . best not to.'

'. . . Beautiful . . .'

She pushes the big glass coffee table out of the way and taking hold of a cushion she places it carefully under his head. As she does so she notices that his lips are tinged with blue and before she can remove her hand from beneath his head she feels startlingly icy fingers wrap themselves around her wrist.

'Oh Michael . . . you're freezing. I'm going to call an ambulance. What do I dial?' He does not answer. Instead he closes his eyes and turns his head away. 'Please, Michael. I think you should be in hospital.'

'9 . . . 1 . . . 1 . . .' Again, it is the whisper, as quiet and soft as a thought and so close she swivels her head around to see.

'What? . . . Oh . . .' A dry despairing groan from Michael draws her back round.

'911 O.K. . . . You have to let go of my wrist now.'

'. . . Dominic . . .'

'What? . . . No . . . it's Maggie . . . never mind . . . just let go of . . .' and the fingers let go. With a splintering crack of her knees she's up on her feet, looking for the phone. She spots it on a small semi-circular table opposite the door. As she arrives to pick it up her temperature plunges and without thinking she

232

turns to look at Michael. She has to move a couple of steps forward in order to see him, down behind the sofa. There is something perplexing in the way that he is lying. She moves closer but cannot pick out the thing that jars.

'Go oonn!' The whisper hisses through her head, leaving a trail of ice that makes her shiver.

'Yes ... yes ... that's wh ... that ... I'm going ... yes!' She crashes back to the phone and jabs out the numbers, saying them as she does so.

'Nine one one.'

The Words

❦

'I'd gladly walk across the desert with no shoes upon my feet to share with you the last bite of bread i had to eat.
i would swim out to save you in your sea of broken dreams when all your hopes are sinking let me show you what love means.
Love can build a bridge between your heart and mine.
Love can build a bridge; don't you think it's time?
Don't you think it's time?'

Luke continues to sing, standing with his back towards her and pulling his tee-shirt down to cover his arse.

She does not need to see it to know that his face is scarlet and the vein that divides his forehead is at full flow. She is still sitting on the brown corduroy sofa but now her knees are drawn up to her chin, her arms wrapped around them, and her eyes are still tight-shut. As his voice settles upon her, so the raging crimson inside her head dulls to nothing.

She no longer hears the words, just the pure plaintive note of his voice, smooth and clear, with a small tired scratch at its edge. It calls at her to go back there. A slow, desperate lament to go back when. To be back where it all began. To be Helen Cake in the attic room of number 48, late on a Saturday night, where after many a drink and tears they had discovered the reason for their bond.

She opens her eyes and looks at him: the protective rounding of his shoulders, the thin legs bent, every sinew of every muscle strained to rigidity; a posture so ugly to elicit a sound so exquisite. Whenever Luke had sung in the past, it was always charged with a feeling that he was mining something rare and precious from deep within himself. It was not an event to be interrupted, because God only knew what might be lost in the process, and so now she rises soundlessly up from the sofa. She stands close behind him, so close that she can feel his warmth and smell the sweet boyish smell of his body: it is of pencils and metal and turned-out pockets. It is a body that has never quite committed to manhood, slim and pale and almost hairless, and she had loved it for this. This body could never crush or scratch or smother. It could never . . .

'Oh Lukey . . .' she whispers beneath his singing and she looks down at the small hands with their grubby bitten nails holding on with stretched knuckles to the hem of his washed-out tee-shirt and, gently, she takes hold of them. They feel cold and knotted, and as if melted by her warmth they soften and let go of the shirt. She steps closer so that her body is touching his, and bringing his hands round in front of him she crosses his arms in front of his stomach and holds on, resting her cheek on the hard knobble of bone at the top of his spine. He stops singing mid-phrase but he does not move. He can see out of the corner of his eye a little tableau reflected in the dark glass of the window. He, half bent over, as if in agony; head thrown back, mouth open, as if screaming something, and she restraining him, wanting to put a stop to the pain but sagging under its weight.

'This is it, isn't it, Helena? This is the dénouement?' he says in a voice Helena feels she hasn't heard in a very long time, if indeed she has ever heard it at all. Still looking at the reflection, he makes an attempt at extricating himself, but she tightens her grip around the wrists.

'Helena . . .' she says in barely more than a whisper. He had dismissed the A tagged on to her original name from the moment she had thought of it, and as for the Cassidy – when she came up with that on the day that they graduated from drama school, he had stormed off in the middle of Oxford Street, saying that it sounded like a bad country and western singer; and then had sulked for a couple of days. Now it sounded to Helena as if he was addressing a character in a play. He looks at the reflection for several seconds and then drops his head down. His legs still bent, he tries to stand up straight, but she strengthens her grip on him, holding him firm, and he hasn't the will or the power to resist.

'Say it . . . please . . . just say it . . .'

'Oh God . . .' she says, and at the base of his neck he can feel her cheek go hot.

'Go on . . . one of us has to . . .'

She tightens her grip again. He sees that the veins on the back of his hands are standing out and his wrists are sore. Tears and snot are soaking through the thin cotton of his tee-shirt to his shoulder beneath, and from the strain of standing with knees bent his legs are beginning to shake.

'Helen . . . my beautiful girl . . . you have to let go . . .'

'Lukey . . . I am trying to.' And suddenly he is free.

He looks down and he can see the imprints on his wrists where her hands had been and his wobbling knees below them, but still he does not move. It is as if he is in freeze-frame and any movement will propel him out of this moment, and then commit him to the rest of his life. He continues to look down at his wrists as the pink marks of her grip begin to fade.

'There, you see? Easy.' And he stands up.

The Shine

❦

'Where's Maggie?'

Maggie turns to see that two nurses are making a bed on the opposite side of the ward. They are standing on either side of it and pulling apart a stiffly laundered bottom sheet. In unison they flap it into the air above their heads with the sound of a sail caught in the wind.

'Maggie who?'

Then with easy synchronicity they wrap the sheet around the mattress, its corners pleated to perfection, and run their hands over its smooth, taut surface with accustomed satisfaction.

'Maggie whoo! ... Maggie! Our Maggie!'

Another sheet, then a white cotton blanket and finally a primrose yellow counterpane are all placed upon the bed with automatic skill.

'Ooh Maggie.'

Now they are shaking and pummelling pillows and one of them is giggling with bright white teeth. Maggie thinks she may have seen her before.

'Yeah, she hasn't been around for a few days now. Is she O.K.?'

But decides that perhaps she hasn't.

'She went away at the weekend.'

For this isn't the same ward.

'Oh ...'

This one has been refurbished.

'A vacation?'

It is brighter, shinier, more relaxed.

'Just needed to get away.'

The patients aren't no-hopers like before.

'Things were getting on top of her, I think.'

Just as Maggie is about to turn back to the man, the bright-toothed nurse fixes a little plastic sign to the head of the bed which reads 'NIL BY MOUTH' and in her mind's eye Maggie sees two apples bowling along on a wet vinyl floor and her mouth waters.

She sits looking at the man and notes the comfort of sitting in the grey plastic chair, how its simple form fits perfectly beneath her own. The man, Michael, looks comfortable, too, and peaceful now, although up until about half an hour or so ago all the indications had been that it was touch and go. He had gone white and rigid like a corpse and his warm brown eyes had become huge and black with terror, and in their unfocused glaze Maggie had seen what she thought was death. People had rushed here and there, firing questions at her that she felt ill equipped to answer. Back at the apartment the police had even turned up; a huge gentle one with red hair, and a dark, rather attractive Heathcliff type who had skulked in the background. The big one had also questioned her and, alarmingly, seemed to know about her own spell in hospital. Then she had been left, sidelined and frightened, until one of the paramedics, a short, wide woman with enormous hips, had said that she, Maggie, had probably 'saved the guy's bacon'. Maggie had stared back at her, thinking that perhaps the woman was joking but hoping that she wasn't. Sure! You did good, the woman had said and had placed a tight, comforting arm around her shoulders, and abruptly Maggie had slapped a hand across her own mouth and relaxed into laughter and the woman had joined her, chuckling and nodding vigorously into her face.

She leans her elbows on the edge of the bed and moves her face as close as she dares to his. She would like to rub her cheek against his but instead she whispers into his ear, 'I saved your bacon.'

'I know.' He hasn't moved and Maggie is not certain of what she has heard. She stays there, taking in his profile; a fine nose and now without the aid of oxygen, the nostrils flaring delicately with every wheezy intake of breath; a full mouth, livid and dry, and as her eyes move up to his, he turns his head and opens them. It is shocking, they are almost nose to nose and, for one brief second, in the dark of one eye she almost sees Beelzebub; and then she laughs because it is just a little fear, and she laughs again for it is her own, not his.

'You're still here.' She smiles and he notices how little her mouth needs to move. 'I thought you'd be long gone.' He takes a tiny snatch of air before pushing each word out with an old man's voice. She notices for the first time the two tracks of dried blood seared across his left cheek and she is overcome by a tiredness that sends her flopping back in the chair.

'Why don't you stay at my apartment tonight?' She does not want to think about this, and lacing her fingers she throws her arms up above her head and stretches, her face grimacing into a yawn. As she releases from the stretch and opens her eyes, the bright-toothed nurse appears hovering over her, her face a sparkle of verve and energy.

'Hi! Maggie ... you're back! Huh! How are you?' Maggie shoots up in her seat. 'Oh yes ... I ... my friend ...' Maggie remembers the cornflower-blue eyes and the eye-watering mint-iness '... He ...'

'Yes, you've been saving folks' lives when you should have been resting up, huh? Now, I have something for you.' And she disappears.

'Thank you.' It is Michael, he is still looking at her, his eyes dragging the rest of his face into a smile. And she is back, holding Maggie's little black boots aloft, level with her cheek. They have been polished with a military shine that causes Maggie to breathe in sharply and exhale with an ecstatic ah! She reaches out for

239

them like a child on Christmas morning and hugging them to her chest she closes her eyes to isolate the smell of leather and polish and hold it to herself.

'These boots were made for walking, huh?'

The Thaw

&

Cissie stands at the door of the apartment; head bent, listening. There is no sound from within. She has walked from the Hotel Apollo, the snow melting under her feet, and a soft wet mist filling her nose and turning her hair into damp, fat little ringlets. Jenny's leaving had been clingy and tearful, but as Cissie watched her being driven away into the fog, she found herself to be lifted by a sense of resolve.

'None of it matters, Ciss. The only thing that matters is what we have, you and I. We all make mistakes, we all fall down. You are properly loved ... know that.' Jenny had said this in a loud, clear voice standing outside the hotel, whilst several other people stood like statues, also waiting for taxis. They were beginning to stamp their feet and cough when she got into her cab, and as she plonked herself down in the seat she boomed, 'Fuck 'em, darling ... fuck 'em ... and the horses they rode in on ... You wicked little lesbian you!'

As Cissie turned to go back into the hotel, avoiding the assembled group as best she could, she had caught the eye of one of them; a thin, middle-aged woman, her face gaunt and pinched with disapproval. Cissie had stopped and looked directly at her, an angry 'fuck you' just waiting to be allowed out, but then she had seen an anxious sheen in the woman's small brown eye, and instead had spoken to her in a gentle but definite voice, like a mother explaining something to a small child.

'That is the woman I love.' With that, a shocked little thrill filling her chest, she had turned and walked in the direction of the Elmscote Hotel, leaving a magnificent silence in her wake. She had then proceeded to skip, high into the air, for a good hundred yards, sending sprays of grey melting snow up in front of her, to land like jewels on her face and in her hair. She had laughed, and laughs now at the thought of it, silently and with glee.

The door is opening, she can smell Helena's amber and lavender bath oil, and she straightens her face.

'Oh m . . . wh . . .?' Helena stands looking at her and although the heavy drape of hair, newly brushed, is partly concealing her face, Cissie can see that both eyes are swollen with a slightly bluish puffiness, and her top lip, inflated to twice its size, has a little dark scab dividing it and another at its corner; its outsized pout giving her what, at first sight, looks like a deliberately smug expression. She doesn't speak but opens the door fully to allow Cissie into the apartment. As she enters she glances into the little kitchen to her right, to see if any evidence remains of their scuffle, but it has been wiped clean. The sink is empty; the tannin brown stain buffed away to reveal the shiny stainless steel beneath. The cupboard doors have been wiped; dried, bubbly smears roll like ocean waves across their painted surfaces; even the floor has been scrubbed and the astringent smell of disinfectant mingles disconcertingly with the bath oil. She walks on into the living room: the coffee table is clear; she notices the plastic ashtray, sitting in the centre, empty and washed, and that it has a logo of a Native American chief which she is seeing for the first time. It is clear and intact except for two little brown craters, dotted in amongst his feathers like shrapnel and another on his chin, burnt in long ago by neglected cigarettes. There is not a cup or a magazine or an item of clothing to be seen anywhere. It is as if everything has been sucked out by a hungry whirlwind; indeed, the window is open wide, a cloud of damp cold air suspended around it, and she peers out half expecting to see one of Helena's shoes hanging from the clutch of pipes that runs diagonally up the building opposite. This building must be no further than fifteen feet away and Cissie can easily see that the snow has now gone from the pipes, just a lone withered icicle remains and, judging from the rapid drips falling from its tip, it won't be long before that too is gone. She stands there for a moment watching the icicle melt and notes that the hum of the building is almost undetectable as if that too has been sucked out and lost in the vast whir and throb of the city. She hears the springs of the sofa and without warning the icicle drops from the pipe and plummets like a tiny missile out of sight. Leaning her stomach on the windowsill, Cissie quickly pushes her head and shoulders through the window to see its descent, but it has gone and not a sound to indicate its fate.

'Don't do it. It's not worth it.'

Cissie hauls herself back in and turns to see Helena, seated to one end of the brown sofa.

'At least choose a more salubrious location . . . Statue of Liberty would be good, or the Chrysler's very pretty.' She says this like a bored travel agent suggesting holiday locations and Cissie smiles with a little snort. Neither speaks for a moment, they simply stare at one another, a slight curl of amusement pulling at the corner of Helena's mouth.

'Who on earth have you been kissing?' Cissie immediately regrets this as she sees the mouth return to its previous po-faced pout. 'Oh my God . . . you're not . . . what on earth . . .? . . . What's happened? Where's Luke?'

Helena slowly closes her eyes. Her head is heavy and she doesn't know what words to speak. She feels Cissie's weight land at the other end of the sofa and opens her eyes to look down at her hands and examine the damage to the blood-red nail polish she had painted on forty-eight hours before and had not checked since. At this moment she cannot look up. Cissie's concerned face would drag the facts out of her before she herself could assemble them in any meaningful order and it would all sound wrong or at the very least it would be inaccurate. It would not properly represent what had taken place and she could not bear any misinterpretation.

'Luke's not here.'

'Oh ... right ...'

'I thought you were going back home?'

'Didn't even make the airport. I'm staying in a grotty little fleapit near the Plaza. Anyway Jenny flew in, just for twenty-four hours ... helped me get things in perspective a bit ... She's gone home now ... so ... I mean d'you want me to go? ... Helena ... I am really sorry about ... what happened ...' Helena does not look up but continues to examine the nails of her left hand and rub at the fingers as if there were a hidden message just below the surface of her skin.

'No, look, no please, I really don't want any more "sorrys". I'm really, really pleased you've come back. I'm just ... a lot has happened.'

'Well I can see that. Do you want to talk ...? Or ... shall I put the kettle on?'

'Yeah that would be nice.'

'... Which?'

'... Pardon?'

'Which? ... Talk? ... Kettle? ... Or ... bit of both?'

'Let's start with the kettle.'

The Dawn

꧁

Maggie has been unable to sleep. She is sitting on the bottom step in Michael's kitchen, having taken up the offer to stay the night in his apartment. She has been there for several hours, slowly eating her way through a packet of marshmallows that she had found in one of the cupboards and staring at the photograph of Michael with the bald child, and then at the crudely drawn little poster that reads 'Dad's Dark Room' and at the trapdoor in the floor with its brass ring-pull. A little balloon of anxiety hovers in her chest as she takes in the cosy ordinariness of it all. Now she steps down, her heart beginning to hammer, and wrenches open the trapdoor, sending the spilled cutlery, that has lain there since God knows when, scattering; and the neatly stacked bottles of Californian and Chilean and Australian wine that she finds there make her laugh out loud and with incredulity.

Slowly and with great care she clears away the cutlery and towels, her heart slowing and the balloon of anxiety shrinking as she does so. And there is something else, something in the careful placing of each knife and fork in its rightful spot and the folding and stacking and putting away of each tea towel that causes her mouth to water and brings a hum to her lips. She then takes the kitchen stairs two at a time, springing into the sitting room where a cold Manhattan dawn sheds a sad pink light over everything, and on up into the study and into his bedroom where she touches and sniffs like a dog in a new space. Then spinning from one room to the other on bare, dancing feet, the hum threatening to become a song, she is caught short by the big steady tick of the clock and starts a jerky, robotic little dance to its beat. She descends the spiral staircase back down into the living space, the image of a long silk scarf floating vertically downwards across her mind's eye as she does so. It is as she reaches the bottom that she hears something indeterminate behind her, something soft against wood, and the hum freezes on her lips. Turning round she notices a door, in a darkened corner of the room; from underneath it, a thin shaft of light glows yellow. It is a door that she cannot recall having noticed before, and from within, another sound, just on the edge of her hearing; an impatient little sigh and then a rustling of clothes and as she walks towards it on tiptoe, not a sound from the maple floor, she is unsure as to whether the rustling had been the swish of her own skirt and that the petulant little breath had not been her own impatience. A freezing draught blows across her toes and up around her ankles as she stands at the door, her hand on the handle. Then with the sudden force of a policeman in a raid she pushes the door open, sending several little plastic figures holding swords and spears flying through the air from the shelf behind and hurtling with daredevil acrobatics to the floor.

The little room is of a deep blue; its temperature several degrees below that of the rest of the apartment. On the floor is a Scalextric track with two tiny racing cars placed ready, side by side, for a burn-up. The curtains are drawn; they are wizard's curtains, navy blue, covered in brightly coloured planets and stars and, judging from the way they fall, thickly lined. In the middle of the room is a single divan: its bedspread is of the same material and is without wrinkle or crease; except to one side, the side nearest the door, where the perfection is disturbed by a crumpled little patch and a dip in the plump softness of the duvet beneath. There is a strong scent in the room that Maggie remembers having smelt briefly on occasion elsewhere in the apartment. It is an uplifting scent and she savours its freshness through flared nostrils.

Then to her left something moves and she turns her head just in time to see yet another little figure plunging head over heels to the floor. She crouches down on her haunches to identify it and there amongst several fierce-looking warriors lying together in drunken disarray is Superman, lying handsome and helpless on his back. She picks him up and places him, standing upright, in the palm of her hand and then she peers hard into the tiny face and something in its square-jawed strength and its blue-eyed integrity makes her giggle, but even as the giggle pops up into her throat, she knows where it is headed. The first sob is short and sharp and causes a shiver to shimmy through her body, and then a warm, now familiar ache to ripple across her lower back. Holding the little hero tightly in her hand, she then wanders around the room, her feet stiff and aching with cold, sniffing back tears and gulping at sobs before they are airborne and, after several aimless tours of the small space half looking at posters of racing cars and space rockets, she throws back the bed-covers and collapses down into their soft folds where the scent of the room is concentrated and heady.

It is as she tries to snuggle down that she feels something hard under the mattress. Reaching underneath it, her fingers find the sharp corner of a book. On dragging it out, she is about to fling it to the floor beside the bed but the writing on its cover stops her dead. It reads THIS IS THE BOOK OF DOMINIC SPENCE AGED 7 YEARS in bright red crayon, then underneath in black felt tip, it reads, KEEP OUT!!!! PRIVATE!!!! heavily underscored in red. On the bottom right-hand corner is a tattered round sticker and on it is a cartoon of a puppy, with huge, sad eyes, holding up a bandaged paw; underneath it, it reads, I HAVE BEEN VERY BRAVE.

Maggie lies there for several minutes staring at the little book, running her fingers over the waxy lettering and pressing the torn edge of the sticker back down. She is considering how numbing a large brandy would be when she turns the first page. Stuck onto the inside cover is a holiday snap of Michael on a beach somewhere, his head thrown back in laughter, one arm nonchalantly draped around the shoulders of a woman who is doubled up, holding her stomach. She is looking up and straight at the camera, her eyes ablaze with mischief, her mouth a perfect dark oval, and Maggie recognises the woman in the night. Underneath, large wavery letters spell out: 'Mommy and Daddy Laughing. Location: Granpy's beach. Photographer: Dominic Spence.'

On the opposite page is a blurred photograph of several soft toys squashed together in an armchair. Maggie can see on closer inspection that it is the green leather armchair from the living space. The inscription reads: 'Geoffrey, Lucien, Corky, Bruno and Mr Fox taking a break. Location: Daddy's armchair. Photographer: Dominic Spence.'

On the next page is a photo of a large black man in a white uniform, standing next to a hospital bed. In the centre of the bed, propped up on several pillows, is one of the toys from the previous picture, a grey rabbit with large floppy ears which appears to be hooked up to an intravenous drip. Underneath it says: 'Geoffrey gets his chemo. Location: Jupiter Ward. Photographer: Dominic Spence'; and opposite in another snap the large black man, still standing by the bed, holds Geoffrey awkwardly in the crook of his arm and the inscription reads: 'Geoffrey gets his cuddle from Mantou for being brave. Location: Jupiter Ward. Photographer: D. Spence.'

So begins a series of photographs in which the toy, Geoffrey, appears to be undergoing various hospital procedures. In one he is lying on a gurney, being wheeled by the same nurse: 'Geoffrey goes for his lumbar puncture ... ouch! In another a kindly looking woman beams at the camera whilst holding a syringe to the toy's arm: 'Kerry takes blood from Geoffrey ... double ouch because he doesn't get to have the magic cream!' After several such photographs, there is one of a boy lying on his stomach on a hospital bed. He is completely bald and is grimacing, his mouth wide and toothless, whilst pointing a spacegun at the camera:

'This is my friend Nathan Pearl. He is nice. He can play chess.'

Maggie then flicks through several pages which again feature the toy, Geoffrey, until she comes across one where Michael is asleep on the same bed with the toy splayed out on his chest. The caption reads: 'Daddy and Geoffrey on Jupiter! Photographer D.S. Geoffrey loves to sleep on Daddy. He can hear his heart beat.' Then opposite Michael is holding the toy in the air and pulling a grotesque face with crossed eyes and goofy teeth: 'Daddy pulling Geoffrey's favourite face. It really makes him laugh. Sometimes till he's nearly sick. Mummy says this is better than medicine.'

After several more photos of Geoffrey engaged in various activities, there is one of an empty bed, with a spacegun placed on the pillow. It reads: 'My friend Nathan Pearl died. I get to keep his spacegun.' There is nothing on the opposite page, but on the next page is a paragraph written in thin, faint pencil. Maggie twists around to place the book nearer the little bedside lamp. It begins with small neat and ordered letters, marching bravely forth in a very straight line across the page, but all too quickly they begin to fidget and jostle one another and then to grow in size, looping and shooting this way and that as if the writer no longer has a say and the words themselves are dictating the form. And it begins to slant from left to right, each line bending more than the one before until the final one almost swoops off the page in a near vertical dive.

When you die your mom and dad can be there but they can't go with you. Mummy says some people have big long lives and other people have tiny little lives. It's the luck of the draw and it doesn't matter if you finish your life quite quickly, it is just as precious. In fact it's probably more special. You might be able to be born again. I would like to come back as a baby. I don't think Nathan will bother coming back, he never laughed at anything. His dad wasn't funny and his mum was always cross.

Maggie reads the paragraph several times over until without warning the little bedside lamp goes out.

'And I brought your favourite Orange Pekoe . . . and wait for it . . . now don't go wild here . . . a pack of . . . OREO COOKIES!'

'OOH! Do you know how many people I would be willing to kill right now for a fresh cup of Orange Pekoe tea and an Oreo cookie to dip in it? Do you?'

'Of course I do!' Elizabeth says in mock outrage and they both giggle, she light and high-pitched, he lower and riper, resulting in an odd harmony, an exclusive little anthem to their life.

Maggie is standing outside the pale primrose curtains which have been drawn around the bed, holding the little book from the night before under her cloak. She is about to part the curtains when she is stopped by the sound of a kiss. The suck of lips on skin; a swift rustle of clothes and a metallic squeak from the bed. At first she had not been sure that it was the right bed but then she had heard Michael's voice.

'Oh thank God! Oh thank God. Lizzie . . . you have no idea.'

'Well thank God you're O.K., Michael. Whoever she was . . . she did good.'

Maggie backs away and sits on a lone grey plastic chair, parked up against the wall. On the nurses' station, in front of her, she spies a pink 'Post-it' pad. Quickly grabbing a discarded pen, she writes in greasy biro scrawl: 'Thanks x' and above this she draws a little pair of wings. She sticks this onto the front cover of the little book and in one fluid movement she wheels round and shoves it with the elegant skill of a crown green bowler underneath the curtains, whereupon the woman cries out and Maggie turns and runs.

The Finger

Without warning the street lamps go out, sending a little flurry of panic across Luke's heart. He is sitting in the window of Carlito's, a tiny coffee house on the corner, half a block up and on the other side of the street from the Elmscote Hotel. He is warming his hands on a thick white cup of black bitter coffee.

'Oh! Here comes the day!' It is a wizened waitress with Mother Teresa skin and shiny black smiling eyes. She is slapping a bright orange menu down on each of the tables and now with the smell of clean ironed linen she stands too close to Luke and slices the laminated oblong between the sugar and the condiments. 'You ready for your day, sir?' She folds her arms, her elbow sharp and pointed just inches from Luke's eye. He stares sideways at it, the little ripple of flesh hanging from her forearm like dough from a rolling pin. She sings:

'Here comes the sun . . . de n de de . . . here comes the sun . . . I say . . . it's alright . . .' He can feel the harmony rising, soft and delicate, from the base of his solar plexus. He turns and tilts his head to look up at her.

'Little darling it's been a lo—' At the same time she twists around with sudden pleasure at the velutinous quality of his voice and the point of her bare elbow whacks into his nose with a fleshy crack.

'Oh my . . . I am so sorry! . . .' The waitress yanks a cotton cloth from her back pocket and shoves it into Luke's face. 'Are you alright? I'll get some ice.' She scuttles off in the direction of the bar. 'Put your head back,' she shouts from somewhere in a far corner.

Luke does as he is told and he finds something like pleasure in the dull throb. He squeezes the bone in his nose between his thumb and forefinger, upping the pain level from dull to shooting, and it makes him grind his teeth and moan out loud. She is back with a second cloth filled with ice.

'Here, put this on. It'll help stop the bleeding. Oh I am *so* sorry. And what happened to your lip? Did I ... I didn't do that ... did I?'

Luke shakes his head.

'Jeez you've been in the wars. Let me get you some water.'

She's off again and Luke presses the icepack down hard on his nose. He closes his eyes and moans again softly as the pain at first intensifies. Then as it begins to abate, and then numb, the little flurry of panic crosses his heart again, followed by a big, empty space. She is back with the water and she places it down in front of him.

'Is it broke? ... Please don't tell me it's broke.' Luke shakes his head. He hears the door open behind him and someone enter, stamping slush from their boots and blowing on frozen fingers.

'Give me a second, sweetheart.'

Luke is surprised by the richness and volume of the woman's voice, given her small, wiry frame. In another lifetime she could have been Judy Garland or Ethel Merman or Edith Piaf.

'... Thank God you're not,' he says into the white napkin.

'What, sweetheart?' His head still back, he lifts the icepack away from his face a little.

'I was just thinking how lucky you are.'

'Oh sure. Has it stopped?' She is now sitting in the seat opposite Luke, trying to see up into his face. 'You in any pain?'

'Not the sort you can do anything about, I'm afraid.'

She laughs, 'Then don't, sweetheart.' He lifts his head up and she laughs again with raised eyebrows and baring teeth too big for her mouth, '... accept,' she says with a single nod. He lowers the icepack from his nose.

'There, you see? It's stopped. Let me get you a fresh cup of coffee,' and she is off. '... on the house!' she shouts from behind the bar.

Luke looks out onto West 77th Street. The thick creeping mist which had hovered a matter of feet from the window is gone, revealing the thin grey column of the Elmscote, its blind windows reflecting a timid morning sun. He counts the floors up to the fifteenth and touches his mouth. He wants to cry, and again he squeezes the bone in his nose and a dull little pain shoots up into his forehead. He removes his glasses and the Elmscote becomes a blur.

'What d'ya mean?' The woman is raising her voice. 'What d'ya mean you have no money?' Luke turns to see. There are only two other customers in the place. 'Why didn't you say you had no money?' One is a red-faced man in a beanie hat, pulled down to his eyebrows, sitting near the door, and the other, sitting further away, the one the waitress is addressing, has her back to him.

It is Maggie and Luke knew it was, even before he turned round.

'You come in here, you order all kinds of crap and then you tell me you can't pay?'

She is saying something back to the waitress that Luke can't quite hear, but he would recognise the lilt and timbre of her voice anywhere. He puts his glasses back on and stares at the back of her head, four inches of black root clearly visible.

He says out loud. 'I've found you!' Then he laughs.

Maggie turns. She stares for several seconds, her face inscrutable, then one corner of her mouth lifts, followed by the other, into a wide grin. 'Hello, Playmate!' They both stand and smile at one another. The waitress places both hands on her hips.

'What is this ... *Brief Encounter*?' Luke reddens and giggles.

'Oh I . . . I'm sorry! Look, there's not a problem. I . . . I'll settle the lady's bill.'

'Never mind the bloody bill! Come and give us a hug!'

Luke moves towards her and she throws her arms around his neck, springing up onto tiptoe.

'Oh Maggie, Maggie, Maggie May . . . what on earth have you been up to?'

'I wish I knew, Playmate.' Gently letting go of her, he takes her hand and leads her back to the seat in the window. They sit there for several easy minutes in silence and then he reaches across the table and smoothes the back of his fingers down the silky pile of her blue velvet cloak.

'I first saw you wearing this in the bar next door to the Royal Court . . . must be ten years ago.'

'Yeah . . . my trusty old cloak. Seen me through a heap of trouble, Playmate.'

'I thought you looked like a fairy princess.'

She throws her head back and he watches the white skin of her neck pulsate with laughter. 'That's because I was, my darling. Now . . . I'm putting off asking, but I can't put it off any longer . . . What on earth happened to your gob, darling?' He brings a hand up to cover it and lowers his head. 'You weren't beaten up or anything, were you?'

'No, I'd give anything for that to be the case.'

'Coffee for the wounded soldier!' The waitress places a fresh cup of black coffee in front of Luke and removes the old one. 'Now, Miss "No-Money"! Is it yet another cup of coffee on the house or are you all caffeined out now, after your previous six cups?'

Maggie takes a huge breath in, her eyes widening and then with a disbelieving snort, she throws her head back again and hoots out a tinkling laugh.

'And how's the schnozzle, sir? I'm taking it we don't have to alert the blood bank.'

Luke manages a smile and something resembling a chuckle.

'I'd love a coffee please.' Maggie touches the woman's arm.

'Hey there! Watch that! These are lethal weapons. I could take an eye out with one of these. Ask your boyfriend. He may never smell the same again.' And she is off.

Luke is looking at Maggie's face as she watches the waitress go back behind the bar. It is an opportunity to search through her features – for what, he is not entirely sure. All he knows is that if she were to look back at him, he would need to look away.

'So glad you're here, Playmate.' She has looked back. 'I'm going to need you to hold my hand if I'm to go back in there.'

He looks down at the large, rough-looking hand that she has pushed halfway across the table. He slides his own across to meet it, fingertip to fingertip. They could almost be a pair, same size, same colour. Her nails are not bitten like his but they are ragged and misshapen and there are withered, grimy little cracks on her thumb and forefinger as if she had gardened all her life without gloves.

'Have I been excommunicated, Playmate? What's the score?'

He looks across at her. She has her other hand up to her face, a forefinger crooked around her right eye partly covering it. It is a gesture of hers that is so familiar to him. He had always taken it as a mark of some kind of dishonesty, of sneaky duplicity, but here he sees clearly that it is simply a gesture of protection, of childish defence against the wrath of the world. He reaches out and takes the hand away from her face and places it next to the other one on the table. He places both of his hands on top of hers and holds her gaze. Like an image in a flawed mirror, he watches as her features appear to change their configuration. It is as if the removal of the finger had caused them to pull infinitesimally in odd directions, removing all evidence of her beauty. It is a face disassembled. Leaving something plain and unspeakably vulnerable.

The Secret

❧

'I have never thought of myself as vulnerable . . . they just came up to us and demanded money . . . well we resisted and . . . we shouldn't have, no . . . We didn't see any point in contacting the police . . . but . . . well yes we ought to report it I suppose . . . O.K. just make me an appointment with the doctor . . . No, no, no I'm fine . . . we're fine . . . O.K. thanks, I'll wait to hear from you. . . . Bye. Why don't Americans ever say goodbye when they hang up?'

'Did they believe you?' Cissie's voice is tentative.

'I've no idea, darling, and quite frankly, whether the slippery little bollock believes me or not is of . . . is of no consequence. The theatre's closed again tonight, so there are seven shows at the most left. The understudy will be having orgasms. There was always something a little bit *42nd Street* about her anyway. All that over-friendliness combined with the whiff of loathing when I rolled in for the warm-up every night. Well . . . now she can finish the run.' She flops back down on the sofa, resuming her position, facing Cissie. They are sitting, like a pair of bookends, their backs against opposite arms of the brown corduroy sofa, their knees drawn up to their chests and each nursing a mug of black instant coffee in both hands. A cigarette is burning another hole into the Indian chief's headdress.

'What are you going to do, Helena?'

'About what?'

'Well . . . about Luke?'

'It's been done, darling. It's over. We both knew that it had got to stop ... somehow ... I suppose that's what it was all about ... putting a stop to it ...'

'God ... wouldn't it have been easier just to split?'

'Obviously not.' She is staring down into her mug. One drape of hair has fallen down from behind her left ear and is covering almost all of her face. The other drape has also fallen forward and the two are touching one another at the tip forming a heart-shaped gap, through which Cissie can see part of Helena's right eye and the very corner of her mouth with its little black crust of blood.

'Yes, but ... do you think he should get away with ... what he's done?'

'He hasn't and he won't. Believe me, it'll be a lot more painful for him than it will ever be for me. Not least because "Little Luke" has got one hell of a carpet burn right on the tip of his helmet.'

'Oh for fuck's sake.'

'... Exactly ... and you can draw your own conclusions from that.'

'... What? ... You mean? ... ooh.'

'Look ... I really don't want to talk about it any more. But I need you to know that there is a piece of me that belongs only to him and vice versa. We just can't do the "couple" stuff. We'll both just have to do that with other people ... End of ... O.K.?'

Cissie puts her cup down and stands up.

'And don't even think about giving me a hug.'

She sits back down. As she reaches for the now cold cup of coffee, the doorbell sounds its jaunty bing-bong and the two women look at each other. Before either speaks, the jangle of keys is heard, followed by the twisting of the lock.

Then shushing and whispers and Luke and Maggie enter the room as if pushed in by some japester. Their faces are pink with surprise as if this was the last place on earth they expected to end up. The two women stare at them. Maggie is wearing Luke's bobble hat, pulled down to her eyebrows, and apart from the dark circles under her eyes she looks refreshed and exhilarated; a person enjoying a wonderful holiday. Luke's hair is pulled up into a strange-looking peak, like a 1950s baby. His eyes are wide and his glasses are not on straight. Helena wonders for a moment if he is drunk. No one says a word for several seconds, then Maggie throws her arms around Luke's middle, pinning his arms to his sides, causing him to squeak and then giggle. Then she squashes the side of her face into his shoulder.

'Look who I've found!' she says as if she had been searching her whole life.

The Epilogue

'Well that was delicious! Do you think the goulash was meant to look like that or had somebody already eaten it? It had that partially digested look.'

'Will all passengers please return to their seats and fasten their seat belts.'

'Oh! And now for some turbulence to really help with the digesting of the truly indigestible.' Cissie makes a circle with her thumb and forefinger through which she belches loudly.

They are sitting on either side of an aisle. Helena and Cissie on one side, Luke and Maggie on the other. Maggie's seat, next to the aisle, is empty. Luke reaches across it and taps at Cissie with long straight fingers.

'Hasn't she been in there rather a long time? I mean supper's been and gone.'

Cissie cranes her head around the seat in front for an uninterrupted view of the toilet and its queue. As she does so someone shouts something. It sounds like, 'That is disgusting!' Now someone is leaving the toilet, one arm raised in front of them, a warning to the rest of the queue to make way. Which they do in silence, flattening themselves against the adjacent seats so as not to come into contact with her.

Helena hears Cissie's sharp gulp, even over the noise of the plane. She unclips her seat belt and half stands to see.

'Oh . . . my . . . God!' Luke doesn't need to move from his seat, he can see perfectly well.

'. . . Oh no.'

Having negotiated the queue, Maggie is walking down the aisle towards them. She has removed her top, to reveal a rather grubby grey-looking bra and she appears to have smeared her body with lipstick for her stomach, chest and arms are smothered in a bright, greasy red substance; but more shockingly, she has shaved great clumps of her hair off. She is almost completely bald, but here and there, long wisps of it, having escaped the razor, float, light as candyfloss, around her head. Loose hairs of varying lengths are flying off her in all directions, so that some of the passengers are brushing them from their arms and heads and whipping around angrily.

'What the hell . . .? That landed in my . . .' Others are turning, with excited, open-mouthed faces.

'Isn't that . . . that actress?' 'Yes . . . Maggie . . . Maggie . . . somebody.' 'Yes that's it – Maggie . . . Smith! . . . isn't it?'

The three friends stare silently as she arrives at and swings down into her seat. After several minutes during which none of the group speaks an ancient woman totters down the aisle and sits in the seat behind. She taps Maggie on the shoulder, leaving perfect fingerprints in the lipstick, and pops a heavily powdered face around the side of the seat.

'Excuse me? I'm from London, dear. Are you that actress . . . Maggie . . . Scott?'

Maggie's head turns with the mechanical speed of a ventriloquist's dummy. Her pupils, vast, all green obliterated, her mouth curled around a strange little smile. The old lady smiles back and makes another set of fingerprints on Maggie's arm.

'I seen you in that thing on telly,' she says, with a conspiratorial wink. 'Are you filming now, dear? . . . you've left a terrible mess in the toilets.'

Cissie and Helena assume the brace position, Luke places a hand gently in the small of Maggie's back, at the same time looking for something to wipe it on.

'No . . .' she says gravely, feeling the warmth of his hand. 'I'm beginning. This is just the first tiny spark that you are witnessing. I'm about to embark on an incredible journey.'

'Well you ought to clear that mess up before you go, love . . . it's not nice.'

Acknowledgements

With thanks for their precious time and help: Sarah Teale, Lorinda Klein, Miriam Gonzalez, Dr Stephen Waxman, Connie Prescott, Joanne Brown, Dr Criton Pavlou; and special thanks to Ian and Jane Livingstone, and most importantly Alan Samson, for his unflagging encouragement, support and of course his patience, and without whom I would not even have started this book let alone finished it.

Maggie's Tree
Reading Group Notes

❧

In Brief

Cissie has brought Maggie to New York. But now Maggie has gone. Cissie and Luke have no idea where she is, and Luke's not impressed. Why has Cissie brought Maggie over with her when she must have *known* the state Maggie was in? Cissie insists that Maggie was OK before they left, but began to slide on the flight. They have come out to see their friend Helena in her moment of triumph on Broadway – and she's certainly not going to spend time searching for her loopy friend when she should be doing the basking she's been waiting for. What should they do? Where is Maggie? Dead in a gutter? Nothing's ever easy, is it . . .?

In Detail

Maggie is in a bar. But the bar seems to be in a very different world from that of her weary and worried friends. There isn't enough air to breathe, the barman's voice is so painful – and what is the matter with her hands? As she finally begins to lose control of everything, she sees the shoes. What lovely brogues; she loves them. And the occupant of the shoes wants to help her. To look after her. But how should she pay him?

The horrible nightmare had come to Michael again in the night. He'd hoped it had left him; but it had just taken a month's vacation. The image of Dominic's body being dragged into the ground hadn't left him all day. But Maggie's pale skin and vivid green eyes had taken his mind away from it in a pleasant enough way, until her behaviour became more extreme and he'd been pulled right in. But Maggie can't read the clues . . . she'll go with him, but what is he: Jesus or Beelzebub?

Helena is determined that Maggie is not going to do it again. It is Cissie's holiday and her own moment of glory, and Maggie is not going to spoil it. It's time for her to take responsibility for herself for once. Anyway, beauty sleep calls. Cissie has her own reasons for running to New York, and could do with a little time to think of herself, without everything being about Maggie. Luke, however, thinks the police should be notified . . . she might need help. But his telephone call doesn't cause the NYPD to burst on to the streets in search of her. In fact, they seem notably underwhelmed.

Michael is finding it increasingly difficult to help Maggie. From a crack of heads to a tussle in the back of a cab, attention is drawn to them. But finally he gets her home. Perhaps herbal tea will help. Now she's cut her head on his precious picture of Dominic – by pressing her head so hard to it that she's broken the glass. He can't leave her alone for five minutes! Finally he gets her wrapped in a duvet and on the sofa, and she's soon asleep.

But in the morning there's so much blood. On the sofa, on the rug, on the floor. Leading to the bathroom. And he can't open the door, something is blocking it. Pushing harder he can see her. Slumped on the floor, and more blood, so much more blood. He calls 911, but she's so cold.

While Michael talks to the police, Cissie and Helena are also down at the precinct, filling in a missing person's report. But Cissie's own worries are increasingly dominating her thoughts. They're on to her; they know. And she's flown out of the country leaving Jenny in the lurch. What has she done? And where the hell is Maggie?

About the Author

Julie Walters was born in Smethwick, Birmingham in 1950. She trained first to be a nurse, but despite her mother's objections she decided to try the career she felt was hers and went to study English and Drama at Manchester Polytechnic, before joining the renowned Everyman Theatre in Liverpool. There she worked with Alan Bleasdale and Willy Russell amongst others, giving her acting the sound base that has led to the success and recognition she has received throughout her career. Her versatility allows her to move from Oscar nomination in *Educating Rita*, via Victoria Wood's creation Mrs Overall, to Mrs Weasley in the Harry Potter films. Julie Walters is 'arguably the nation's best-loved actress' (*Sunday Times*) and is rightly regarded as something of a national treasure.

For Discussion

- The first words of the book are 'Maggie is missing'. What did that make you think? How did the first paragraph set up your expectations, and were you on the right track?

- How did your knowledge of the author affect your experience of the book? Did you come to it with preconceptions due to Julie Walters' profile?

- 'He dabs carefully at the cut with the towel, inadvertently turning the cross into a smudgy-looking swastika.' How is this image significant in our developing understanding of Michael? Is it a prediction of his actions to come?

- Images of mothers throughout the novel often lack a face. What does this tell us about the characters?

- The characters come to us with no backstory. How is this important to our understanding of the unfolding plot? It is, in itself, rather filmic. Do you think the writer's history has a part to play in the style of the novel?

- How important are smells in the novel?
- Boots seem important too, don't they?
- 'Swinging the foot up on to her knee she can see the tiny red crescent dangling from the sock like a miniature sickle and she breathes out a long, rushing roar of breath.' What is the significance of the 'red crescent' to Cissie?
- The author's experience as an actress has helped her to describe the movements of her characters with great fluency. Is this immediacy always a help?
- What is Maggie's tree?
- Maggie's 'madness' serves to highlight the 'sanity' of the other characters. But how sane are they? And how mad is Maggie?

Suggested Further Reading

The Ghost at the Table by Suzanne Berne
The Story of You by Julie Myerson
The Wrong Boy by Willy Russell
Arlington Park by Rachel Cusk
The Vanishing Act of Esme Lennox by Maggie O'Farrell